The Gypsy
In My Soul

The Gypsy
In My Soul

A gripping wartime story of love, loss, hope, and survival

A Novel

Christine Harris

iUniverse, Inc.
New York   Bloomington

iUniverse books may be ordered through booksellers or by contacting:

iUniverse
1663 Liberty Drive
Bloomington, IN 47403
www.iuniverse.com
1-800-Authors (1-800-288-4677)

Because of the dynamic nature of the Internet, any Web addresses or links contained in this book may have changed since publication and may no longer be valid. The views expressed in this work are solely those of the author and do not necessarily refl ect the views of the publisher, and the publisher hereby disclaims any responsibility for them.

ISBN: 978-0-595-47434-9 (sc)
ISBN: 978-0-595-71337-0 (hc)
ISBN: 978-0-595-91711-2 (ebook)

Printed in the United States of America

iUniverse rev. 12/23/2009

In memory of my parents, Maggie and Ole … for being just who they were.

In the journey is the reward.

—Chinese Proverb

Acknowledgments

This journey from idea to publication has been made possible by the help of numerous encouraging people. My special thanks to author Elizabeth Ridley who was my teacher, book doctor, and friend throughout the writing of this novel.

I would also like to extend my appreciation to Dr. Ian Hancock, faculty member with the University of Texas and member of the United States Holocaust Memorial Commission. Dr. Hancock, recognized as the most eminent scholar on the Roma, was most generous in sharing with me his writings and insights.

Thanks go to my husband, Ron, who patiently carried files, computers, and books all over the world for me while I worked on this project, and then carefully and courageously critiqued the final draft of *The Gypsy in My Soul*. And thanks also to my Olson siblings and my friends who read the unpublished draft and provided input.

And I could not go without recognizing my children, their spouses, and my grandchildren. What they have taught me about living and loving has immensely impacted my writing. Thank you, Brett and Jan, Jenny and Kelly, Bailey; Jagger, Ryder, Nicolas, Nathan and Tyler.

Author's Note

The author of this novel uses the term *Gypsy* where it is applicable to the historical era. However, the term *Gypsy* is no longer the scholarly or preferred name for this population. Linguistic and genetic studies indicate that this population has its origins in northern India, and not in Egypt, as it has been long believed. Today the preferred name for Gypsies is *Roma* or *Romanies*.

The Roma began their exit from the subcontinent of India more than a millennium ago, first migrating into Asia and Eastern Europe, and eventually dispersing throughout the world. Although they share a common historical past, the Roma cannot be generally identified by physical appearance, dress, or lifestyle. Like other modern populations, they have integrated with various societies while striving to maintain their own unique cultural roots and values.

CHAPTER ONE

Grandview, Nebraska
October 1972

"It wasn't just Jews who were murdered; it was Poles, Russians, and Gypsies. Millions died in concentration camps."

Beth Karmazin, who had been idly doodling in the margins of her spiral-bound notebook, stirred and sat upright at her desk. Mr. Henry's words captured her attention as he began his lecture, the fourth in a series on the Holocaust. A crisp autumn breeze blew through the open classroom window and lifted her long black hair as she focused on the aged instructor, observing his stooped shoulders and his ever-present bifocals balanced precariously on the end of his nose.

"Today we will focus on the Gypsies, who, like the Jews, were specifically targeted for racial extermination," continued Mr. Henry, who at sixty-seven had been lecturing to classrooms full of listless students since well before the start of World War II.

"The Nazis considered the Gypsies to be asocial, criminal misfits."

Looking slightly unsteady on his feet, Mr. Henry pulled down the projection screen at the front of the room and locked it into position. "Mr. Terrian, the lights, please," Mr. Henry asked, nodding toward a long-limbed blond-haired boy at the rear of the classroom. With the flick of the switch the room went dark, and a loud "whoosh" filled the air as the creaky film projector sputtered to life. "THE GYPSIES: HITLER'S OTHER VICTIMS" appeared as a dark caption on the screen.

Beth liked history, and she had been fascinated with Mr. Henry's World War II lectures, but she didn't know much about Gypsies beyond the ones she had seen working the carnival at the Nebraska State Fair. Long ago, her Grandpa Sullivan had warned her to stay away from them. He swore it was a band of Gypsies traveling through the Nebraska countryside during the Depression that had stolen his blacksmithing tools. He said someone forgot to ring the church bell to warn the town that a caravan was on the way.

With a jerk, Mr. Henry advanced the filmstrip, and Beth's attention was drawn to horrific images at the front of the room. For the next fifteen minutes she watched in awe as photo after photo of stick-thin bodies, wooden carts piled high with corpses, and boxes of tattered shoes filled the screen. Several times she wanted to turn away from the spectacle of victims who suffered from torture, starvation, and disease. Yet Beth could not take her eyes from the screen. These shocking photos didn't belong to the distant past or to a dry lecture out of a dusty old textbook; they belonged to real life, and Beth felt compelled to know the story behind them.

Abruptly, a map of Europe appeared on the white projection screen, illustrating where the Gypsies had lived before the Holocaust decimated their numbers in Eastern and Western Europe. Another click and the map disappeared, replaced by a photograph of three terrified Gypsy children clinging arm in arm as a Nazi soldier with a bayonet marched them toward a cattle car. The children's frightened eyes pierced Beth's soul. Her stomach churned and she gripped her pen tightly as Mr. Henry again advanced the filmstrip.

Now Beth was looking at a single photograph of a tall, angular woman. Beth stared at the woman, mesmerized by her beauty and her dark, haunted eyes, and strangely, Beth felt a connection to the woman—but why? Was this some kind of subliminal manifestation that Beth simply couldn't understand? Suddenly Beth's face flushed as she became acutely aware of herself: her long, black hair, her almond-shaped eyes and olive skin. She realized she looked like the woman on the screen. She looked like all of the doomed faces in the filmstrip. But how could that be? She was an American girl of Polish-Irish ancestry. What connection could she possibly have to these faraway foreigners?

In the darkened classroom with the flickering filmstrip throwing intermittent flashes of light, Beth now saw several pairs of eyes peering back at her. They had noticed too. Even her cousin Matthew Karmazin had turned in his seat. Beth tried to shrug off their stares by focusing more intently on the screen, but she couldn't pretend that she didn't notice. She blinked nervously and fidgeted with her watch, hoping the filmstrip would end soon.

During the remaining minutes of class Mr. Henry lectured about the war crime trials at Nuremberg, but Beth didn't hear him. She couldn't shake the image of the Gypsy woman in the filmstrip with the dark, penetrating eyes. When the bell rang, signaling the end of fifth period, Beth hurriedly gathered up her books and headed out the door for the band hall, a short walk from the high school's main building. She was relieved to get out into the sunlight, away from Mr. Henry's classroom, and away from the thought that she was somehow linked to the Holocaust victims. Autumn leaves crunched under her sandals as she walked briskly down the sidewalk. The cool breeze felt good on her hot cheeks. She loved the fall: the fresh smell of the air, the changing colors of the leaves on the trees, and the excitement of football.

Beth was completely unaware her cousin Matthew was behind her until he called out, "Beth, hold up."

"What did you think of the filmstrip?" Matthew asked when he caught up to Beth.

"It was very disturbing," Beth responded somberly.

"Yeah, yeah, it was. Mr. Henry gets away with showing a lot of disturbing stuff. But no one ever seems to complain."

"I guess not," Beth replied with a shrug, hoping Matthew would get the hint that she didn't want to talk about history class.

"Maybe it's because he has been around so long. You have to admit he has a way of getting your attention. Beth, do you mind if I ask you a personal question?"

Beth was five feet seven inches tall, taller than most girls her age, and as she glanced sideways at Matthew she was seeing him at eye level. She considered his grim expression now and suspected she wouldn't like his question.

"Sure, go ahead," Beth said, as she swatted away a persistent honeybee that had landed on her arm.

Matthew looked down at Beth's clothing with a dismissive glance that narrowed his wide brown eyes. "Why do you dress that way?"

Slowing down, Beth thought about how she looked. She wore her dark hair straight to the middle of her back, large hoop earrings, and silver eye shadow. Her fitted black bolero jacket stopped at her waist, and her colorful patched peasant skirt fell to her ankles. She wore open-toed sandals. It was the fashion of the counterculture, popular on the East and West coasts. Perhaps it wasn't the standard in Grandview, Nebraska, but Beth liked the way she looked, and Matthew had no damn right to insult her about it.

"If you're planning to ask another question like that one, Matthew, screw off. I don't have time for it."

Matthew was forced to skip a step now to keep up with Beth's accelerated pace. "Don't get mad," he pleaded.

"Well, how do you expect me to react?" Beth responded without looking at him.

"I'm sorry; I didn't mean to hurt your feelings. It's just that you don't fit in dressed like that."

Beth had never worried about fitting in. She was an "A" student, a member of the debate team and the band, and she wrote for the high school newsletter. What could be wrong with that?

"What do you mean, I don't fit in?"

"Well," Matthew said, shifting his books from one arm to the other and biting his lip nervously, "you look like a Gypsy."

So that was where Matthew had been headed with this discussion.

"Is that why you were staring at me in class? You think I look like a Gypsy?" Beth looked at Matthew as if seeing him for the first time. His eyes were dark, but his skin was much lighter than Beth's, and his hair was blond and curly. He was her first cousin, but they looked nothing alike. Beth's father, Karl Karmazin, and Matthew's father, Dimitri, were brothers from Poland. But Beth's dark-haired, light-skinned mother was Spanish-Irish, while Matthew's mother was Nordic, a woman with platinum hair and very pale skin. Beth had obviously inherited the darker features of her mother and father, while Matthew had received a heavy dose of his mother's Nordic genes.

Matthew cocked his head. "I just thought that after what happened to our grandmother, you would be more careful. Not that that would happen here, of course, but people can be very cruel."

Beth turned. "What do you mean, 'what happened to Grandmother?'"

"You know, taking her off to that Nazi camp."

"What? A concentration camp?"

Matthew put his finger to his lips. "Shh, not so loud. Yes, one of those," he whispered.

Beth kept walking, trying to digest what Matthew had just told her. Her father had never mentioned a concentration camp. He had told Beth that his mother died of pneumonia during the war.

"That's ridiculous," Beth said, regaining her composure. "Why would Grandma Karmazin be taken to a concentration camp?"

"You don't know?"

"Matthew, enough of these games. Know what?"

"Grandma Sasha was a Gypsy."

Beth and Matthew approached the door to the band hall, from where Matthew would go on to biology. But Beth wasn't about to let him get away, not after dropping this bombshell. She grabbed his arm and forced him to face her. "Did your father tell you this?"

Matthew's father and Beth's father were not only brothers, but also business partners in Karmazin Electric. As teenagers, Karl and Dimitri had escaped Warsaw together during the Nazi occupation of Poland. They were as close as brothers could be, and Dimitri was Beth's favorite uncle. She trusted him completely. He wouldn't make up something like this.

"Settle down a minute, and let's go over there," Matthew suggested, nodding toward a bike rack away from the student congestion at the band hall door.

Beth folded her arms and leaned against one of the half-empty racks as Matthew explained. "No, my dad didn't tell me," Matthew said quietly. "I overheard him relating the story to Father O'Reilly after Mass one day. I guess that was after you quit going to church."

Matthew never missed an opportunity to mention the church to Beth. She had given up going to Mass more than a year earlier. Her parents were immensely disappointed, but they accepted her decision. It wasn't that she didn't believe the scriptures, she explained to them; she just couldn't handle the repetition and rules. But Matthew, now an altar boy, thrived on the practices of the church, and, like her parents, he didn't understand why she stayed away.

"What else did Uncle Dimitri say about Grandma?"

Matthew paused and watched a squirrel cross the sidewalk and run up the large oak tree. "Nothing really, only…"

"Dammit, Matthew, tell me. She was my grandmother too."

Tersely, Matthew replied, "I was going to say—before you interrupted and swore at me—that I didn't hear what else my dad said because he began whispering to Father O'Reilly at that point. Later, when I asked him about it, he told me I shouldn't eavesdrop on other people's conversations, and that was it."

"Why didn't you tell me about this sooner?"

"My dad told me it was up to your dad to tell you. So please don't be mad at me; I'll be in trouble enough at home for spilling the beans."

The Grandview High School band was getting ready for state competition and the band director had scheduled a two-hour practice that afternoon. Unable to keep her mind on her music, Beth missed several notes on her clarinet during the practice. Ghastly images of what she had seen in the filmstrip in history class loomed in her head. If Matthew was right, her own grandmother might have been one of those prisoners she had seen on the screen, or worse, been one of the corpses.

After practice Beth left the band hall through the back entrance, avoiding her classmates, who typically stopped to chat outside the front door of the building. Walking briskly down Elm Street, she dodged several youngsters playing hopscotch and took a shortcut through the alley between Alice's Café and the John Deere parking lot, arriving home on Locust Street just before dusk.

In the kitchen, the evening news blared through static from an old Bakelite radio next to the stove, where her mother was wiping up spots of splattered tomato sauce from a pot of chicken cacciatore.

"Hello, honey, how was school?" Margaret Karmazin asked cheerfully.

"Fine, Mom, fine," Beth responded anxiously. "Where's Dad?"

Beth knew he was home from work. She had seen his white pickup in the drive as she was coming up the walk. Her mother wiped her hands on her apron, and reached over to tune the radio.

"In the den, dear, reading. Did you—?"

Beth had already started toward the den before her mother could finish her question. But on the way she was compelled to stop and look in the hallway mirror. What she saw was not the same person who had looked back at her that morning before school. *My God! My face, my hair. Matthew was right—I do look like a Gypsy.*

Beth found her father, Karl, sitting in the same overstuffed chair that had been his favorite as long as she could remember, all the way back to the family's first house on Arnold Street. The evening paper, proclaiming dismal news about casualties in Vietnam, lay disheveled on the floor beside the chair, and the smell of pipe tobacco permeated the room, a smell that had annoyed Beth when she was younger, but which she had eventually come to associate fondly with her father's presence. Quiet classical music came from the record player behind the recliner. Beth stopped and kicked off her sandals before she stepped onto the beige carpet, but she didn't bother to excuse herself before interrupting her father's reading.

"Dad, was Grandma a Gypsy?" she asked breathlessly.

Karl's skin paled. He lowered the journal he was reading and looked up over the top of his glasses. "Where did you hear that?"

"Matthew. Is it true?"

Karl caught his daughter in an unflinching gaze and stroked the faded rectangular scar on his left cheekbone. "It is true," he replied.

Beth dug her toes into the plush carpet and met her father's eyes. "And was she sent to a concentration camp?"

Karl sighed and ran his fingers through his sandy hair. His face tensed. "Yes, she was."

"Why didn't you tell me? Look at me; I even look like a Gypsy. You told me Grandma got sick and died. Didn't I have a right to know the truth?"

Karl leaned forward and flipped his glasses onto the end table. There was a spark of anger in his hazel eyes. With a Polish inflection that became more pronounced when his emotions were inflamed, he responded, "This isn't about rights, Beth Ann, it's about tragedy and death."

"But—"

Karl interrupted. "Listen to me. I told you a long time ago your grandmother died during the war, and that is the truth. There is nothing more to discuss."

Beth watched silently as her father rose and stalked out of the room. She didn't understand. She was the one who should be angry. She had been lied to. Well, perhaps her father hadn't exactly lied to her, but he hadn't exactly told her the truth either. And why not? Was he ashamed of his Gypsy heritage? How could he be ashamed of his own mother?

Beth wasn't used to her father being angry with her. She fought back tears as she put on her sandals and trudged into the kitchen, where her mother was putting a tin of cornbread into the oven. "Mom, why didn't you and Dad tell me Grandma Karmazin was a Gypsy?"

Margaret Karmazin turned, her eyes wide with surprise, as she looked at her oldest daughter. Then she responded tenderly, wrapping her arms around Beth. "Oh, honey, we were only trying to protect you."

"From what? The truth?" Beth asked as she felt her mother's embrace.

"No, we wanted to protect you from carrying a burden you didn't need to carry, from a story so horrible that you might become angry with the world. We just wanted you to be happy. That's what parents want for their children."

Beth knew she was lucky to have two loving parents, but Karl and Margaret didn't realize they couldn't completely shield Beth from the world. They couldn't protect Beth from the way kids had made fun of her when she was younger, calling her "Injun" or "Darkie." And they couldn't protect Beth from other parents who sometimes looked at her quizzically when she went to a classmate's birthday party, or from her boyfriend's sister, who asked what country she was from.

Beth pulled away from her mother's arms. "Mom, tell me about Grandma."

Margaret sighed as she motioned for her daughter to sit down at the kitchen table and pulled up a chair across from her.

"I never met your Grandmother Karmazin, but this is what your father told me. Your dad's mother, Sasha Lacatus, was a full-blooded Gypsy, born at a Gypsy camp in eastern Poland. Your dad's father, Henryk Karmazin, was a Polish citizen from the small city of Lublin, Poland, where your grandmother's clan often came to sell their crafts. They met in the town square and after a short courtship were married and moved to Warsaw, where your father and your Uncle Dimitri were born. So, your father is half Gypsy and you and your sisters are one-quarter Gypsy."

Margaret smiled. "But this is America. Everybody is a little bit of something or other—Swedish, German, Czech—it doesn't matter really, we're all the same inside …"

Beth was annoyed. She swore her mother could hum her way through a tornado. She had the damndest way of trying to make everything seem just fine when it wasn't. She supposed this quality gave Margaret strength during tough times, but right now it irritated the hell out of Beth. "But my friends here in Grandview don't have dark skin and they're not Gypsies. Gypsies are different, Mom; you can't tell me they aren't. How did Grandma die?"

Margaret bit her lip and looked away before replying, obviously unhappy that Beth had asked the question. "When Heinrich Himmler, the commander of the German SS and Gestapo, ordered the deportation of Europe's Gypsies to camps under German occupation, your grandmother was arrested and taken to Auschwitz. We don't know exactly how she died, only that she died at Auschwitz. There's no way to know for sure what caused her death."

"Then how do you know she's dead?" Beth asked, moving forward in her chair.

"Listen, Beth, there were twenty-three thousand Gypsies sent to Auschwitz, and when the camp was liberated by the Russians, only a few sick Gypsies remained alive, and your grandmother was not among them."

"So she was sent to this camp just because she was a Gypsy. Didn't Dad want to kill the Nazi bastards?"

Margaret flushed. "Beth, don't talk that way in this house."

"I'm sorry, Mom," Beth responded contritely, wishing she hadn't used that word. Beth knew Margaret hated to hear her swear.

"Of course your father had those thoughts, over and over. After the war, your father wanted to see every last Nazi dead, hung until they turned blue in the face, but he couldn't live his life obsessed with such a thing. Justice has to be done according to the law. You know that."

"But how do you know justice was done for Grandma when you don't even know what happened to her? You can't even be sure she's dead. Maybe she escaped; maybe—"

Margaret tossed her hot pad on the table, exasperated, and turned and looked hard into Beth's face, intending this to be her last word on the subject. "She's gone, like millions of others who went to the camps, and nothing will bring her back."

Beth responded with yet another question. "Matthew said Uncle Dimitri whispered something about Grandma to Father O'Reilly, but when Matthew asked his father about it, he wouldn't give him an answer. Is there something else about Grandma that Dad and Uncle Dimitri aren't telling?"

Margaret rose from the table and moved toward the refrigerator, saying nothing.

"There is something; isn't there?" Beth pressed.

Margaret didn't turn around. "Let things be, Beth. Just let them be," she said with finality.

First it was her father, now her mother was shutting her out. Beth picked up her books from the table and stalked out of the kitchen and up to her bedroom.

At dinner later that evening, Beth was quiet. She closely observed her two younger sisters as she had observed Matthew earlier that day. Ellen and Lilly were brunettes with light skin; Ellen, the older of the two, had blue eyes like her mother, while Lilly's eyes were hazel, like Karl's. Neither looked Gypsy, Beth thought. The only obvious physical features that bonded the three sisters were their high cheekbones and straight noses.

Ellen and Lilly's prattle over the dinner table seemed like nonsense to Beth, compared to the thoughts she had spinning around in her own head. Lilly whined over not selling her quota of Girl Scout cookies, while Ellen effusively described the dress she was going to wear to the sophomore dance. Beth couldn't handle it. Before dessert, she pushed her plate away and told her mother she would be back later to dry the dishes. Then, grabbing her iced tea from the table, she left the dining room and went out to the back patio.

Aside from the occasional chirping of a cricket and the low rumble of a coal train in the near distance, Beth was glad to be away from the noise at the dinner table. Still, she couldn't relax; she paced the patio until abruptly the screen door opened and her mother stepped out.

"Beth, are you okay, dear?" she asked gently.

Beth glanced down at her long bronze-colored arms, and then looked back up. Her eyes burning with passion, and her voice resolute, she answered her mother, "Maybe you and Dad can forget about Grandma Sasha, Mom, but I can't. I will never forget. Someday I will find out what happened to her."

CHAPTER TWO

Warsaw, Poland
February 1943

Seventy-year-old Jan Karmazin banged his cane on the back door of Karmazin Watch Repair. Jan had slipped away from his tailoring work that morning to see his nephew Henryk Karmazin, to try to talk some sense into him, make him understand that he had to act quickly. Jan, a widower and childless, no longer cared so much for his own life, but he was determined to save his nephew and his nephew's family. He and Henryk had been close since Henryk was a young boy and more so since the early death of Jan's brother, Buk; Henryk's father. Jan prayed his nephew would hear him out today and move quickly.

Receiving no response to his banging, Jan used a key Henryk had given him years ago and let himself into the shop. Clutching Warsaw's dissident newspaper in one hand and his cane in the other, he hobbled into the work area, where he found Henryk hunched over his worktable peering through a heavy magnifying glass at a disassembled watch, his lunch of cold pierogi and sauerkraut sitting half-eaten on the bench beside him.

Without looking up, Henryk greeted Jan with a nod of the head. "*Dzie_ dobry*. Good morning, Jan. I recognized your knock; must be something about your cane. Out for a stroll?"

Jan was annoyed by Henryk's question. How could Henryk be so ambivalent about what was happening around him, or was this his nephew's idea of a joke? *Lapankas*, Gestapo dragnets, were conducted regularly now in Warsaw. One might be walking anywhere, perhaps to see a friend or neighbor, when suddenly the street was closed and the Gestapo was on all sides asking for papers. If you couldn't prove that you were working to support the German war effort, you were arrested and shipped to a labor camp.

"Come on, Henryk, when was the last time anyone in this city felt safe enough for a stroll? I brought a watch with me."

Henryk spoke as he continued looking down at his work. "Sorry, Jan, I won't be able to get to it until this afternoon; it's the damn Nazis, you know. Seems there is no end to this. But I promise I'll squeeze it in as soon as I can."

"I don't want the watch fixed. I brought it, should some Nazi pig question what I am doing here."

"So you have come for a visit?" Henryk asked, setting his magnifying glass down on the table and picking up his narrow half-rimmed glasses.

"Not exactly. I have advised you of this before, Henryk, but now I have come to plead with you. You must get Sasha and the boys out of here. Look at this." Jan tossed the underground newspaper onto Henryk's worktable.

Henryk grimaced and pulled a flop of his chestnut-colored hair away from his brow as he glanced at the headline: "Fourth transport of Gypsies made from Lublin to Auschwitz."

"Soon they will be rounding them up here in Warsaw, Henryk," Jan said harshly, waving his hands in the air.

Henryk put his finger to his lips. "Jan, please, lower your voice and sit down. Let's talk—quietly."

A frustrated Jan acquiesced and shuffled to the stool across from Henryk's worktable. "You must get your family out of here while you still can," Jan continued. "They are doomed if they stay here. Your brother Manny can help, he has connections. Do it before it's too late; Poland is no place for a Gypsy wife and two half-Gypsy children."

Henryk removed his glasses and rubbed his tired grey eyes. He knew there was truth in what Jan said. Since the German invasion in 1939, hundreds of thousands of Poles had been executed as political prisoners or had died of starvation or disease. But it wasn't just the Poles. The German policy had targeted Jews and the Gypsies as well, with the clear intention of enslaving or exterminating both populations. In the summer of 1942, Heinrich Himmler, the commander of the German Schutzstaffel, or SS, as it was commonly referred to, and the Gestapo, the secret police, had ordered all Gypsies in countries under Nazi occupation to be relocated to ghettos. In December of 1942, just two months earlier, the mass deportation of the Gypsies to concentration camps had begun. Yet Henryk refused to believe Sasha was in danger.

"Jan, you're overreacting; Sasha never registered with the Gypsy Center and she has no birth certificate. She is safer here in Warsaw disguised as a Polish housewife than she would be anywhere else. All we have to do is survive the war. It will be over soon."

"I wouldn't be so sure of that. Keep reading." Jan pointed to another headline at the top of the newspaper: "Russian offensive slowed by early thaw. Troops and supplies stymied by gorging rivers on Eastern Front."

"This war is a long way from over, nephew. God forbid that I would ever hope for the Russians to come, but if they don't get here soon, who will save us?"

Abruptly Henryk grabbed Jan's arm and put a finger to his lips. Jan's gaze followed Henryk's to the window and out to the street. Two black-booted Nazi soldiers on patrol passed down the cobblestone street of the Stare Miesto, the old town of Warsaw. In the previous few weeks, this had been a more frequent occurrence. There were rumors of an uprising brewing in the ghetto, and the Nazis were responding with vigilance.

When the soldiers were out of sight, Jan and Henryk breathed easier. *How could things have come to this?* Henryk asked himself as he rose from his bench to get coffee for Jan and himself. He had known eighteen years ago that marrying a Gypsy wife would pose complications, but he had never imagined this. His parents were furious when he announced his intention to marry Sasha. "No one will accept this union," his father had said. "Not God or anyone. Your children will be criminals."

"Our grandchildren, our poor grandchildren, will be despised," his mother had wailed. This attitude toward Gypsies had been prevalent across Europe for centuries, but the Nazi policy was different; it was more than discrimination or even persecution, it was mass extermination; the plan of men gone mad.

Henryk couldn't bear the thought of losing Sasha. He had fallen in love with her the first time he saw her. She was eighteen; Henryk was twenty-four. It was unusual for a Gypsy girl to be single at eighteen. Most Gypsy girls married much younger, to boys chosen for them by their families, but Sasha had refused every boy her parents had tried to match her with. He had seen her one Saturday, standing on the back of a Gypsy wagon on the street in Lublin, holding up for sale a watercolor of wildflowers she had painted. Henryk was struck by Sasha's beauty: her dark flashing eyes, her dazzling smile, and her black hair whipping in the wind. She wanted more money for the painting than Henryk had ever spent at the market. He bargained with her just to have an excuse to talk to her, but she refused to bring the price down, so Henryk finally agreed to the price she asked, with one condition—that she meet him for coffee that afternoon.

Three months later Henryk proposed marriage to Sasha, and she accepted. Henryk's parents warned him that he would never be able to tame Sasha's wild side, that their children would be ostracized in conservative Warsaw. Sasha's family was no happier than Henryk's. They insisted Sasha's spirit would die if she tried to live the life of an ordinary Polish housewife and Mar Dep, the Shero Rom, king of the Keldari Gypsies, banned Sasha from her clan. Marriage between Gypsies and *Gadje*, or non-Gypsies, was forbidden by tradition.

Both Henryk's parents and Sasha's refused to attend the wedding, and the parish priest refused to marry Henryk and Sasha, forcing Henryk to leave the church until years later when a new priest was seated in the parish. Henryk and Sasha wed in a civil ceremony at the Warsaw town hall, with only the mayor and his secretary as their witnesses.

Henryk stared into his coffee. "Jan, I can't send Sasha away. I love her; she is my life, the air that I breathe. I can't live without her. And my boys? They are my own flesh and blood. How can you ask me to do this?"

Jan looked sympathetically at his hardheaded nephew. He knew how much Henryk loved his family. Yet it was time for Henryk to think with his head rather than his heart. "I am telling you—"

Before Jan could finish, the front door rattled, and two young German soldiers entered the shop. Jan grabbed the underground newspaper and threw it under the table. *"Heil Hitler,"* the men in the uniforms announced, raising their arms stiffly and approaching Henryk's workbench.

"Ja," Henryk responded as he stood, squaring his shoulders and swallowing the trepidation that tightened his throat.

Jan found his cane and struggled from his stool to stand also. Under occupation rules, the Poles were not required to salute Hitler, but they were required to stand in the presence of a German soldier. The foot soldiers of the Third Reich were barely more than children now, conscripts from the eastern provinces who had no great love for the Fuehrer. Yet they had been schooled in an enemy mentality and had been taught contempt for Poles. These men, young and inexperienced as they were, were still to be feared.

"My watch needs repair," the younger soldier said in German, tapping his wrist with his index finger. He stepped closer and his face came into focus beneath Henryk's powerful overhead lamp. The soldier couldn't have been more than seventeen years old. He was fair-skinned with a splash of freckles across his nose, and his soft downy cheeks appeared untouched by a razor.

The other soldier appeared to be a little older, probably in his early twenties, with dark hair, heavy eyebrows and pockmarked skin. Both men carried rifles and wore Wehrmacht uniforms with gleaming swastikas pinned to the front of their oversized jackets.

"Armbanduhr. Kaputt," the younger soldier said simply, again tapping his watch. Henryk had learned German in the years since the invasion, but he pretended to understand nothing beyond a few basic words. He found that this feigned ignorance gave him a tactical advantage. He could listen for strategic information and later pass it on to the intelligence wing of the Polish Resistance.

"Ja," Henryk said again, motioning for the soldier's watch.

The young man removed the watch and handed it across the worktable. Henryk held it up to the lamp and looked at it beneath his powerful magnifying glass, turning it so that he could see it at various angles until he found the problem. The glass over the watch face had cracked, and a shard was pressed against the watch hands, stopping them precisely at ten minutes to one. It would be a simple repair, taking five minutes at the most, but Henryk didn't tell the soldiers this; he chose to stall. He wanted the two young men to linger in his shop and talk, so that he might eavesdrop on their conversation.

As Henryk removed the watch's back with a tiny screwdriver and pretended to explore the watch's inner workings, the two soldiers walked around the shop, surveying the crowded shelves and peering into the locked glass cases. They admired a six-foot-tall grandfather clock which Henryk had just returned to its nineteenth-century glory, a job that had taken him several months.

Henryk listened closely to the soldiers' casual conversation. Their accents were heavy and guttural, and they spoke hurriedly, making the discussion difficult for Henryk to follow. Even so, Henryk was able to pick up a few key words and phrases—*troops were moving to the north along the Vistula River, and east toward Bialystok, a big push of at least ten thousand soldiers, and these two among them. Movement would begin Thursday.*

Henryk's hands trembled at this news; since the German retreat from Stalingrad, the Poles had been counting on the Russians to oust the Germans from Poland. He took a deep breath and tried to still his insides, then he looked up at the soldiers. *"Wann …?"* he intentionally stumbled, pretending to search for the correct words. *"Wann brauchen Sie die armbanduhr?* When do you need the watch? *Sroda?"* he used the Polish word for Wednesday.

"Mittwoch!" the soldier said curtly. Wednesday.

Henryk nodded. This seemed to confirm what he had overheard, that the "big push" would happen on Thursday. Henryk set the watch aside, turned to his rolltop desk behind the front counter and typed up the work order on his aged typewriter. The soldier signed his name at the bottom, *Leutnant Detlev Niemann*, in a loose, flowery hand. Henryk took the paper and nodded.

"Danke schoen, Herr Leutnant Niemann," he said evenly, tearing off the carbon sheet and handing the bottom copy to Niemann, who folded it neatly and placed it in his breast pocket. *"Kommen Sie zuruck …"* Henryk pointed to the date in the middle of the calendar week. *"Sroda. Mittwoch."*

On the way to the door Niemann glanced over at Jan, who was still standing near the stool with the watch in his hand that he had brought into the shop with him. He pretended to be waiting for help. Niemann nodded to him and said, "Your turn now, old man, and you had better hurry. You don't look like you have much time left." Then both soldiers laughed derisively and walked out, slamming the door behind them.

When the soldiers were gone, Jan let out the deep breath he seemed to have been holding since the soldiers' arrival. Color quickly returned to his pale, withered cheeks. "What did they say?" he asked Henryk anxiously.

"I guess they didn't get enough of a beating at Stalingrad. They said they are launching a counteroffensive along the great rivers to the east." Henryk paused. "I must alert the Armia Krajowa. They will get word to the Red Army on the other side of the Vistula."

That evening in their apartment above the shop, Henryk Karmazin shared supper with Sasha and their sons, seventeen-year-old Karl and sixteen-year-old Dimitri. In spite of food rationing, Sasha had managed to prepare a filling meal of beetroot broth with dumplings and a side dish of one sliced hard-boiled egg. Karl watched with a mixture of sadness and pride as his two hearty sons slurped down their broth and wagered for the largest slice of egg.

To this point the Karmazins had been one of the luckier families in Warsaw: lucky to be alive and still living in their home. The Germans had deported or executed virtually all of Warsaw's teachers, religious leaders, professionals, and intellectuals, but many of the city's merchants and craftsmen were deemed essential support to the Third Reich, and they were allowed to live and continue working. For once, Henryk was grateful he didn't have an advanced education; he had a skill that the Germans needed, and it allowed him to put food on the table.

The family ate by candlelight, using their limited electricity to run the small black-market radio perched on the corner of the dining room table. The curtains were drawn and the radio turned low, tuned into the BBC World Service broadcast from London. Sasha was one of a small percentage of literate Gypsies. She was adept at languages; she listened to the radio whenever she thought it was safe and learned English in this way, while Henryk and the boys learned the language late at night with textbooks bartered for on the black market.

The news that evening was not good; the British RAF had temporarily halted its air strikes against Germany due to the heavy losses of RAF planes and pilots. Henryk feared for his sons. Soon Karl would reach the age of conscription in Poland, and Dimitri was only a year behind—they were potential recruits for the Armia Krajowa, Poland's underground army. Henryk had dreamt of college for the boys. He had put money away for it, never imagining his children might instead go to war.

Sasha and the boys were still eating when Henryk excused himself from the table. "I'm sorry, I have to go." Sasha rose to see him to the door while motioning for the boys to stay seated.

"Do you really have to go?" she asked, her voice shaking. "It has been such a short time since you saw the doctor and he warned you about putting strain on your heart. These meetings are stressful and dangerous, Henryk. I would be lost without you."

Henryk put his hand on his wife's waist and bent to kiss her. She was a tall woman at five-foot-eight, but at six-foot-three Henryk still towered over her. He gazed into her deep, dark eyes that reflected the flickering candlelight, while he stroked her hair gently. Sasha's hair had been her pride. Before the occupation it had been long and luxuriously black. Now, to hide her Gypsy heritage, she had cut it to shoulder length, and bleached it to a drab chestnut brown. She had changed her way of dressing too. Her long colorful skirts, fitted jackets, and gold jewelry had been replaced by sturdy white blouses, thickly knit cardigan sweaters, and shapeless boiled wool skirts in plain earthen colors. When she left the apartment, which wasn't often, she wore a common babushka and no jewelry beyond her plain gold wedding band. Her naturally bronze-toned skin had paled from lack of sunlight and poor nutrition. No one who saw her now would think she was anything other than the ordinary Polish housewife her parents so feared she would become.

Henryk missed what had been his beautiful Gypsy wife, but it was more than Sasha's physical beauty that Henryk missed: it was her spontaneity, her passion, and her spirit, all of which had been dulled by endless enemy restrictions and fears for her family.

Sasha held tight to her husband as they kissed tenderly. This moment of intimacy did not pass unnoticed by Karl and Dimitri. The boys shot each other knowing glances. They liked the fact that their parents were different. Most of their friends' parents were dour and undemonstrative. Henryk himself had come from such a family, but fortunately for the boys, Sasha had freed him from his reserve.

"Henryk, be careful tonight," Sasha implored him. "You said two soldiers visited the shop this afternoon. They may be suspicious."

"Those two today were just children. There is nothing to fear from them."

"If anything happened to you … and me, a Gypsy? Who would protect the boys?"

Henryk gently pushed Sasha away and grabbed his coat and hat from the wooden peg beside the door. "I have to go tonight. I have information that must be passed to the AK as soon as possible."

Henryk had started down the steps, when he was possessed to return to the warmth of the apartment. He went to his sons and placed a hand on Karl's shoulder, while tousling young Dimitri's curly hair. "Don't stay up late boys; chores start early tomorrow."

Later that evening Karl and Dimitri brought out their schoolbooks, which, except for evenings when they were using them, were kept hidden under oak planks in the floor of Karl's bedroom. The Nazis had forbidden education in Poland; schools, universities, and libraries were closed soon after the invasion. Schooling was determined by the Nazis to be a waste of time for the inferior minds of the Poles, never mind that Poland had produced many of the world's greatest artists, musicians, and scientists.

Like many parents, however, Henryk and Sasha allowed their children to continue their studies behind closed doors. Tonight, as with every other night since the occupation began, Sasha cleared the table so that the boys could spread out their books, then she went to the sink and began cleaning the dishes with bar soap and cold water. When she had dried them and put them away, she pulled out the broom, and as she swept the floor she absentmindedly began humming the tune of an old Gypsy song.

Dimitri looked up from his books. "Mama," he asked, "would you sing that song for us? I haven't heard you sing for such a long time."

Sasha faced the table as a stern Karl warned his brother, "You know it's a Gypsy song; it's dangerous for her to sing it."

"It seems like we can't do anything anymore," Dimitri complained. "Sometimes I just don't care. I hate the damned Nazis. Sing it; please Mama, just once."

Dimitri's dark eyes were huge and pleading in the low light and Sasha's heart melted. While Karl was tall and fair, Dimitri was olive-skinned with a head of light brown curls. He reminded Sasha of her beloved brother, Stefan. She could never tell Dimitri no.

"Very well then, just one song," Sasha relented. "Then you boys must finish your studying and go to bed."

Sasha cleared her throat, hummed a few notes, and then began to sing softly in a sweet, melodic voice. *"Prohasar man opre pirende, sa muro djiben semas opre chengende …"*

The boys did not speak the Gypsy language, but they understood the words to this Gypsy lament, having heard it many times. At the end of the second verse they chimed in, "Bury me standing, I've been on my knees all my life …"

Suddenly Sasha's voice caught in her throat and she stopped singing. "What was that?" she asked in a whisper.

Dimitri was confused. "What?"

"That noise."

The three of them held their breaths. In the distance, moving closer, was the precise clip-clop of hobnailed boots. A cold chill ran up Sasha's spine as she listened to the eerie pings striking the ancient, uneven cobblestones of the Stare Miesto.

As the sound of the boots came closer, Sasha could hear voices, but the soldiers were talking too low for her to distinguish their words. She could only hear the language's sharp echo. The Gestapo and SS were on the street more often now, routing out Jews to be deported and Poles who were suspected of anti-fascist activity. Their presence was terrifying. Abruptly, the sound of the boots stopped.

"Mama?" Dimitri asked.

"Shush," Sasha said, pressing a finger to her lip. Sweat beaded her forehead, and adrenalin shot through her body. It seemed a lifetime before the soldiers once again began their marching and the danger passed.

"That was too close," Sasha said when they were out of earshot. Then, wiping her brow with a dishtowel, she continued. "I won't do that again. I can't sing, Dimitri; it's too dangerous for all of us." She heard the rough edge in her voice, and she didn't like it, but Dimitri had to understand the jeopardy that singing placed them in. A German soldier hearing a Gypsy song would ruthlessly track down those persons giving voice to it. Perhaps they had heard the singing, Sasha thought with a start. Perhaps they would come back later. Silently she vowed never again to be so careless.

Klaus Broza brooded over his situation as he wiped down the counters of his shop, *Broza Sklep Miesny*, a small family butchery in Stare Miesto, just a block from Henryk Karmazin's watch repair shop. It was nine o'clock in the evening. He had worked later than usual.

Hans Frank, the German governor-general of the occupied areas of Poland, had come in unexpectedly from his headquarters at Krakow that day and sent an attaché to the butchery demanding ten orders of venison be cut for cooking by eight o'clock that evening. Klaus had just made the deadline. He had taken care of the bastard Nazis, while in the back of the shop his sixteen-year-old son lay critically ill with pneumonia. Klaus and his wife Eva were filled with worry over him. Eva said he would die by the end of the week without some kind of miracle. But Klaus didn't believe in miracles. What the boy needed was penicillin, and that was almost impossible to come by these days in Warsaw. Klaus could not afford the black market prices for it, and the only ones who had free access to the drug were the Germans. However, for something of value, like the right information, a German soldier might be bribed.

As Klaus opened the front door of his shop to sweep the step, he gazed up Mokotow Street to his friend Henryk's watch repair shop. He had known Henryk and Sasha Karmazin since he had moved to Warsaw. They were friends: they had taken communion together for years, and their sons had gone to school together. Klaus could not believe he was thinking of betraying Henryk, but Klaus's son was dying, and there was money in turning over Gypsies to the Gestapo.

Henryk had never admitted to Klaus that his wife was Gypsy, but when Klaus had asked him one day, Henryk had not denied it. It had been obvious to Klaus from the beginning that Sasha was not Slavic. Her dark coloring, her mannerisms, and her accent were Gypsy. Also, Klaus had seen her in the town square talking to Emil Dep, the son of one of the Gypsy kings. No married Polish woman would speak to a Gypsy. Now Klaus pondered as he swept the step. *Which was of greater value—the life of a Gypsy woman or the life of a strong, young Polish boy?* When he went back into the shop he found his Eva standing near the cash register, weeping. Dark circles lined her eyes; she had not slept in days.

"He is delirious, Klaus, and burning up with fever. I can't bear it." Eva's weeping now turned to sobbing as she threw herself on the century-old sofa in the entryway.

Klaus walked past her to the back of the shop and returned with his cap and jacket.

Eva raised her head and sniffling into her handkerchief asked, "What are you going to do?"

"I am going to do the only thing I can do," Klaus replied solemnly, his brow furrowed under his bushy, gray-white hair. Then, grabbing his wool cap, Klaus opened the door and stepped out onto the street.

Karl and Sasha were alone in the apartment above Henryk's shop. Dimitri had gone with Henryk to deliver the repaired antique grandfather clock to a once-wealthy family on the other side of Warsaw. Travel such as this was risky. If the Germans stopped them, they would confiscate the clock, and it would undoubtedly end up in some German officer's billet. And it was impossible for Henryk to know how he and his son might be punished for their effort to deliver the clock to a Polish citizen. While Henryk and Dimitri would have committed no crime under the current laws of the occupation, Henryk had learned long ago that Nazi decrees were changed on the spot and new ones concocted every day. But Henryk needed the money, so he had committed to making the trip.

Karl was at the kitchen table repairing a broken wing on Dimitri's model airplane, while Sasha was hanging drapes that she had fashioned from surplus fabric bartered for on the black market. They would be less transparent then the lace that had covered the windows since before the occupation.

It had been a quiet afternoon, and Sasha was feeling relaxed, when suddenly the door rattled in the shop below. A few seconds later, there was a loud crash as the locked door gave way to the intruders. "Karl—run–leave out the back door!" Sasha whispered roughly.

But Karl was too proud to scamper away like a frightened child, and he wouldn't think of leaving his mother alone with Nazis. A second later, the sound of heavy steps coming up the old wooden stairs was followed by another crash as the door to the apartment flew open, and in rushed two Nazi officers. "Sasha Karmazin," one barked in a deep voice.

"Yes," Sasha said, nodding slowly.

One of the officers rushed toward her, grabbing her arm and pulling her away from the half-hung curtain. *"Komm mit uns."*

Karl stood up and tried to grab the other officer's arm. "No!" he screamed. "Leave her alone, Nazi *Schweinhund.*" Karl spat on the man's uniform, and the man reacted quickly, thrusting the butt of his rifle into Karl's face, hitting him beneath the eye and knocking him to the floor.

Splayed on the ground, his head throbbing, Karl held a hand to his face, and felt the warm trickle of blood seeping between his fingers. "Mama!" he screamed, watching as the soldiers pulled Sasha toward the door. When she didn't move quickly enough, one of the soldiers grabbed her by the back of the neck and pushed her forward, breaking her gold necklace. The thin chain slithered to the floor, while the jeweled gold cross, made by Sasha's father, landed beside the table leg.

"Karl, stay away!" As the soldiers pulled her toward the door she grabbed the doorframe, digging into it with her fingernails, but her struggle was useless.

"Let her go! Let my mother go!" Karl cried, reaching out to grab his mother's hand. One of the Nazi soldiers kicked Karl in the stomach, doubling him over in pain and knocking the air out of his lungs. When he was able to breathe again, he heard his mother's cries moving down the staircase. He looked up at the open, empty doorway and feared that he would never see her again. He crawled a few inches, still struggling for breath. Reaching his mother's golden cross on the floor, he curled his fingers around it, picked it up, and cradled it tightly to his quivering chest.

CHAPTER THREE

Warsaw, 1943

Henryk was frantic and filled with remorse. He had gone to the Gestapo station and been told there was no news regarding Sasha, beyond her arrest, and when he persisted with questions, he had been spat upon and thrown out. His contacts in the Armia Krajowa had turned up nothing. Unfortunately, their intelligence was limited to military and political movements; they had little information on individuals.

Henryk had one last hope. While most of the Gypsies in and around Warsaw had been deported or gone into hiding, a few troupes of Gypsy musicians continued to entertain the Nazis in exchange for their freedom. These Gypsies would listen in on Nazi conversations and sometimes, with enough vodka, soldiers would divulge information about specific Gypsy prisoners and prisoner transports.

Emil Dep, the son of Mar Dep, king of the Keldari, was a violinist who regularly played at a Nazi club on the edge of Stare Miesto. After these engagements, he hung out at the Taverna Cava and partied with some of the disreputable locals. This bar was located below street level in the underbowels of the city and was either unknown to, or ignored by, the Gestapo. Henryk had to go there. Emil might have heard something about Sasha.

As Henryk prepared to leave his apartment, he thought of what he knew about Emil. Sasha had never liked him. Emil professed to follow the strictest standards of Gypsy tradition. In fact, it was said that when in the presence of his father, he mimicked the king's behavior so expertly, one might have thought him a clone. But Mar Dep was well respected; Emil was not. Stories slipped out, even from the tight-lipped Keldari, that Emil Dep was not his father's clone by any means. Rumor said that he was cowardly, that he had a weakness for alcohol, and that he liked boys in a way that one should like girls. Before the occupation, he was often seen drunk and wielding a knife in the taverns, flanked by a couple of toughs from the settlement, who took care that Emil didn't get himself in so deep that he couldn't be dug out.

It was Emil's poor character that Henryk was counting on tonight. It was midnight Saturday, and if Emil were true to form he would be hanging out with his bawdy friends at the Taverna Cava, where Henryk hopefully could elicit information from him about Sasha.

Under protest, Henryk sent Karl and Dimitri to his brother Manny's for the evening. He then placed his identification in his breast pocket and retrieved a pocket watch from his work cabinet, so that if he were stopped by the Gestapo or soldiers on patrol questioning why he was out after curfew, he could say that he was attempting to deliver a repaired watch to someone who hadn't shown up. It was a very feeble excuse, but Henryk was willing to try anything—he had to get Sasha back.

Henryk bundled warmly and slipped out into the bitterly cold night. The city was dark; the electricity to the streetlights had been switched off for three years. Still, a spattering of candles and oil lamps burned in some of the windows, possibly illuminating a person trudging the icy streets alone. Not wanting to be seen, Henryk hugged the walls of the concrete and half-timber buildings as he made his way through the Old Town.

He was only a block from the Taverna Cava when he heard voices. He jumped into a window well and scrunched down as far as he could. When he was sure they hadn't seen him, he peered out to see where the voices were coming from. Two German soldiers, on either side of a civilian man, were coming up the stairs of the tavern. "*Raus, schnell*—Move, fast," one of the officers yelled as he pushed the man across the street and into a jeep.

Henryk ducked down again as the driver turned on the headlights. But this time Henryk's foot went out from under him and he kicked the well, making a rough noise. The jeep crept forward; just short of the window well, it stopped. Henryk held his breath; his heart thumped so loud he was sure the soldiers would hear it. A flashlight slowly panned the building above his head, and then finally went off. Henryk didn't look out again until he was sure the jeep was well down the road, and then he took a deep breath, and lifted himself to the sidewalk.

After answering several questions through a hole in the door, Henryk was allowed to enter the tavern. "What are you doing out on the street at this time of the night?" the tavern keeper asked Henryk when he was securely inside. "It's after curfew, and the Nazis have just been here."

Henryk quickly scanned the room, and then nodded toward the bar. "Looks like I'm not the only one who has forgotten curfew."

The balding tavern owner replied gruffly, acknowledging the men at the bar, "Them? They come in before curfew and don't go home until morning, after curfew." Then, in a more friendly tone, he offered Henryk a drink. "Come, sit down, it's on the house."

Under the circumstances, Henryk knew he should not accept, but he was cold and tired, and a glass of vodka sounded good. He sat at a small table in the corner, away from the bar. The tavern owner brought the drink and asked again, "So, tell me now, why are you here?"

Henryk looked up at the large, heavy-jowled man. "I am looking for Emil Dep. Have you seen him?"

"Certainly I have. He just left, accompanied by two Nazi Gestapo officers."

Henryk's heart sank. "Where were they taking him?"

"I presume the station. Oh, you mean after that? I don't know. Maybe they just wanted information. They know Emil; they have talked to him before. Maybe this time they will send him away. He said they cleared the station and deported a large number of Gypsies yesterday, so maybe they will get what they want from him and send him out with the next bunch. I won't miss him; he was too much trouble. The good Gypsies go down the street, but me, I get Emil."

Henryk was motionless, paralyzed with fear. He could hardly get the words out to ask the next question. "Did Emil say where yesterday's train was going?"

"Yes, but I can't remember where," the tavern owner said, rubbing his forehead. "Let's see, was it Treblinka?"

"Think, man, think. Please. This is very important."

"Yes, it must be, for you to come here against the rules. Maybe it was …?"

Suddenly a very thin man with hollowed cheeks and a heavy scarf wrapped around his neck turned in his seat at the bar and faced Henryk. "It was Auschwitz."

"Yes, yes," the bar owner said, "That was it—Auschwitz."

Henryk's Uncle, Jan Karmazin, and Manny Karmazin, Henryk's brother, made their way down the alley to Karmazin's Watch Repair. It was just after six in the evening; a cold drizzle was changing to freezing rain. The blowing precipitation had persisted for days, augmenting the demoralized and tense mood of the oppressed city. Rumors of an uprising were rife; neighbor mistrusted neighbor. Food was scarce and medicine even scarcer. The citizens of Warsaw were terrified, exhausted, and running out of hope.

Using Manny's key to the back door, Jan and Manny entered the darkened watch repair shop and stood for a moment in the cold, stuffy air. Neither Jan nor Manny had seen Henryk since Sasha's arrest several days earlier. It was increasingly dangerous to be out on the streets. Fierce raids were occurring regularly. The Gestapo would round up a dozen citizens on minor charges and then execute them in a public forum just to show the Poles that they could kill anyone, anytime, for little or no reason. It was the insanity of a war without rules; of evil men without souls.

Slowly Jan and Manny ascended the steep and narrow steps leading to the apartment upstairs. At the top of the stairs they knocked, and hearing no response, pushed open the door to the Karmazins' apartment. Jan, hunched over with arthritis, passed through under the opening easily, while Manny's curly hair skimmed the archway.

"Henryk? Boys?" they called out, but received no answer.

The apartment was eerily silent. They paused for a moment to take in the modest living room with its sofa, two armchairs, and a coffee table. The room was orderly, suffering only from a light coat of dust. Then, through a set of French doors, Jan and Manny entered the dining room, a space much larger than most dining rooms. A box of yarn on the dining table sat beside Dimitri's model airplane, nearly complete, missing only a propeller. Atop a side table next to Henryk's easy chair sat Henryk's pipe and a pouch of tobacco.

It was a nostalgic scene. For years, after church, Jan and Manny had come to Henryk and Sasha's for Sunday dinner. Afterwards Jan, Manny, and Henryk would smoke in the living room and play cards, while Karl and Dimitri put together puzzles or studied at the dining room table. And Sasha, after cleaning the kitchen, would paint in the corner near the window, where she caught the light on sunny days. But that had all changed with the fall of Poland and the arrival of the Nazi police and soldiers. Now one took a chance even to visit family.

Manny and Jan checked the smaller bedroom shared by the boys and, finding it empty, proceeded down the hallway to Henryk and Sasha's bedroom. They knocked softly before opening the door.

At first glance this room also appeared empty. The curtains were pulled closed; pillows were piled in the middle of the bed; the air was stale. Jan and Manny strained to see in the darkened room. Then from a rocking chair in the corner of the room came a weak and scratchy but familiar voice asking, "What are you doing here?"

"It's me, Uncle Jan, and your brother, Manny." His voice was soft and soothing. "We've brought you something to eat."

Henryk Karmazin opened his swollen eyes and looked into the concerned faces of his brother and his uncle. "Manny, any news of Sasha?" he whispered anxiously, lips trembling.

Manny was forty-five; three years older than Henryk. He worked for the resistance as a messenger. Posing as a poor farmer, he carried clandestine information from unit to unit between Warsaw and Krakow. Occasionally, he heard stories from his compatriots about the fate of arrested citizens. But he had heard nothing of Sasha. He shook his head. "No, nothing."

Henryk closed his eyes, sinking back into the dark comfort of sleep. "Leave me be," he mumbled, pulling the threadbare blanket back up to his gray-stubbled chin.

Jan and Manny looked at each other, shaking their heads. Henryk was thin and clearly not taking care of his hygiene. He was unshaven and his body odor indicated he had not bathed in days. Jan questioned him about how the family was surviving. His response was grim. Henryk was out of money. He hadn't worked since Sasha's arrest. He hadn't completed any of his customers' orders, not even the Nazis', but they had been too busy on the front to harass him.

Finally Jan posed the question he had most dreaded asking since entering the apartment: "Where are Karl and Dimitri?" Jan had been sick with worry that the Nazis would come back for them once they confirmed that Sasha was a Gypsy.

"I don't know. They have been going out every night, without my permission."

"Henryk," Manny said, "you've got to get a hold of yourself. We can help you get out; I have contacts, but you have to act quickly. The Nazis will be back for the boys, and if you fight them, which you surely will, they will take you too."

Henryk's eyes filled with tears of anger and pain. "You are crazy. Don't you see? I can't leave without Sasha."

"Then send the boys away. You will find them after the war."

"But escape is no guarantee. I've lost my wife; I don't want to lose my boys. How many have we lost who tried to flee?"

"You are right," Manny replied gruffly, his hands on his hips as he grimaced at Henryk. "But if they stay here, they have no chance."

Suddenly there was noise at the foot of the stairs. Jan and Manny turned quickly, eyes widening. They feared it could be Nazi soldiers, or maybe someone who, passing by, had seen the darkened watch shop and decided to rob it. Manny slipped quietly out of the bedroom and to the staircase. Footsteps quietly inched up the stairs.

"Who goes there?" Manny asked in the strongest voice he could muster.

There was a pause, then a tentative question, "Uncle Manny?"

Manny broke into a smile. "Karl, Dimitri. Yes it's me and your Uncle Jan."

As the boys bounded up the stairs and into the apartment Manny took both boys into a warm embrace. "Where were you?" he asked, relieved to see them.

"We were out," Karl responded, breaking away from Manny and removing his cloth cap and his coat.

"Out doing what?" Jan asked, now joining the trio on the landing. "You shouldn't be on the streets after curfew."

Dimitri opened his mouth to answer, but Karl motioned him to be quiet. That was all right; Jan could guess where the boys had been: on the streets looking for food and firewood, trying to sell whatever they could from the apartment to get money.

Jan looked closely at his grandnephews and despaired. Karl was still nursing a black eye and the gash on his cheek where the cheekbone had been broken from the brute force of a Nazi rifle butt.

"Come to the dining room; we have brought you a loaf of rye bread and some cheese," Jan said as he dipped into his rough burlap bag. Both boys tore hungrily at the food and chewed quickly. When they had finished, Manny motioned Karl closer to the light. He tilted the boy's head back to get a better look at his cheek. When Manny touched the raised welt, Karl flinched. Manny suspected that the injury hurt worse than the boy was letting on, and he worried that infection might be setting in.

"Karl," Manny said gently. "Do you have some alcohol? We need to clean this wound."

"I'll be fine," Karl answered, clenching his jaw. "Have you heard anything about our mother?"

Karl had always been a serious boy and very dutiful, but with a friendly sparkle in his eyes. Now his manner was brusque; his eyes were hard.

"I'm afraid not," Manny replied. "But you shouldn't give up hope."

"Bastard Krauts," Karl said, anger seething out of his tall, thin body, while his eyes brimmed with hatred. Dimitri, in contrast, perhaps because he had been spared the horror of actually seeing his mother taken away, appeared more lost and confused than angry. He seemed to have reverted to a more childlike state, which had left him solemn and quiet.

"Boys, we have come to talk to you. You must go into hiding."

"Go into hiding! Never!" After several moments of bantering with his uncle and great-uncle, Karl brushed past them and headed toward his father's bedroom with Dimitri close behind.

Jan and Manny had no choice but to follow the boys, hoping for one last chance to convince a mentally fragile Henryk to flee the country with the boys. But as they stepped into the room, they were surprised; Henryk appeared from the bathroom, clean-shaven and in a fresh change of clothes. ➝

"Papa, you're up and—" Karl began, before he was interrupted by Henryk.

"Let me speak, Karl. I've been silent too long. Manny and Jan are right. You must leave; I want you to pack your bags tonight and be ready to go. I have some family gemstones and silver you can take to get cash. I'll join you later."

Karl didn't move. He stared at his father with incredulity.

Henryk's face tightened, and his eyes narrowed. "Karl, did you hear what I said? This is the best chance this family has. Now go, do what I say, and take care of your brother."

Sullenly, Karl turned, and taking Dimitri by the shoulder, left the bedroom.

Henryk had tried to be strong for the boys, but now, alone with Jan and Manny downstairs at the worktable in the watch repair shop, he held his head in his hands. "I can't believe this is happening. I'll never see my family again. We all know it. But if the boys survive, I guess they will have each other and that is better than nothing." Tears flowed down his cheeks and onto the table. Manny turned on the small oil lamp and offered him a drink from a bottle of Czech ale he had bought on the black market. They sat away from the front window to avoid detection by the Nazi foot patrol soldiers, who by this time of night would be winding their way back toward the center of Old Town.

Manny explained his plan for Karl and Dimitri. They would be hidden in Warsaw until they could be smuggled to Gdansk, where they would be given forged German papers, indicating that they had been assigned to work on a German freighter running from Gdansk to Sweden. Once in Sweden, the Swedish connection would take over and scuttle them off the boat. "They will then be given new identities. The boys will be safe in Sweden; it is a neutral county," Manny assured Henryk. "And when the time is right, our friends in Sweden will get the boys to London."

"Henryk," Manny asked, changing the subject, "the underground must know who deceived you, who turned Sasha in. If it happened to you, it could happen to others. It had to be someone amongst us."

Henryk pulled a handkerchief from his pocket and dried his eyes before responding. "But there were so few who knew Sasha was Gypsy. Someone might have suspected, but other than the family and closest friends, no one knew for certain."

"What about the Keldaris? Would anyone in the clan want harm to come to her, or would anyone be shameless enough to barter her life?"

"Only the worst kind of Gypsy would do that."

"Well, someone did, and someday we will find out who it was, and they will pay."

Karl and Dimitri entered the dining room with their bags.

It was time to say good-bye. Henryk gave the boys a small bag of items to barter with and two small keepsakes. Then, at the back door, Henryk pulled one son and then the other close, tears again flowing down his cheeks.

"Papa," Dimitri started, "perhaps we should stay and—"

At once, Henryk gained control of himself and released his grip on the boys. "No, you must go. I will come for you later. Quickly now, you have to stay ahead of the patrol." Henryk gave the boys a push and signaled to Jan and Manny that it was time. He watched until they reached the corner, and then he turned and went into the shop and walked slowly up the apartment steps.

When he reached the landing, he peered across the living room and through the French doors to the dining room, where he and his loving Sasha and Karl and Dimitri had spent so many hours, days, and years together as a family. Unable to control his agony any longer, he ran to the dining room table and flung Dimitri's model airplane against the wall and scattered the schoolbooks to the floor. He then picked up the curtains Sasha had been hanging, intending to tear them to shreds, but suddenly something stopped him. It was the familiar scent of Sasha. He pulled the panels tight to his body and face and kissed them all over, and then, still clutching them in his hands, he sank to the floor and convulsed with sobbing.

Manny took Karl and Dimitri to the modest apartment on Dobra Street that he shared with his wife, Helenka, and their infant daughter. But it would not be safe for long. The Nazis would undoubtedly be back for the boys, and not finding them at the apartment, would begin a search of family homes.

In a matter of two days Manny was able to broker a hiding place for the boys in an old bicycle warehouse on the outskirts of Warsaw, where they could stay until Manny secured rail tickets to Gdansk. From there he would have false identities arranged that would allow them passage to Sweden and eventually on to England.

Under the cover of darkness, Manny bundled the boys out of his Dobra Street apartment and to the bombed-out warehouse where many Jews were also hiding. Manny and his nephews traveled in the back of a horse-drawn cart over unpaved roads to avoid detection. Manny kept a tense lookout through the wooden slats in the cart, watching for Nazi tanks and troops.

"When will Papa join us?" Dimitri whispered halfway through the cold, bumpy ride. "I'm afraid."

"Dimitri, I know you're afraid; so am I," Karl whispered in reply, "but it doesn't help anything. We have to get through this if we ever want to see Mama and Papa again."

"Your father will join us soon," Manny promised. "As soon as he can."

When at last they reached the warehouse, conditions were even worse than Manny had expected. He nearly wept when he took in the stench of sickness, waste, and decay that filled the ramshackle building, but he swallowed his disgust and put on a brave face for his nephews. "It's only for a little while," he promised, tying his own scarf around Dimitri's neck for warmth and stuffing a packet of dried meat into Karl's pockets. "Until my friend Pietr in the Resistance can get me your papers. We will get you out of here as soon as we possibly can."

For several days Karl and Dimitri stayed in the warehouse, sleeping side by side in a closet with little food or water. Rats ran through the building day and night and sometimes crawled over them as they slept. Nazi soldiers in armored tanks drove past the warehouse several times a day, searching for Jews and Gypsies. Often they were close enough that the boys could hear their voices.

After the boys had spent ten days hiding in the warehouse, Uncle Manny came for them early one morning. "Good news, boys: I've gotten your papers, birth certificates, and cards that identify you as full-blooded Polish citizens," he explained, fanning out the documents. "And I've got you second-class one-way train tickets to Gdansk and tickets on a freighter to Sweden. But we must leave now, before the sun comes up. I will take you as far as the train station at Serock."

"And where will Papa meet us?" Dimitri asked innocently, grasping his older brother's hand.

"He won't," Manny said gently. "Not now."

"What?" Karl exploded. "We can't leave Poland without our parents. We won't go without them."

"Your father will stay in Warsaw and wait for your mother's release," Manny said. "Then they'll both join you in England. But you must go on ahead, and Karl, you must take care of Dimitri. It's up to you."

Karl, always an intelligent boy, had matured quickly in the weeks since his mother had been taken. He grasped immediately what his Uncle Manny was really saying, and he knew it would be a long time before he saw his parents again.

"I'm going to come back to Poland someday," Karl said, with fire in his eyes. "When I'm old enough I will come back here as a soldier, and I will kill Nazis."

Manny accompanied the boys to the rural train station in the town of Serock and bid them good-bye. He made certain that each boy had a small amount of money and each carried something to remind him of his parents. Karl had his mother's gold cross on the broken chain, which had been repaired with a knot that Henryk soldered in his shop. Dimitri was given his father's antique pocket watch to carry in his vest.

From Serock, the boys traveled alone to Gdansk and then on to Stockholm on a Swedish freighter ship. In Stockholm, they were met by one of Manny's contacts who placed them on another ship. Finally, Karl and Dimitri arrived, very homesick, but safe, at the port of Southampton, England. Here they were housed for six weeks at a refugee shelter, sponsored by the Polish-American Alliance. Then eventually they learned they were going to the United States, thousands of miles from their home in Poland, to live with a foster family in Nebraska.

The boys were disillusioned; would they ever see their parents again? Karl's emotional strength was waning; he didn't want to go to Nebraska, but he had promised his father he would watch over his brother, and as long as he and Dimitri stayed together, Karl would have a chance to keep that promise. He had to hold on.

Henryk Karmazin stayed behind in Warsaw, alone with his sorrow. As the weeks passed, rumors increased, saying that Sasha, along with a number of other Gypsies, had been deported to Auschwitz. Henryk lost hope that he would ever see his wife or sons again. The Resistance movement was failing, underground meetings were increasingly rare, and it wasn't safe for either Manny or Jan to visit him. Henryk removed all the watches from his shop window and locked up all his windows and doors. The Nazis didn't bother him about watch repair, nor did they ever come back for the boys; they had their hands full now with the Russians and trying to crush the Armia Krajowa.

At the age of only forty-two, Henryk's weakened heart finally gave in to his grief, and with Warsaw in flames around him, he died alone in his apartment, sitting at his tiny kitchen table clutching the small wildflower painting he had purchased from his beloved Gypsy wife in Lublin so many years before.

CHAPTER FOUR

Grandview, Nebraska, June 1973
Charleston, South Carolina, July 1975

Karl Karmazin, forty-seven years old, with thinning gray-blond hair and a slight middle-aged paunch that had settled around his waist, stood in the bedroom doorway of his home on Locust Street and, full of pride, watched his eighteen-year-old daughter, Beth. She was dressed in a black gown with a gold valedictorian's sash, while her black cap with its golden tassel rested on the bureau in front of her. *Could it really be graduation day?* he wondered. How had his lively oldest daughter grown up so quickly? Just a few years earlier she had been wearing pigtails and playing with paper dolls.

Beth brushed her shiny waist-length black hair in the mirror, carefully placing every strand in its place and scrunching up her nose in dissatisfaction when a few stray hairs went askew. Karl's heart filled with joy.

Without thinking, Karl lifted his hand and rubbed his weathered cheek, massaging the crooked old scar from the long-ago rifle butt that had shattered his cheekbone. The scar, once so prominent, had faded with time and sunk into a small net of wrinkles that surrounded it so completely that it was barely visible now. But it pained him to remember how it had gotten there.

"Dad?" Beth was startled, and she put down her brush as she noticed her father's grim reflection in the mirror. She turned and looked at him, wide-eyed. "Is something wrong?"

Fumbling, Karl plunged his hand into his pocket and withdrew a gold chain with a jeweled cross on it. Beth was surprised; she and her father disagreed about religion, and it had been several years since she'd attended Mass. She couldn't imagine why he was giving her a cross for graduation.

"The time has come for you to have this," Karl said, his voice husky, as he stepped closer and motioned for Beth to turn so he could place the necklace around her neck. "This belonged to your grandmother, Sasha."

Beth was both thrilled and confused as she turned and lifted up her length of long black hair. "But Dad, why are you giving this to me? Ellen and Lilly are Sasha's granddaughters too."

Karl's strong hands shook as he secured the clasp around his daughter's neck and positioned the chain. Beth felt the cross settle against her breastbone and she lifted it to look more closely at the design. It was made of a burnished gold with a deep red stone set at the juxtaposition of the cross' arms.

"Is it a garnet?" Beth asked as she looked up at her father.

"Yes. Your grandmother's father made the cross. Garnet was Sasha's birthstone, as it is yours. So it is appropriate that I am giving it to you. I know she would want you to have it. And I want you to have it. It is the only remembrance I have of either of my parents, and I know you will take care of it."

Beth fought back tears as her fingers tested the chain's tight little knot and the solid gold cross. "Did she wear it always?" Beth asked in a whisper.

Karl stepped to Beth's bed and sat down. "My mother was wearing this cross on the day the Nazis took her away," he said softly, folding his hands in his lap.

"Why is the chain knotted?"

Karl sighed, shaking his head at the painful memory. "As the soldiers grabbed her, the chain broke from her neck and the cross fell to the floor. I grabbed both the cross and chain and later gave them to my father. He knotted it and soldered the knot with his watch repair tools so that when Sasha came home, she could wear it again. But he must have soon realized that wasn't going to happen, because before I left home, he passed it to me."

Karl didn't tell his daughter that her tall, trim figure and angular bone structure bore such an incredible resemblance to her grandmother that it sometimes made Karl's breath catch in his throat.

"My mother would be so proud of you today, not only graduating high school, but graduating first in your class." Karl's hazel eyes crinkled as he admired his daughter's gown-draped form. "Most Gypsies in Mama's day didn't believe in formal education; they felt it restricted their freedom. But Mama was different; she believed education was the only way to find freedom. She desperately wanted Dimitri and me to go to college."

Beth smiled and blushed slightly, before her face took on a worried frown. "Dad," she said slowly, "Are you angry about my speech?" Beth had already informed her parents that she planned, as class valedictorian, to give a commencement speech that included speaking out against the ongoing war in Vietnam.

Karl's hazel eyes darkened, and his face turned stony. "I don't like that you are speaking out against our government," he said honestly, measuring his words. "You are attacking the very country that saved my life and gave me refuge. Your Uncle Dimitri and I would have been killed if we had stayed in Europe. Thank God that the Olsons took us in. One of the proudest days of my life was the day I took the oath to become an American citizen."

"But, Dad," Beth interrupted, preparing her argument in her head.

"No, let me finish." Karl held his daughter firmly in his gaze as his carefully modulated speech once again revealed traces of his old Polish accent. "I don't agree with you on this issue," he insisted. "But I support your right to say what you want to. The right to free speech is sacred. Living under Nazi rule, I learned firsthand what life is like without free speech."

Beth relaxed at this olive branch of a truce offered by her father. Today was not the day to argue politics. They had already spent countless nights doing that at the dinner table, to no avail. If there was one trait that father and daughter shared, it was stubbornness.

Beth's eyes grew misty. "I wish Grandma Sasha could be here," she said sadly, brushing a hair from her gown.

"So do I," Karl agreed. "If she were alive today she'd only be sixty-six. She would enjoy this day. But it's been so long now, I barely recall her face. Her voice, yes, her beautiful voice, that has stayed with me. I can still hear her singing her Gypsy songs." Karl closed his eyes and nodded in time to the music that only he could hear.

Beth was delighted. This was more than she had ever heard her father speak about his mother, or about the terrible day that she had been taken away from her family.

"Sing one for me," Beth asked impulsively.

"What?" Karl opened his eyes and looked up at her in surprise.

"One of Grandma Sasha's Gypsy songs. Sing one for me. I want to hear how the language sounds. Please?"

Karl fidgeted and glanced down at his watch. "We need to get going," he said evenly. "It's already eleven-thirty. We can't have the valedictorian late for her own graduation."

"Yes, I suppose you're right," Beth replied, silently aware that her father always set his watch ten minutes ahead. If he had wanted to sing, time would not have been an obstacle.

Later that afternoon Beth sat with over one hundred of her classmates at the outdoor graduation ceremony behind Grandview High School. Summer had come early, but the humidity was unusually low for the middle week of June. A warm prairie breeze coming from the west blew across the outdoor arena, carrying with it scents of corn and grain and cattle.

Beth's stomach fluttered as she sat upright in the folding metal chair, waiting to stand and deliver her speech. She worried about how it would be accepted, and considered cutting out the political commentary. "Maybe this isn't the time or the place," she thought, biting her lip.

Suddenly Beth heard her own name called, and she strode up to the podium and took her place behind the microphone. She cleared her throat and looked out at the dizzying sea of people spread out before her. Rows of wide, expectant faces met her eyes. Clearly visible, in the second row, were her mother, father, and two sisters, alongside her Uncle Dimitri and his wife, Lorraine, and her Grandmother Sullivan. Taking a deep breath, Beth launched into her speech, holding nothing back.

Two years later, in the summer of 1975, Beth Karmazin, at the age of twenty, found herself between her sophomore and junior year of college at the University of Nebraska, where she was majoring in journalism and communications. She was dating Andy Weinberg, a history major from Chicago who was two years her senior. Andy appeared to be a perfect match for Beth, sharing her love of spicy food, social causes, and classical music.

They were planning to spend the summer break volunteering at a shelter for the homeless in Omaha, but before beginning their service they took up an offer from their friend and classmate, Shelly Moyer. Shelly had invited her boyfriend, Milo Hardage, along with Beth and Andy, to visit Shelly's new home in Charleston, South Carolina. Shelly's mother, who was from Lincoln, had married a pediatrician two years earlier and moved to Charleston, where her new husband had practiced for more than thirty years.

Beth and Andy, having spent their entire lives in the Midwest, couldn't wait to experience firsthand the Old South with its classical architecture, deep cultural history, and slower pace of life. Andy, who was Jewish, joked about his friends protecting him from "The Klan," but none of the four actually expected to experience any real racism or anti-Semitism as they piled into Milo's VW bus and headed out from Nebraska to South Carolina. This was 1975, after all. Saigon had fallen, the war in Vietnam was over, and it had been more than ten years since the Civil Rights Act had passed.

They were about a hundred and fifty miles outside of Charleston, in Buckhead County, when Beth, Andy, Shelly, and Milo stopped for gas at a station along a dusty two-lane highway. The four piled out of the van and into the station, stopping at the bathroom and buying cigarettes, candy, and pop. Beth had just purchased a Milky Way bar and a Pepsi when she glanced up and noticed a sign that said GYPSIES STAY OUT! on the back wall above the clerk's head.

"What?" she thought. "Did I just see what I think I saw?" She blinked, shook her head, and looked up again. This time each word on the handwritten sign felt like a slap in her face. GYPSIES STAY OUT.

As far as she was concerned, that meant her. She had never felt so shamed. She was aware that Gypsies had been emigrating from Europe into the eastern United States since its early settlement; many of these groups had come in as indentured servants. At one point a small number came through the port in Charleston and eventually settled in Appalachia. While less persecuted than they had been in Europe, the Gypsies were still not openly welcomed in America.

But Beth had never imagined that today they would be victims of such flagrant discrimination. The teenage boy behind the counter looked at her suspiciously, but she said nothing. She handed him a five-dollar bill and then quickly pocketed the change and turned away.

As the four friends got back on the road Beth was too embarrassed to ask if the others had noticed the sign. Maybe they had and, like her, were too embarrassed to respond. Then again, of the other three only Andy knew that Beth had a Gypsy grandmother, and maybe he thought he was protecting Beth by not saying anything.

Beth tried to get the nasty experience out of her mind, but a couple hours later when the four college students stopped for lunch at a local dime store counter, Beth was refused service. Beth's olive skin had gotten very tan in the two weeks since school had let out, and with her hair pulled back in a ponytail and secured under a baseball cap she could easily be taken for a Black or a Gypsy. It didn't matter which: Beth's darker complexion, whatever its origin, made her unworthy of service. Andy, Milo, and Shelly had already gotten their food by the time they realized that Beth was being refused service.

"Come on, let's go," Andy said in disgust. "I don't want to eat this deep-fried crap anyway."

"No, it's okay," Beth said, shaking her head and feeling her cheeks blush. "You guys are hungry. Don't let me stop you."

Even more embarrassing than being denied service was the thought that Beth, through no fault of her own, was preventing her famished friends from eating. It would probably be at least another half hour before they got to Charleston and could find somewhere else to eat. And, Beth realized, the next place they stopped might not be willing to serve her either.

"Come on then, share my lunch with me," Andy said, pulling Beth onto his lap and hugging her tightly around her narrow waist. She relaxed a little, enjoying the feel of his hands on her body.

Andy held up a French fry and she snatched it between her teeth. "Everybody knows that having this milkshake with my burger is anything but kosher," he announced loudly, pushing the edge of his grease-soaked plate.

Every head in the restaurant snapped up at that comment, and then quickly looked away, back to their newspapers or the mounds of food in front of them.

"Hey, maybe your rabbi can give you dispensation," Milo joked loudly. "Or whatever it is you people do."

Beth tried to smile at Milo's gauche attempt at ethnic humor; she knew he was trying to lighten things up, but her insides were still stinging and she felt a burning sensation across her face.

It wasn't long before prejudice raised its ugly head once again, and Beth started to wonder if their whole trip had been cursed. It felt like *bibaxt*, or unavoidable bad luck, as the Gypsies called it. On their third day in Charleston, Shelly invited Milo, Andy, and Beth for lunch and a swim at her stepfather's country club.

Western Lakes Country Club was a palatial estate on the outskirts of Charleston, set against a backdrop of stately sycamore and magnolia trees and dark-suited valets parking the luxury cars that lined the club's circular drive. Beth had committed herself by now to salvaging a good time; she began to picture herself by the country club pool in her new striped bikini, a drink in one hand, and a trashy Harold Robbins paperback in the other.

Milo and Shelly had arrived earlier and had told Andy and Beth to meet them at the pool. At the front entrance to the club Andy and Beth were required to give their names and to register in order to get their day passes.

"I'm Andrew Weinberg, and this is Beth Karmazin," Andy said formally, pushing up his glasses and hiking his duffel bag over his shoulder. "We are guests of Dr. Charles Longhurst."

The attendant, a tall blond woman with a long face and pointy nose, glanced down a long list and, seeming to find what she was looking for, made a small notation in pencil.

"I'm sorry, what did you say your names were?" the woman asked, staring at the sheet.

"Andrew Weinberg and Beth Karmazin," he replied. "Is there a problem?"

The woman looked up and raised her haughty chin. "I'm sorry, Mr. Wein-berg," she said, emphasizing each syllable of his last name. "But this club is restricted."

Both Beth and Andy were shocked. "But ... but our friends are already here," Beth protested. "We have an invitation."

"Beth, don't," Andy implored, grasping Beth's hand and giving it a firm squeeze. "I know where I'm not wanted."

Beth was furious; she wanted to stay and fight. But she saw the dark look on Andy's face and she retreated. She understood his shame, having felt a similar thing herself only three days before.

Beth and Andy walked a half mile in the searing South Carolina heat to a nearby ice cream shop, ordered one banana split, and sat together in a booth eating it, each taking one end and working toward the middle. "It's good to know there are at least a few places where we can both get served," Andy joked, digging into the strawberries. "Just think how fat we'll get if we only eat ice cream for the next two weeks."

"Andy, it's not funny," Beth said sadly, twirling her plastic spoon. "I had no idea shit like this still happened. Do you go through this often?"

In the year and a half since she had known Andy, Beth had never seen him victimized by anti-Semitism, nor had he ever mentioned any incidents of it. The University of Nebraska had an overwhelming majority of white Christian students, yet attitudes seemed tolerant toward other races and beliefs.

"I can't say it happens often, but it happens," Andy admitted, nudging a cherry toward Beth's end of the dish. "That's how I ended up at the University of Nebraska, in fact."

Beth was confused. "What do you mean?"

"When I graduated from high school I had the grades for the Ivy League, but the East Coast schools have strict quotas on Jewish students.

Lots of my friends ended up in Minnesota, Wisconsin, and Michigan. The universities and state schools in the Midwest have always been more liberal in regard to registrants. But the fraternities—now that's a different matter."

"What about the fraternities?"

"Well, why do you think the Jewish boys have their own fraternity on campus?"

Beth was not a member of a sorority, and she had never paid much attention to the organization of the Greek system. "I don't know. I guess I always thought they wanted their own fraternity."

Andy smiled cryptically but said nothing. Wide-eyed, Beth stared at Andy. "Are you suggesting they couldn't get into other fraternities?"

Andy didn't have to answer the question. Beth turned away. The shame she had felt earlier in the day was gone; something inside her was changing. Since high school she had felt a commitment to fighting social oppression and economic deprivation, but she had always seen herself as being separate from the fight, and perhaps even a little bit above it. Now, her focus was changing. Now the fight was not only humanitarian, it was personal—it was about her and about Andy.

CHAPTER FIVE

Auschwitz, Poland
March 1943–April 1944

As the long line of cattle cars rattled through the cold, windswept Polish countryside toward the town of Oswiecim, Sasha could see through the small opening between the wooden doors what lay ahead—rows of brick buildings, roughly the same size and color and spaced an equal distance apart. From a quarter mile away it looked like an ordinary army encampment, but as the train moved closer Sasha could see that this camp was surrounded by electrified barbed wire and a number of watchtowers that stood like silent sentries, rising from the flat ground every hundred meters or so and looming over the barren landscape.

Within the dark, crowded, foul-smelling cattle car a flurry of nervous voices rose in intensity, crying for help and asking what was happening. Several people crowded around the narrow opening, forcing the doors further apart and letting in a welcome rush of cold fresh air. As the largest watchtower came into view it was clear that the journey would soon be over. No one knew it at the time, but the numerous buildings surrounding the central watchtower served as the living quarters for the seven thousand Schutzstaffel, or SS soldiers, who were assigned to the camp. Ahead of the largest watchtower was an arched metal gate with an inscription that read, "Arbeit Macht Frei," in sharp black letters.

"*Arbeit Macht Frei?* What does that mean?" several people asked, crowding around the door.

Sasha, fluent in German, was quick to translate. "It says, 'work will make you free,'" she explained.

"It's a work camp!" an older man shouted in delight. "See Edith, it's not a death camp, it's a work camp! As long as we can work we will survive." A number of other people murmured in agreement and in relief.

Sasha had grave doubts, but she kept them to herself. She did not trust anything the Germans said or did, not even something written on a sign in arched black letters. After all, hadn't the Germans lied when they brought her to the Gestapo office in Warsaw and promised that she would be released to her family after "questioning?" Instead, the Nazi officers had grilled her for hours, depriving her of food and water and forcing her to sleep on the cold concrete floor of a jail cell. First they demanded, then they threatened to kill her if she didn't tell them, the names and locations of her fellow Gypsies living in and around Warsaw.

Sasha tried to explain that she had left the Gypsy community behind when she married a Pole. Still the officers were not satisfied; they threatened to bring in her sons for questioning and deport them to a work camp if she refused to talk. Sasha insisted that no Pole would have children with a Gypsy woman and that the boys who lived with her belonged to her husband and his first wife who had died years ago.

After Sasha had been in custody for ten days, the Gestapo decided she was either telling the truth or she wasn't going to talk. Finished with her, they designated her for deportation to Auschwitz.

The train that Sasha was assigned to was filled mostly with Jews, but there were a few other Gypsies and a number of Poles who had obviously done something to offend the authorities. It had been a wretched two-day journey. They had been packed in like animals with no food or water, very little air to breathe, and the thick stench of urine, sweat, and excrement, along with the cries and sobs of the terrified passengers.

As the massive gate to the camp slowly opened, the train lumbered through and ground to a halt, wheels squealing sickly on the metal tracks until the train was still. Nazi camp guards, aided by their enormous, vicious German Shepherds, marched up to the cattle cars and threw open the doors. The guards began screaming and shouting at the passengers to get out. *"Raus! Raus! Raus!"*

When the sick, the injured, and the elderly failed to move quickly enough, the guards grabbed them by the arms, legs, and hair and dragged them from the cars, throwing their frail bodies onto the hard-packed ground. Sasha watched in horror as several passengers were shot, either by a pistol pressed to the forehead or a rifle shot which rang out from a short distance.

The shocked, dehydrated, and hungry former passengers, now officially prisoners, huddled en masse in front of the train from which they had just emerged. An amalgam of sickly-looking male prisoners in striped pajama-like uniforms, carrying violins, cellos, and woodwinds, showed up on the raised wooden platform and began to play waltzes.

Sasha's first thought upon witnessing this surreal scene before her was to flee, to run away, but how far could she get? Where would she go? The camp was surrounded by electrified barbed wire and guards in watchtowers with binoculars and rifles, in addition to the soldiers of the Third Reich armed with batons and pistols and stationed every few yards. There would be no escaping from here. "Stay strong," Sasha told herself. "You must stay strong to survive and go home. You will find a way out of here."

The prisoners were quickly ordered into a line and made to parade before a high-ranking SS officer stationed behind a wooden desk atop the platform. This officer visually inspected each prisoner, asked several questions, examined their passports and ID cards, then quickly ordered them *links* or *rechts*—left or right—and then on to barracks located further within the fortified camp ground.

Watching the procession, Sasha quickly realized that those being sent to the right tended to be less fit: the elderly, children, the weak, injured, or disabled. Those being sent to the left appeared to be younger, stronger, and healthier: teenage to middle-aged men and women. Even so, there seemed to be no definitive criteria for being sent one way or the other. A healthy-looking middle-aged man on the dock was sent to the right because his hat was too big, and another because his jacket was too narrow. Families were broken up without a second thought; a father was sent to the right, while his wife and children went left. A mother separated from her teenage sons broke from the line to go back to them, and as she took them in her arms and held them close, all three were shot to death and their limp bodies dragged away like animal carcasses.

Sasha's position was toward the end of the long line, and after she had waited an hour or more, the line ahead had thinned enough that she could make out individual faces in the crowd. Some of the people Sasha saw looked as if they were going on a luxury holiday with their shiny new suitcases, expensive clothes, and heavy winter coats. Some of the women even wore long dresses with diamonds and fur.

But others waiting in the line were thin and full of sores, wearing rags for clothes, their hair unruly and skin pale and sallow. No doubt they had already been imprisoned for many months before their deportation, or they had been transferred from another camp.

Suddenly, the sun broke through the heavy clouds, and the rays of light caught a glint of gold toward the front of the line. Sasha squinted, looking for the source of the flash, and what she saw stopped her heart. *Could it be? Oh no. It couldn't be.* There was a black-haired man in his early forties wearing a colorful embroidered vest and a woman about ten years younger, equally dark-haired, in a long striped skirt and gold hoop earrings. It was Sasha's brother, Stefan, and her sister, Melina.

Sasha wanted to cry out and get their attention but she didn't dare, for fear all three of them would be shot and killed on the spot. Sasha had not seen her brother and sister, her only siblings, in nearly five years. When she had married Henryk, almost twenty years earlier, her parents had disowned her. Stefan and Melina were more accepting and had visited Sasha and Henryk until the occupation, when it became unsafe. The last time Sasha had seen Stefan and Melina they told her that their parents had died, and that Melina had married and had two children. Their extended family, the *kumpania*, was planning to live more settled lives near the Baltic Sea coast.

Since they did not read or write or have access to a telephone, Sasha had no means of keeping in contact with Stefan and Melina. After the Nazis invaded Poland in 1939, Sasha prayed that her brother and sister had escaped before the war began. She pictured them living in England or Ireland or some other part of Europe yet untouched by Hitler's master plan. Yet here they were, on the same transport to Auschwitz as Sasha was. Tears filled her eyes, but she bit her lip and drew in her breath. There was nothing she could do now but watch, wait, and pray.

Another fifty or so Gypsies passed through the line as Sasha kept her eyes peeled for those she might know. Suddenly she jumped back as she spotted two familiar faces—Mar Dep, the Shero Rom of the Keldari, and his son Emil, now a grown man. Mar had aged immensely since she had last seen him eighteen years earlier. His hair and his mustache were white and his face craggy. He looked tired and confused. Sasha respected Mar, even though he had banned her from the Keldari clan when she chose to marry Henryk. Mar had done what he had to do, sticking to Gypsy law and tradition. But his son Emil was another matter.

When they were children, Sasha had confronted him often about his unscrupulous behavior. He was a disgrace to the Keldari clan and to his father. Sasha said a quick prayer for Mar to go to the left. What happened to Emil, she didn't care.

Sasha was deeply relieved when she saw both Stefan and Melina sent in the line to the left, along with the stronger, healthier prisoners. She vowed to find them, provided she too survived the selection. She closed her eyes and said a silent prayer for their safety.

Finally, a freezing and exhausted Sasha reached the front of the line. She was bone-tired, having not slept for nearly two weeks now. She'd had almost no food or water and her stomach was twisted in a knot. Her legs were weak and noticeably shaking, yet she knew she had to look strong if she were to have any chance of being sent to the left. She saw that a number of women in the line ahead of her were pinching their cheeks and biting their lips, trying to draw color into their ashen faces. Sasha immediately did the same thing, and began stretching her arms, and taking deep breaths. She rubbed her eyes, hoping to brighten them.

When she reached the front of the line, her heart was pounding in her chest and she could hardly breathe. Unlike many of the prisoners, she did not have a passport or identification card. All she had was the *Z* on her clothing that identified her as a Gypsy. The Nazis in Warsaw had simply thrown her onto the train and there didn't appear to be a written record of her transport, or other identification. Should she lie? Pretend to be someone else? Might that protect Henryk and the boys back at home? Or would it in fact make her situation worse if she was found to be lying?

She didn't have time to think it through before she stepped up to the desk. "Name?" the officer barked.

"Sasha Lacatus Karmazin," she said, standing up straight.

"Your papers?"

"I have none," she replied.

"None?" The officer looked irritated, and Sasha feared she might faint.

"I was put on the train at Warsaw. I am a Gypsy," she said, looking the guard straight in the eye.

"Where and when were you born?" he asked, making a note in his ledger.

"I was born in Rzeszow on February 3, 1907," she said. She didn't know the actual place of her birth, but she had learned long ago, when she entered the non-Gypsy world, that life was easier if she was able to supply some vital statistics when asked, even if they weren't accurate.

Meanwhile, in the line next to her, an old woman was being questioned by a different guard. "Name?" he asked.

She looked at him blankly.

"Name?" he asked again, growing angry.

The woman shook her head and muttered something in Polish.

"She says she is waiting for her husband," Sasha volunteered. Sasha knew that speaking up might get her killed. On the other hand, it might also save her life. "He was supposed to meet her at the station but she lost him in the crowd."

"You speak Polish?" the guard asked.

"*Ja,*" Sasha replied. "I am fluent in Romani, Polish, German, and Russian. I know a little French as well." Sasha did not mention that she could speak English, as she was afraid they might want to know how she had learned it.

"Can you read and write these languages?"

"*Nein.*" Her voice caught in her throat. "I read and write only Polish."

"Ask this woman her name and where she is from," the guard ordered.

Sasha did as told and relayed the information to the guard. The old Polish woman thanked Sasha profusely, then the woman was sent to the right, along with the others designated for extermination. Sasha was devastated, wondering what she might have said differently that would have spared the woman's life.

"You will work as an interpreter, a *Dolmetscherin*," the guard said to Sasha, stamping something in his ledger. "We need more interpreters. Go to the left."

Sasha, still dazed by what had happened, stepped down from the platform and went to the left with the others, where she soon endured a humiliating orientation process. The Nazis took an electric razor to her scalp and shaved her head; her hair fell in sheets to the dirty concrete floor. Afterwards, Sasha was given a health inspection, standing naked beneath a bright light in a cold, damp, drafty room. Then she was sent to the showers and deloused, and her inner forearm was quickly and crudely tattooed with the letter *Z*, for *Zigeuner*, the German word for Gypsy, and a permanent identification number. The Nazis at the office in Warsaw had taken away her jewelry. But here, to her surprise, she was allowed to keep the clothes she had worn on the train, and she was given a long burlap sack dress and open-toed sandals. As she would learn later, Gypsies were allowed more privileges than the Jews.

Following the orientation process, Sasha and the other Gypsies were sent to the Gypsy enclosure at Auschwitz I, better known as Birkenau. Unlike in the Jewish section, here families were allowed to stay together, and the accommodations were slightly better. Still, Sasha was forced to sleep in a bunk constructed of hard wooden slats and stacked three high.

There were no showers or bathing facilities, only a toilet area which was a large open barn-like structure with two rows of latrines, just two long lines of wooden holes positioned over a drainage ditch. The space between each latrine was no more than a few inches, and toilet time was severely limited, with no hope of dignity or privacy.

That first night, as Sasha climbed up into her wooden bunk, which was no bigger than the overhead luggage rack on a normal train, her head was spinning. Some of the other Gypsies seemed not to appreciate the gravity of their situation, and they sang lusty songs and danced with their children on the cold, sawdust-covered floor. Someone had captured and killed an enormous rat just outside the barracks, and someone else used contraband matches to make a small fire on the barracks floor and roast the rodent. People clapped, sang, and stomped their feet as strips of meat were torn from the creature and shoved into hungry mouths.

Sasha tried to ignore the commotion and go to sleep, knowing she had to keep up her strength if she had any hope of survival. Her arm burned and ached from the crude tattoo, which she couldn't even bring herself to look at. Her stomach, which had been painful for days, now felt even tighter and more unsettled after the small meal she'd had of stale bread and broth. "Think of Henryk and the boys," she told herself as hot tears slid down her cheeks and peppered the straw beneath her head. "You've got to stay strong."

After her first few days at Auschwitz, Sasha's life fell into a predictable routine, a routine whose boredom and predictability was broken only by random moments of sheer terror: when someone was called into the offices unexpectedly, or shot on sight for working too slowly, or for insubordination. Life was cheap; death was common. If a man fell over dead while digging a trench, his body was kicked over the edge and the other workers simply dug around him. Suicide was common; nearly every morning, while marching to the mess hall, Sasha could see dead bodies hung like scarecrows on the electrified barbed wire. It was the only way to truly escape the misery.

She learned to avert her eyes from the smokestacks that fired up on a daily basis, spewing human ash high into the air, the remnants of people Sasha might have spoken to, might have eaten with, might have met just hours before. Sasha tried not to think ahead; she tried not to remember her life before Auschwitz. She learned to live only in the moment, moment to moment, knowing that if she survived one more day, she might one day be free.

Sasha was very useful to the Nazis at Auschwitz, and she knew that increased her odds of survival. Soon she was moved to the barracks for "essential prisoners" at Auschwitz I. In the mornings she worked in the munitions depot or the gunpowder room, interpreting directions to the other workers. Then she would report to administration, and would be sent to wherever an interpreter was needed. In the evenings, she worked at the SS officers' mess hall, interpreting instructions to cooks and servers. Sasha often worked eighteen to twenty hours a day, seven days a week, and even though weak with exhaustion, she knew her usefulness was critical to her survival.

Sasha had been a prisoner at Auschwitz for nearly two months when she first saw Leutnant Gerhardt Klinsmann. He had transferred to Auschwitz from the concentration camp at Bergen-Belsen and was going to be in charge of operations for several of the barracks. That meant that Sasha would be working in very close contact with him.

Klinsmann was a tall man, at least six-foot-four, and appeared to be in his mid-thirties. He was heavyset with a thick build, although more muscular than fat. He had thinning reddish-brown hair combed straight back and hazel eyes with light eyebrows. His complexion was freckled and he had strong, angular facial features. His thin, colorless lips hid small, uneven teeth.

The first time that Sasha encountered Klinsmann a chill went through her body. It was the way he looked at her. His expression wasn't leering; it wasn't wolfish. It was arrogant, haughty, confident, possessive, and ruthless. He would have her; it was just a matter of time. She would, of course, have no say in the matter. Sasha felt sick to her stomach but made a conscious choice: *I will do what I have to do to survive.*

During the first few weeks of working for Klinsmann, Sasha found him tolerable. He rarely spoke to her directly, and never addressed her by name. She was most useful in helping him communicate with the *Sonderkommandos*, the prisoners who worked at the crematories, helping to make certain that this "factory of death" ran smoothly and efficiently. He had a way of grunting his satisfaction: quick, guttural, and low in his throat, like a dog.

Klinsmann expected perfection from her, especially in her new task of cleaning his office and preparing his lunch. But as long as she did what he wanted, he basically ignored her, which was a relief. Sometimes Sasha found herself wondering what Klinsmann would have been in the outside world. Was he a career soldier, a military man even before the war? Sasha doubted that. She pictured him as a banker, a postal supervisor, maybe a mid-level bureaucrat—a man desperate to move up, but never quite reaching the top position.

Klinsmann's pursuit of Sasha unfolded slowly. At first, he would rub his hands over the stubble on her scalp, or he would pat her bottom as she walked past. Twice he grabbed and squeezed her breasts, leaning in so close she could feel and hear his heavy breathing. Each time it happened she forced herself to smile, while being careful not to look him in the eye for fear he might see her revulsion. Sasha tried to stay still and focused inside herself, knowing that he could not touch her soul if she did not let him.

Eventually he began to address her as *"du,"* or "you." *"Du kommst,"* he would say. *"Komm hier."*

"Lieutenant, my name is Sasha," she would say. "Please call me Sasha." She hated the thought of him using her name while he used her body, but she had another motive. *If he sees me as a human being, it will be harder for him to kill me or have me killed. When it comes my turn to march to the gas chamber, he may argue for my life.* She knew it was a long shot, but she was determined to do everything possible to increase her chance of surviving the war and returning home to her family.

Klinsmann rarely spoke to her other than to bark orders, but he surprised her one day by asking, while she dusted his desk, "Where are your husband and children? Your Gypsy husband and children?"

Sasha, caught off-guard, was nearly speechless. "Sir?"

"Are they here at Auschwitz? You must have married young and had many dark-skinned children," he continued, his eyes moving wolfishly up and down her body, lingering at her breasts and hips.

Sasha panicked and did not know how to respond. Should she lie and say they were here? Klinsmann could look it up and if he found she lied, she would be killed immediately. But if he knew the truth, that she married a Polish Catholic and possibly had "mixed-race" children, that might offend him even more.

"Sir, I married young and my husband died, thrown from his horse. We had no children," she added quickly.

That answer seemed to satisfy him and for the next several days he didn't ask her anything about her family, her background, or her life before the concentration camp. Sasha was relieved and grateful and hoped she could handle the next situation as well.

But she was caught completely off-guard a week later. She was coming from the officers' mess hall with Klinsmann's daily rations of coffee grounds, fresh bread, butter, sliced sausage, a hunk of cheese, and the fresh-cut flowers that he liked to have on his desk. Realizing she was a minute or two late, she ran through the camp as fast as she could, knowing that she could be executed for arriving late. The Nazis hated tardiness almost above all else. So when Sasha entered Klinsmann's office and the drapes were drawn and the lights off, she was relieved. She thought he must have been called away to a meeting.

Sasha put down the things she had brought and set about tidying Klinsmann's desk. Suddenly she heard a noise, two or three heavy boot steps, and a shadow behind her crossed the floor, further darkening the room. Before she could turn around, one hand grabbed her shoulder, while the other clamped tightly over her mouth. "Do not make a sound," a harsh voice whispered roughly in her ear, "or I shall kill you right now."

The hand on her shoulder spun her around and forced her to the floor, tearing her skirt. Then the huge body was writhing on top of her and she nearly suffocated beneath the weight. It all happened so quickly that she didn't even know for certain that it was Klinsmann until he raised his head and she saw clearly his cruel, vacant eyes and his mottled face with the fair skin burning red and purple from exertion.

Sasha's heart pounded and she wanted to scream, to cry for help, to push his huge heaving body off her own and break free. But she knew she couldn't. To fight back would mean certain death. "I must imagine that I am somewhere else," she told herself. "My body may be here but my spirit, my soul, is somewhere else."

At first she tried to see herself at home with Henryk, Karl, and Dimitri, but that image brought tears to her eyes, and she didn't dare cry. She then tried to imagine strolling through Warsaw's Lazienki Park in the spring when the apple trees were in blossom, but this didn't work either. As she tried to hold her body still and loosen her muscles against Klinsmann's violent thrusts, to make the attack less painful, she felt him struggling to reach climax. As his anger and frustration mounted she feared he would blame her for not "satisfying" him and kill her on the spot. She prayed frantically for it to be over.

With a loud grunt he finished and sat back on his knees, still straddling her body. He looked at her, glassy-eyed, then curled back his thin upper lip and spat upon her naked abdomen. Sasha was shocked. Her first impulse was to lash out and slap his face, but she held back, praying for her life.

"Zigeunerunrat," Klinsmann muttered, "Gypsy filth." Then he grabbed her skirt, balled it up in his fist, and threw it in her face. "Get out of here," he ordered. "Gypsy whore. Get out of my sight."

Terrified, Sasha grabbed her torn clothing and ran from the office. She spent the rest of the day huddled in her bunk bed, holding her knees to her chest and sobbing. She was bleeding vaginally, her back ached, and her thin arms were covered in dark bruises that had already risen to the surface of her skin. Some of the other women in the barracks sneaked Sasha some bread from supper, but she found she had no appetite; she could only manage small sips of brackish water. When she closed her eyes she saw Klinsmann's hulking figure pressing on top of her, nearly cracking her bones with his weight and his hands and knees and mouth tearing into her, as if he were trying to devour her flesh. As she drifted into sleep at last she allowed herself one small indulgence: she let herself remember what it was like to have Henryk's loving arms around her, protecting her in the night. Her heart ached for him.

When Sasha awoke the next morning before daybreak, and said her prayers, she fully expected to be dead before the sun went down, sent to the gas chambers with the thousands of others who were destined to die that day. She could not imagine that Klinsmann would want her around anymore. She would be seen as "Gypsy filth," a reminder of his disgust, his lust and his sin, his violation of the rules of the Third Reich that forbade sex between Aryans and non-Aryans.

She went to the mess hall, where as usual she picked up Klinsmann's rations. Then, not knowing what else to do, Sasha went as always to Klinsmann's office. When she arrived, he behaved as if nothing had happened the day before, or as if he had no memory of raping her. Sasha tidied his office, prepared his lunch, and then accompanied him on his rounds of the barracks, translating orders from Klinsmann to the Sonderkommandos.

After a few days Sasha began to hope that Klinsmann's attack had been a one-time thing and that he would not assault her again. But then it did happen again. This time he did not jump out at her from behind his office door. Instead he grabbed her while she stood at the small sink rinsing his lunch dishes. This time the rape was quicker; he labored less before reaching climax, yet Sasha found it more painful. After several more rapes she finally learned to disconnect her mind from her body, imagining herself as a vibrant young woman running through a meadow of wildflowers, her long black hair flowing in the breeze. Only by sending her mind to this "special place" could she survive the assaults that she now knew would come on a regular basis.

Knowing that there was nothing she could do to stop the rapes, Sasha decided over time to try to use her connection to Klinsmann to better the lot of her fellow inmates. When Sasha brought Klinsmann his fresh lunch every day she would ask if she could take the stale scraps and rotten fruit from the day before back to her barracks. Oftentimes Klinsmann said yes, and so Sasha became a saint to many in her barracks. But there were also those with treacherous tongues who whispered that she was secretly Klinsmann's lover, enjoying an illicit affair with him.

A few weeks after Klinsmann began his assaults on Sasha, she began to notice changes in her physical condition. One night as she returned from the women's common latrines, she waited before climbing into her bunk, bent slightly forward with her hands on her thighs, waiting for the cramp to pass. It felt like a menstrual cramp, but she hadn't had a period for several months. That was not unusual; most of the women in the camp had stopped menstruating due to stress, malnutrition, and emaciation.

But there was something else now, something different about the vomiting and stomach cramps. She didn't want to believe it; she didn't dare believe it. Still, she could no longer deny it. She was pregnant with Klinsmann's child.

When she had been pregnant with Karl and Dimitri she had experienced the same symptoms—the strange dreams, the intense hunger and cravings, the fluttering in her womb that made her dizzy and breathless. She imagined she was close to one month along. Klinsmann had raped her so many times now she had lost count. At first she did keep count, scratching out with a sharp stone one line in the wooden frame of her bunk for each rape. But the lines had begun to run together and sometimes now she was so exhausted, so demoralized, and so spent after being raped that she didn't have the strength to carve any more lines.

"How can I be pregnant?" she thought. She was thirty-six years old and thought her childbearing days were finished. It had been fifteen years since Dimitri was born, and even though she and Henryk had a passionate love life, there had been no further pregnancies following an early miscarriage almost ten years ago. Now she was pregnant? Why now, of all times?

Sasha lay in her bunk with silent tears coursing down her face as a cold draft circled her shaven head. How she would have loved to have had another child with Henryk, especially a daughter. He would have doted on a daughter. "This could be a daughter I'm carrying," she thought. "If I survive the war and return home, could Henryk and the boys ever accept me and this child? This bastard Nazi child, half German, half Gypsy? Where would we live? Who would accept us? We could never return to the Old Town of Warsaw. But Henryk is such a kind man; he loves me with his whole heart. He will know I did not choose to have sex with another man. He will know it happened against my will, and he will love the child as his own."

Sasha stopped and chastised herself. "No. Do not think that. If you start to think of this pregnancy as a baby, you will die. There is no chance that this child will survive Auschwitz. Other women, Gypsy women and Jewish women, have been pregnant here, and not one child had survived. Not one! Many mothers were murdered as soon as their pregnancies became visible. The others either died in childbirth along with their babies, or, if miraculously, both mother and child survived, they were sent to the gas chambers together soon after the baby's birth. No, Sasha, you cannot think of this thing growing inside you as a life. The only thing you can do is survive each day, do everything possible to survive. Make no mistakes, and do nothing to call attention to yourself. All that matters is surviving one more day."

But what would happen when Klinsmann noticed? He seemed to be almost completely unaware of her body when he was raping her, and after he used her he invariably pushed her aside in disgust. He never touched her except to hold her down, and then his hands were on her neck and upper arms, never around her stomach.

Still, he will see me eventually, when he tears off my clothes and my midsection is round and distended. Then what? He will know he is the father and will be disgusted by what he has created. No doubt I will be killed immediately, with the child still inside me.

"No, Sasha," she told herself, "don't think those things. That will not happen today. Today you know only that you are with child. No one else can see it. You will live to the end of this day, and that is all that matters."

CHAPTER SIX

Lincoln, Nebraska
Chicago, Illinois
Summer 1976

Thunderclouds loomed in the far western sky, threatening to ruin a perfect Fourth of July day; high winds with hail and heavy rain were forecast for late afternoon. But for now, the crowds that lined O Street for the Bicentennial parade were celebrating under sunshine and confetti. As the elaborate parade worked its way through downtown Lincoln, a giant George Washington on stilts loomed into Beth and Andy's view. Behind the giant George Washington came an equally enormous Abraham Lincoln, a glowering figure with black top hat and fuzzy beard.

Dozens of children ran out from the crowd as the presidents reached into their burlap sacks, pulled out handfuls of candy and began showering them on the crowd. Kids squealed with delight as they scooped up sugary treats and shoved them into their pockets and mouths.

Following close on the heels of the presidents came a trio of young men reenacting the Spirit of '76, complete with a drummer, flute player, and flag bearer. Overhead the Goodyear blimp carried a banner proclaiming, "Happy 200th Birthday, USA!"

"This is really incredible," Beth said, her voice cracking slightly.

"What's wrong?" Andy asked, wrapping an arm around Beth's shoulder and pulling her close. He had just finished his first year of law school at the University of Michigan but had returned to Lincoln for the summer to be near Beth and to intern at a local law firm. Meanwhile, Beth, between her junior and senior years of college, had stayed in Lincoln to volunteer at a shelter for abused children and to work part-time at a feminist bookstore.

"There's so much focus on fun," Beth said, shading her eyes from the bright mid-afternoon sun. "I wonder if the real story behind the celebration is somehow being lost."

Andy turned and faced Beth, puzzled by her comment. Beth's long black hair was cut shorter than usual, falling just above the shoulders, parted down the middle, and feathered back in a trendy style. She wore faded bell-bottom jeans, a tight white halter top with spaghetti straps, and cork wedge sandals. Her makeup was simple: blue eye shadow, coral blush, and clear lip gloss.

"Now, why would you say something like that?" Andy asked. Andy, even though he was interning at a law firm, had grown out his curly hair to a short Afro, and he wore faded blue jeans with a Keep On Truckin' T-shirt.

"My father was a refugee, and this country gave him a home and opportunity," Beth explained, watching a cortege of children ride by on their red, white, and blue-beribboned bikes. "Your grandparents came here to escape the pogroms in Russian in the nineteen-twenties, and this country gave them refuge. Do you think the people watching this parade really appreciate that?"

Andy smiled widely, a glint in his eye. "Why, Beth Karmazin, you sound positively right-wing. Is this the same girl who told me she made veiled criticisms of the Vietnam War in her high school valedictorian speech?"

"I've always loved America," she proclaimed. "The war in Vietnam just never made sense to me."

"Hey, let's lighten up. It's a celebration."

"But shouldn't people understand what they're celebrating?"

"Okay," Andy replied, gesturing with his hand to the crowd across the street. "If you want to get serious, take those two little ladies over there with the kerchiefs on their heads. I see them every morning on my coffee break, together in Miller's Deli. They escaped from Latvia at the onset of World War II with only the clothes on their backs. They were lucky to make it out of Europe alive and then to America. And see that middle-aged couple over there waving the American flag? They are clients of the firm. They lost their son in Vietnam three years ago when his helicopter was shot down. Don't you think these people understand the price of freedom and love of country?"

Beth briefly peered into the crowed where Andy had gestured, then looked down at her parade program. "Yes, I imagine they do." Andy had made a point, and she didn't see a reason to debate the subject further. "Okay, the clowns are coming," she said, making an effort to sound light-hearted. "They're the last entry."

Andy kissed the top of Beth's head and slid his hands down to her hips. "When did you say your roommates would be back?" he whispered in her ear.

Beth was sharing an apartment with two other college girls, while Andy rented a room from an older couple who lived nearby. Andy and Beth had wanted to share an apartment for the summer, but Beth couldn't bear the hurt on her father's face when she told him what she and Andy were thinking. It was apparent she would be driving a deep wound into his heart if she so blatantly snubbed the traditional values he had tried so hard to instill in his children.

"They won't be back until late," Beth said with a smile. "Sheila is at her parents' in Omaha and Nancy has a hot date with Artie." She placed her hand over his and pressed it more tightly to her hip.

"And the Sandersons aren't expecting me back until midnight," Andy offered. "I told them I'd be at Love Library doing research for one of the partners."

"On the Fourth of July?"

Andy shrugged. "I had to tell them something."

Beth and Andy made out on the bus the whole way back to Beth's apartment, but when they got there and found Beth's roommate Nancy busy in the kitchen, their ardor quickly cooled.

"Nancy, weren't you going out with Artie tonight?" Beth asked as she came through the door, smoothing her halter-top and trying to fan the redness out of her face.

"Not anymore. The jerk. I found out he's been stepping out on me." Nancy stood at the stove, morosely heating some soup. "With a girl from Iowa, no less." Nancy's long blond hair, pulled back in a barrette, hung down between her shoulder blades. Her head drooped as she stirred the soup with more intensity.

Beth looked at Andy and raised her hands in a gesture that said, "Sorry."

"Oh, by the way, Beth, your dad called," Nancy said. "You're supposed to call him back when you get in."

"My dad?" Beth responded worriedly. Her dad never called; he wrote to her once a week. Her mother did the calling, but only on Sunday, and this was Saturday. Something must have happened. "What did he say? Is everything okay?"

"I don't know. Your dad's not one to rap. He just said for you to phone him as soon as you got home."

Beth's worry now turned to fear. Her face paled. "Something must be terribly wrong."

Andy lifted the phone from the wall and dialed Beth's parents' number. He knew it by heart. He had called it numerous times during school breaks. As the phone began ringing he handed the receiver to Beth.

"Hello, Karmazin residence. This is Margaret speaking." Beth's mother's voice was calm and precise.

Beth felt a flutter of relief. At least her mom was okay. "Hi, Mom." Beth's voice sounded shaky.

"Beth, how are you? Did you enjoy the parade?"

"It was great. Mom, is something wrong? Nancy said to call Dad right away."

Margaret paused. "We're all fine, dear. I'll put your dad on."

Beth flashed Andy a tentative thumbs-up as she waited for her father to pick up the phone.

"Hello, Beth."

"Hi, Dad. I got your message. What's going on?"

"Everything here is fine. I just wanted to remind you that the warranties on your car expire next month and I thought you might want to have it serviced before that happens."

Beth grabbed a kitchen chair and sat down beside the sink. "Oh, sure, thanks; I'll do that."

Beth and Karl chatted a few more minutes about home and school, then as their conversation was closing, Karl said, "By the way, there is something I have been meaning to tell you. A professor in Chicago is writing a book, a narrative history, about the Gypsy Holocaust. In the book, the author, this Professor Peter Mavik, claims that my mother, Sasha, collaborated with the Nazis."

"Collaborated with the Nazis? That is incredulous," Beth replied indignantly. "Collaborated to do what?"

"I don't know, but he says he has testimonies to the fact." Karl paused. "I wanted you to hear this from me, Beth, before you heard it or read it somewhere else."

Beth exploded, jumping out of her seat and nearly tipping the chair. "Testimonies? What kind of testimonies?" she demanded.

"He says he has interviewed survivors of the war who have firsthand knowledge of your grandmother's activities."

Beth's mind raced. "When is this book coming out? How did you find out about this?"

"Beth, calm down," Karl warned. "Just calm down. Mavik contacted me a few years ago and told me he had information that my mother was a Nazi collaborator. I refused to talk to him, and didn't hear from him again until his secretary called the other day. She said it was a courtesy call to let me know the book was coming out next year."

So that was what her father had been keeping from her since Matthew first told her about her grandmother. That's what Uncle Dimitri had been whispering to Father O'Reilly. Sasha had been accused of being a collaborator. But why hadn't her father told her? Did he perhaps think his own mother was a traitor?

"Dad, I'm shocked," Beth said, cupping the phone to her mouth. "I can't believe this and surely you don't. Grandma Sasha would not collaborate with the Nazis. I don't care what kind of testimony he has—they're lies."

"Beth, there's nothing you can do about it. I just wanted you to hear it from me."

Beth motioned for Andy to hand her the pad of paper and ballpoint pen from the cupboard drawer. "What did you say this professor's name was? Mavik? M-A-V?" she asked, pinning the phone between her ear and shoulder as she grasped the pen.

"Dr. Peter Mavik, from the University of Chicago. Beth, there's nothing you can do, okay?" Karl's voice held an edge, and Beth understood that it was a warning.

"Sure, Dad. I promise." She scribbled Mavik's name and the university on the notepad. "Don't worry about me."

After saying good-bye to her father and hanging up the phone, Beth quickly filled Andy in on the details, while Nancy poured herself a cup of soup and hunkered down on a beanbag chair in the corner of the room to read the *Rag*, the university student newspaper.

"I don't like the way you look, Beth. What are you thinking of doing?" Andy asked, scratching his bristly chin.

"Stopping him, of course. But first, I've got to call Amanda and tell her I need a few days off from the bookstore. Then I have to scare up some cash for bus fare. Tomorrow's a holiday, so that might be hard …"

The next afternoon Beth boarded a Greyhound bus and headed for Chicago, against the passionate protestations of Andy, Beth's boss at the bookstore, and just about everyone else who knew her plans. She settled back in her seat and watched out the window as the bus crossed the bridge over the Missouri River and entered the vast farmland and lush cornfields of western Iowa.

By early afternoon her enthusiasm was fading and she began to have second thoughts. "This is stupid," she told herself. "I've probably just wasted a bus ticket. It's summer break. He might not be on campus, or even in Chicago, for that matter." But as she thought this, she saw in her mind's eye a photograph of three terrified Gypsy children clinging arm in arm as a Nazi soldier with a bayonet marched them toward a cattle car, an image she had first seen in a filmstrip back in high school.

"Grandma Sasha couldn't possibly have collaborated with the Nazis or even sympathized with them," she thought, as she ran her fingers along the gold cross suspended from her neck. "Sasha lived her whole life in Poland; her husband and children were Poles. She wouldn't do such a thing."

The long bus ride gave Beth a chance to think back on how she had come to be so passionate both about her grandmother and about her Gypsy heritage. After having learned from her cousin Matthew that she was one-quarter Gypsy, Beth had begun to search for information about the Gypsy culture. She had scoured the high school library but had come up with almost nothing beyond some children's books about fanciful, free-spirited traveling groups who read cards, performed magic, or taught bears to do tricks.

Then one Saturday afternoon during her senior year of high school, Beth's mother had asked Beth to join her on a drive to Lincoln to shop for a holiday dress. For Beth this was a perfect opportunity. While her mother shopped Beth went to the nearby campus of the University of Nebraska and rushed to Love Library. It was here, surrounded by stacks of reference books, that Beth began to understand what made the Gypsy people unique. Gypsies were not instinctively wanderers, nor did they choose to lead a nomadic lifestyle. And, according to modern scholars, the Gypsies did not originate in Egypt as had been widely believed. Their origin was actually northern India, which had been their home until Islamic barbarians forced them out more than a thousand years ago. Following this mass exodus into Europe, the Gypsies were compelled to keep on the move by governments and people who rejected them for their dark skin color. No one would hire them for steady jobs and their children were not allowed to attend school. Eventually, traveling became the Gypsy way of life and the overriding characteristic of their cultural identity.

Journeying on horses, in wagons, and often on foot, the Gypsies spread like a many-fingered web, weaving their way through the European continent over hundreds of years. A fiercely independent people, they developed their own skills and trades and sold their wares to the lighter-skinned populations, or *Gadje,* as the Gypsies called them. The Gypsies suffered epics of persecution, genocide, enslavement, and eventually the apocalypse of the Holocaust, which claimed more than a million Gypsy lives. In modern times, because their language was found to have roots in a dialect of Hindustani known as Romany, the Gypsies are known among scholars as *Roma.*

This was all good information, but to Beth's dismay, in all of her research she found nothing written from a Gypsy perspective—no narratives, chronicles, annals, or even personal accounts of their lives—none of the records essential to preserving and passing on the history of a culture. Because the Gypsies were not allowed into the European educational systems until the advent of communism in Eastern Europe, they were largely illiterate. Stories were handed down from century to century by word of mouth, until eventually the Gypsies preferred illiteracy as a way of life, and literacy became an evil linked to the *Gadje*.

Beth hadn't meant to become immersed in the Gypsy plight; she was only looking for answers to her heritage. But gradually, as she learned more about the stigmas and stereotypes affixed to the Gypsies, she began to empathize with their struggle and connect with their uniqueness, until being Gypsy—if only part Gypsy—became integral to her identity. And she became even more determined to find out what had happened to her Gypsy grandmother, a thirty-six-year-old wife and mother who was torn away from her family and never heard from again.

A noisy bump in the road brought Beth's focus back to the bus trip at hand. She rolled up her denim jacket to use as a makeshift pillow and felt something lodged in the pocket. She unbuttoned the pocket and found five twenty-dollar bills, along with a note from Andy that read, "My crazy Gypsy girl, please be careful!! I admire your courage, but at times it scares the hell out of me. Use the money to find a good hotel. Your Loverboy, Andy."

Tears welled up in Beth's eyes as she held the note tightly, hoping that Andy's heartfelt words would give her some strength. She watched out the bus window as the miles ticked by on Interstate 80 and the gently rolling hills of eastern Iowa gave way to the flat grassy prairie of northern Illinois. Everywhere Beth looked she was overwhelmed with Bicentennial memorabilia, from the commemorative Bicentennial license plates to the high-flying stars and stripes, to all the fire hydrants and rural mailboxes painted in varying shades of red, white, and blue.

Once Beth reached Chicago, she found a room at a Holiday Inn and stayed the night, rising early the next morning to take the "L" train to the Hyde Park campus of the University of Chicago. "This is stupid," she told herself. "Why am I here? He might not even be on campus. He's probably teaching summer school somewhere else."

Beth found the administration building and asked for Professor Mavik's office. She was directed to a small building on the southern edge of the urban campus. She walked up the two flights of stairs, turned a corner, and saw the door with the small typed tag on yellowed paper that said, "Dr. Peter Mavik, Chair, Department of History." Beth knocked confidently on the door, while her heart pounded in her throat.

"Come in," a male voice replied.

He IS here. Beth took a deep breath and opened the door.

Dr. Mavik's office was small, poorly lit, and stuffy. Books were piled everywhere: on the desk, the chairs, the top of the file cabinet, even on the seat of the old bicycle balanced beside the door.

Mavik was perched behind the wooden desk, typing on an electric typewriter. He was younger than Beth had expected, and not bad looking. Tall and thin, he was probably in his early forties, with graying brown hair parted on the side and hanging almost to his eyes, thick, dark-framed glasses, olive skin, a thin nose and narrow jaw. He glanced up at Beth briefly and, seeming to decide that she was just another student, resumed his typing.

"My summer office hours are Thursdays from 3:00 to 4:00 PM. Please come back then," he mumbled, as his rapid typing grew more intense.

Beth cleared her throat. "Dr. Mavik, I'm not a student," she said. "At least not at the University of Chicago."

He shrugged and continued typing. "Then what can I help you with?"

"I'm here about your book."

"My book?" He still didn't look up from his typing.

"I'm Elizabeth Karmazin."

The name caught his attention and the clattering hum of the typewriter ceased. "Karmazin?"

"Yes," she said steadily, stepping closer to his desk. "I'm the granddaughter of Sasha Lacatus Karmazin. The woman you claim collaborated with the Nazis at Auschwitz."

Mavik's face flushed slightly, but he kept his composure. "I'm sorry, Miss Karmazin, but I'm busy right now. If you'd like to make an appointment for later in the week—"

"No. I can't," she interrupted. "I came all the way from Nebraska to talk to you."

"I'm sorry you made a wasted trip, but I can't speak to you right now," he said, returning to his typing.

"Please, just tell me," Beth pleaded. "I heard that you have witness testimonies. What sort of testimonies?"

Mavik seemed to soften a little. "Look, I understand that this must be difficult for you and your family." He ran his fingers through his thatch of hair. "I am writing a historical narrative, so I have the liberty to tell the story the way I see it; based on fact, of course. And I am not obligated to spare peoples' feelings, especially concerning the Holocaust. It is the defining event of the twentieth century, after all, and as the few remaining survivors grow older and die, their stories die with them."

Mavik motioned for Beth to take a seat in front of his desk. She lifted a dusty stack of books from the chair, set them on the floor, and pulled the chair forward. Beth was sure that the professor had to have some sort of verification of his research. To maintain the reputation of the university history department and certainly to keep his tenure, he dare not fictionalize characters and events in his narrative. But it would be easy to misinterpret information or stretch the truth about Gypsies, since almost the entire Gypsy population from the war era was illiterate. And it had been three years since Mavik had published anything significant; under pressure from the university he may have applied less-than-scholarly standards to the veracity of his manuscript.

"Doctor Mavik, all I'm asking is that you tell me the source of your information," Beth said, sitting down. "You could at least do that."

"All right," Mavik responded, as he leaned back in his chair and laced his hands behind his head. "You see, I have been working on this book for more than ten years. I've traveled to Poland, and I have been to the Auschwitz camp, spending hundreds of hours poring over records and documents. By the way, I'm fluent in German, Polish, and French, and not bad at Romani, the Gypsy language. Although they have far too many dialects for even me to master. Also, I do my own translations. The official translations often contain numerous errors in syntax."

Beth resisted the urge to roll her eyes at the professor's obvious high regard for his competencies. "My research on Sasha comes from several sources."

Sasha? Mavik dared to call her grandmother "Sasha" as though he knew her! He had no right to refer to her with such familiarity.

Mavik turned in his chair, pulled open the drawer of an old metal file cabinet, and withdrew a ragged ream of onionskin paper. THE PORRAIMOS: THE GYPSY GENOCIDE IN WORLD WAR II, BY DR. PETER MAVIK was typed in capital letters and underlined on the front of the manuscript. Beth was familiar with the word *Porraimos*, the Gypsy name for the Holocaust. It literally translated to English as "The Devouring." While Mavik flipped through the document looking for a specific page, Beth fought off the impulse to grab the manuscript from his hands and run from the office, throwing the whole thing under the "L" train.

"Sasha's first accuser was a man named Klaus Broza," Mavik said, tilting his head to see better through his thick glasses.

"Klaus Broza?" Beth immediately recognized the name. The butcher from Warsaw, her grandfather Henryk's neighbor. That he would accuse her grandmother of being a collaborator made Beth feel ill. Her father had told her that Klaus and Henryk were good friends, that they had lent each other money during the tough times in Poland, and when currency was hard to come by they had bartered with one another. Klaus would bring meat to the Karmazin family, and Henryk would repair the Broza family's watches and clocks. The families regularly attended Mass together. Yet this friend of Henryk's, Klaus Broza, had accused Henryk's wife Sasha of being a collaborator.

"Why would Klaus Broza accuse my grandmother of being a Nazi collaborator?"

"Well, that isn't exactly how he put it. He didn't say she was a collaborator, but, based on what he did say and other witnesses' stories, that is what one must conclude. Broza said that he had seen Sasha in Stare Miesto, the old town square, talking with the governor general of the occupied Poland, the notorious Nazi, Hans Frank. Although his headquarters were in Krakow, Frank came to Warsaw often, sometimes bringing his wife, a terrible woman who had a reputation for stealing from the Jews in the ghetto."

"I know who Hans Frank was, and the fact that Sasha was seen talking to him means nothing. My father told me that Nazi soldiers were always stopping residents and demanding to see their papers. It was their nasty little game of harassment and intimidation."

There was a sudden look of admiration in Mavik's eye, as if he wished his own students were so bright. "You are correct," he acknowledged. "However, I understand your grandmother had no papers, so why wasn't she arrested? Never mind, I would never publish conclusions with information only from one source. I have other sources, witnesses who give credence to Broza's story."

Beth's stomach sank. She wasn't sure if she wanted to hear more. Mavik leaned forward and paged through the manuscript again until he found what he was looking for. "Read this," he said, handing the manuscript to Beth and indicating with his finger the middle of the page. "This is the testimony of a woman I interviewed in London in 1972, a Polish Jewish survivor of Auschwitz, named Rebekah Levy."

Beth took the manuscript, cradled it in her lap, and began to read:

"The Gypsy woman Sasha Karmazin lived in a block for prisoners whose jobs the Nazis labeled as 'essential.' As much as possible, these workers were kept away from the diseased prisoners, and they were generally better fed. The Gypsy woman worked as a *Dolmetscherin*, a translator, so she was quite valuable to the Nazis at the camp. She was also very striking to look at—a face I shall never forget. She was tall and thin with huge dark eyes. Her eyes were made more striking by the contrast to her shaven head, which had only a shadow of black growth. She was dressed in a long skirt and a tattered jacket. The Gypsies were allowed to keep some of their personal possessions, while we Jews were forced to wear the hideous gray and white striped prison uniforms.

"I myself saw the Gypsy woman twice, and spoke to her just once when she was called into my block, where I was held with many other Polish Jewish women. She was ordered by the SS guard to find musicians for Alma Rose's famous orchestra that was coerced to entertain Nazi officers. Because the Nazis did not speak Romani or Polish, they needed the *Dolmetscherin* to find them their musicians. When Sasha asked me if I were a musician, I told her no. 'But you can sing, can't you?' she asked me in Polish. 'I'm certain just by looking at you that you can sing.' Her dark eyes were glowing, insistent, pleading, as if my life depended on the answer, which of course it did.

"'I have no musical training,' I replied, shaking my head. 'I used to sing to my children when they were babies, but they are gone now.'

"'That is good enough,' she replied, taking my arm and pulling me out of the crowd. '*Hier Herr Kommandant, sie singt, sie singt*,' she called to the Nazi officer, then leaned close to me and said, 'You will do fine. Now, go with this officer.'

"Then she said something else to the officer in German and he wrote my name and my number down on his list. Before he led me away with the other musicians, Sasha took me aside and whispered in my ear so the guard could not hear, 'You must keep singing, no matter what. Just keep singing and you will survive.'

"I did not see the Gypsy woman again until the spring of 1944. She had been correct; singing in the orchestra kept me alive long after those who entered Auschwitz with me had died. I was assigned to the Jewish women's barracks at Birkenau, a large addition to Auschwitz and the site of the crematories. When I wasn't practicing or performing with the orchestra I was assigned to the *Kommando für Erdarbeiten*, the digging unit. We prepared the land to build the railway tracks to the crematories, laying the way for the deaths of hundreds of thousands of our Jewish brethren and others as well. Can you imagine living with such a remembrance and with such guilt? I was working with my unit; we were pulling stones out of the earth with our bare hands, when I saw two soldiers escorting the *Dolmetscherin* away from the Gypsy complex where she had recently been moved.

"She was pale and haggard, her bare arms looked thin as knobby twigs, but clearly she was pregnant. Her belly protruded from her slim body. Even when malnourished, a pregnant woman's physique gives away her condition. I asked the worker beside me if she knew what was going on, and she explained that the Gypsy *Dolmetscherin* was the mistress of Hans Frank, the governor general of Poland, who often visited the camp. His headquarters were just up the road in Krakow, and although he had no authority over the camp, he often came there to visit. Probably, she said, the guards were taking her to see him.

"I said a small prayer on the spot for the Gypsy woman's soul. More than anything I wished I could sing for her, just a verse or two, as an offering of thanksgiving for my life. I knew that if she had been impregnated by Hans Frank, it was not of her own free will, and I refused to judge a person who had saved my life. After that day, I never saw the woman again."

Beth's hands were sweaty; her lip trembled as she looked up at Mavik. "This is a haunting story," she said softly, "but still I am not convinced."

"Turn the page and you will find an Auschwitz survivor named Adolf Synovec. His story is the most damning. He claims that Sasha Karmazin leaked information that led to the deaths of thousands of Gypsy prisoners."

"That's ridiculous. What proof does he have?"

"Unfortunately, Mr. Synovec died shortly after this interview, but he claimed that he had a good Gypsy source who told him that Sasha knew the Gypsies at Auschwitz were stealing and stashing weapons in preparation for a revolt and she knew where the weapons were. She divulged that information to the Nazis, and in retaliation they liquidated the entire Gypsy camp."

"Liquidated?" Beth was not familiar with this term.

"*Exterminated*, to be precise. Of the twenty-three thousand Gypsies who were deported to Auschwitz, three thousand remained alive on the morning of August 1. Then the SS soldiers moved in, seized their weapons, and herded them to the gas chambers."

Beth was stunned by this piece of information, but she managed to maintain her composure. "Let's go back to the previous witness, Rebekah Levy," she said. "There is no proof that Sasha was escorted away from the camp and given refugee status as Frank's mistress. God forbid, the guards may have been taking her away to be executed."

"I would agree that that is a possibility, except for one thing," Mavik argued, removing his thick glasses and rubbing his eyes. "There is a record of Sasha's arrival at Auschwitz." He paused. "But there is no record of her death. To me, that suggests she left the concentration camp by some other means. No one ever escaped from Auschwitz, so we must assume she had help from someone in a position of authority. That someone was likely Hans Frank, who was planning to rendezvous with her in Switzerland after the war, except that he—"

"Except that he was arrested by the Allies, made to stand trial at Nuremberg and was executed in 1946," Beth interrupted, completing his sentence.

Mavik smiled briefly, his lips tight. "You've studied your history, Miss Karmazin," he said with some admiration.

"That is exactly the point, Dr. Mavik." Beth looked him straight in the eye. "This is *my* history we're talking about here. It is my family you are seeking to defame."

Mavik sighed heavily, stood up, and stepped to his crowded bookshelf. He pulled down a dusty, leather-bound book, opened it, walked over to Beth, and placed the book in her lap. As he leaned over her shoulder, Beth caught an unpleasant whiff of his rank cologne. He pointed to the narrow columns lining the book's yellowed pages. "These three volumes are copies of the Auschwitz-Birkenau concentration Gypsy camp registry," he explained. "This volume covers the female Gypsy population. Two very clever Polish lads who had been clerks at the camp buried them in a bucket as the Nazis were evacuating the camp. They were dug up several years later. This one is the female registry. Here you can see the prisoner's last name, first name, date and place of birth, identification number, occupation, date of imprisonment, and date of death. As I said, the Nazis were very thorough and organized."

Beth shuddered. Mavik sounded almost admiring of the Nazis' brutal efficiency.

"The final column," he continued, "is for special notes and dates referring to things such as transfers to the punishment unit or transfers to another camp."

Beth looked at the neatly organized columns and felt like she'd been punched in the stomach. These were the names of real people; real human beings, she realized. Each notation represented a precious human life that could never be replaced. Names of wives, mothers, daughters, and sisters were listed here. This particular list was from 1944; doing some quick math in her head Beth realized that the youngest victims listed as *gestorben*, or dead, had been only two or three years old.

"Were any Gypsy babies born at Auschwitz?" Beth asked softly, thinking that perhaps Sasha's baby, if it survived birth, might be listed in the registry.

Mavik, still hovering over Beth's shoulder, cast a thin shadow over the pages of the registry. "Yes," he replied. "A statistic noted after the war by one of the Zentralat staff at the Gypsy center in Heidelberg said that three-hundred-seventy-one Gypsy births were recorded at Auschwitz-Birkenau during the time the camp was operating."

Beth swallowed hard, fearing to ask the next question. "How many of the babies survived?"

Mavik blinked. "None."

Beth's throat tightened and her eyes pinched, but she refused to cry in front of Mavik.

Mavik leaned forward and turned a few pages until he found the listings for the letter K. His finger traveled down the furthest left-hand column until it stopped at Karmazin.

Name: KARMAZIN

Vorname: SASHA LACATUS

Geburtsdatum:—07

Geburtsort: Rzeszow

Beruf: Dolmetscherin

Eingang ins Lager: 27.3.43

Beth was stunned, literally speechless at this stark black-and-white reminder of her grandmother's life and her imprisonment in a Nazi concentration camp. Beth had studied German in high school and college and was able to translate the entry. Her grandmother, Sasha Lacatus Karmazin, who was said to have been born in Rzeszow in 1907, worked as a translator at the camp, and had entered Auschwitz on March 27, 1943.

"If you look here, the final column is blank," Mavik said, tracing across with his long, thin index finger to the other side of the page. "There is no record of Sasha's death at Auschwitz, nor is there a record of her being transferred to another concentration camp. And she was not among the handful liberated when the Allies arrived in 1945. Therefore, my conclusion is that Sasha was taken to a safe place before the Russians liberated it."

Beth had had enough. She could see she was not going to persuade Mavik to change the manuscript. "When does your book come out?" Beth whispered, struggling to find the right words and restrain her anger.

"The end of next year. December 1977," he replied smugly.

"I can't stop you from publishing these lies," Beth said evenly, realizing the enormity of that task. "I'm only a college student. I don't have the experience or resources to chase this down. But I can promise you this: I know that you are wrong, and someday I will prove it. Someday you will have to retract this story and print the truth about Sasha Karmazin."

CHAPTER SEVEN

Auschwitz, Poland
April–May 1944

Sasha continued to hide her pregnancy while she worked as an interpreter and as Klinsmann's assistant. One sunny afternoon in mid-April she was summoned to translate at a work site where a number of Gypsies were said to be causing trouble. The first groups of Gypsies deported to Auschwitz hadn't been made to work; the Nazis considered them untrainable, but as The Third Reich increased and sped up importations from the occupied areas, a much larger labor pool was needed to build and maintain the camp and crematories. Eventually, even the Gypsies were subject to work selections. But the Nazi guards had a hard time controlling them. Even the threat of imminent death often didn't intimidate the Gypsies into compliance.

When Sasha reached the work site, she couldn't believe her eyes. In the crowd she spotted her sister, Melina. Sasha's heart leapt with joy. Melina appeared thin and sickly, but clearly it was her. Having not seen her brother or her sister since the day they had all arrived on the same transport to Auschwitz, Sasha had feared the worst. Yet, here Melina was, looking haggard but still well enough to work.

Sasha was distracted, her gaze constantly drifting toward Melina at the back of the crowd, but she continued translating for the guards. "This project is very important," she said, translating their words. "If you do the job well, you will be rewarded with additional food rations and a lighter workload. Just work quickly and quietly."

In time, the Gypsies calmed down. Sasha hated manipulating her own people; she hated being the organ for disseminating the Nazis' boldface lies. She knew that there would be no rewards, and that the less productive workers would be exterminated as soon as the project was over. But how could she tell them the truth? If she did, they would confront the soldiers and they would be beaten to death or shot dead on the spot. Better to keep them alive and pray for the Allies to come soon.

As the Gypsies resumed clearing the ground of stones and breaking through the hard-packed earth, a guard dismissed Sasha and ordered her to return to Klinsmann's office. Sasha nodded and briefly scanned the crowd for one final look at her sister. Just as she was about to give up her search, Melina rose from her bent position, stood on tiptoes and caught Sasha's eye. Melina waved, pointed to herself and began a series of gestures, tapping her chest over her heart. "I am alive," she was demonstrating. Sasha nodded. Then Melina raised her hand and held it level, high, and flat above her own head for a moment, then drew both index fingers down from her nose on either side of her lips. Tall. With a mustache. *She is characterizing Stefan*, Sasha realized. Then Melina nodded and tapped her heart again. *Alive.* She was showing Sasha that their brother, too, still lived. Sasha wanted to shout with joy, but she only nodded and turned, hurrying back to Klinsmann's office with an unexpected lightness in her step.

As the weeks went by, Sasha was more frequently called to work at the officers' mess hall, interpreting directions from the Nazi chefs to the mostly Polish and Gypsy kitchen workers and cooks. Several times during this period Hans Frank, the governor general of Poland, visited Auschwitz and he would take his meals in the mess hall with the other officers. Sasha tried to stay out of his sight. He and another officer had stopped her on the street in Warsaw one day more than a year earlier and asked her for her papers. Had they not been distracted by a sudden nearby explosion, Sasha was sure she would have been arrested.

Hans Frank had no authority over the camp; all of the Nazi concentration camps, including Auschwitz-Birkenau, were under the command of Heinrich Himmler. But Frank, who was envious of Himmler's elite status in the Nazi inner circle, would often intimidate whoever was the Auschwitz commanding officer at the time into allowing him to visit the camp. And at this particular time, the commander was SS Major Richard Baer. Baer, of course, would not mention Frank's visits to Himmler, and Frank would not record these visits in his official journal, as he wanted no responsibility for what took place in the camps. He only wanted to know what Himmler was up to.

The sight of Hans Frank in the mess hall each time he came gave Sasha the chills. She knew his reputation, and she remembered him stopping her on the street in Warsaw to question her. He had been Hitler's chief legal advisor before being assigned as governor general of Poland, and he had grossly manipulated the law to justify the criminality of the Third Reich. Under his command, millions of Polish civilians starved to death, were murdered, or were deported to work camps where they had little to no chance of surviving. His main office was in Krakow at the Wawel Castle, a stately monument of Renaissance architecture and only a mere fifty kilometers down the road from Auschwitz. Here, Frank and his wife often entertained the Nazi elite and favored celebrities, hosting lavish parties, while, just outside, children starved in the streets and soldiers harassed civilians.

Frank had dark hair receding at the temples, a high forehead, a straight nose, and smooth skin. His dark, deep-set eyes were shifty and unsure, unlike the steely cold blue eyes of many of the other SS officers. Of all the Nazi hierarchy, Frank was more dangerous than most because he was unpredictable; he was an equivocal man who on the one hand touted justice and sensitivity and on the other gave orders that resulted in the slaying of thousands of innocent Polish citizens. And he was an anguished man, doing everything on the outside to please or impress authority, while on the inside he writhed in self-pity and frustration because he was not accepted into the Fuehrer's most intimate inner circle.

As Frank's visits to Auschwitz increased in frequency, Sasha became aware of the fact that she had caught his eye. At first she wondered if it was her growing pregnancy that he noticed. If he mentioned that to Klinsmann, or to anyone else for that matter, she would surely be killed. Whatever the case, he said nothing to Sasha; he just stared at her as she moved about the officers' dining room, directing the prisoners and making certain that all the foods and drinks were served at precisely the right time and at the proper temperature.

On one visit, after dinner, Frank followed Sasha into the kitchen and stood behind her as she supervised the dishwashers. She could feel him watching her, inching closer and closer. Suddenly he reached out, grabbed Sasha's shoulder and turned her away from the sink and toward him. Lust burned in his dark eyes and Sasha ached to run away. But where could she go? A room full of Nazi officers, smoking imported Cuban cigars and drinking expensive port, waited just beyond the kitchen's swinging door.

Stepping closer, Frank pushed Sasha up against the big steel sink, then pressed his rotund body to hers and began kissing her neck and her face. She felt she might vomit, but she struggled to stay still. He tore the front of her shirt and reached in and grabbed and fondled her breasts, which were swollen and tender from the pregnancy. She felt tears sting her eyes, but she held her breath. *"Liebchen,"* he said, *"Sehr schoen."*

The dozen or so workers in the kitchen went about their business, scrubbing, rinsing, and stacking dishes as if nothing were wrong. Sasha feared Frank would rape her right there against the sink. She closed her eyes and held her breath, trying to force down the bile rising in her throat.

Suddenly Frank stopped his molestation, and then, inexplicably, he pulled closed the two torn sides of her shirt. "Repair that," he said, then wiped his mouth with his handkerchief, turned, and walked back to the dining room with steady, even steps.

Sasha twisted back to the sink, turned on the water and began scrubbing her hands, her arms, and her face. Several of the kitchen workers eyed her with unsympathetic expressions as they continued working. Undoubtedly, they thought she had asked for this, or even deserved this. As Sasha turned to find a pin to hold together her shirt, she noticed Emil Dep standing across the room leering at her. She had not seen him come in.

Emil had been recently made *kapo* of the Gypsy compound, the equivalent of a foreman. Like many of the *kapos* he was ruthless in the way he executed his power. He would severely beat any Gypsy who challenged his authority, and he took more than his share of the complex's food and medicine, often selling it on the Auschwitz black market to other *kapos* and lower ranking SS guards. His father, Mar Dep, one of Gypsy Shero Roms, was the only one who might have curbed Emil's corrupt behavior, but he had been sick for weeks with typhus and in and out of consciousness.

Just a month earlier Emil had requested membership in the Auschwitz underground, a network of prisoners scheming to defeat their Nazi captors. They bribed guards and stole gunpowder and metal equipment for fashioning weapons to use in an ultimate revolt. Although Sasha's pregnancy placed her at a disadvantage recently, she had been a member of the underground for months, and she had blackballed Emil Dep's request to belong, citing incidences of his vicious and deceitful character. As his eyes, menacing and full of hate, met hers now, Sasha was certain she had made the right decision.

The final time Hans Frank came to Auschwitz, just a few weeks later, it was, surprisingly, at the invitation of Heinrich Himmler. Sasha knew that this was an especially significant meeting; all week she had overseen deliveries of steak and veal and Danish butter; fine German wines and French champagne, along with bounty from the sea: crabs and lobster, smoked salmon, and tins of caviar. The refrigerators were so overfull that big blocks of ice had to be stacked in an outbuilding, creating a makeshift icebox. Meanwhile, all the meal and party preparations were being handled by prisoners who each day consumed less than one cup of broth and one thin slice of bread. Anyone caught stealing, or even sampling, the food, was immediately taken out and shot.

During the meal Alma Rose's orchestra performed, and all the attendees, officers and their wives, were dressed in their finery. When the meal was over, four high-ranking Nazi leaders, Heinrich Himmler, Adolf Eichmann, Rudolf Hoess, and Hans Frank, gathered alone in the officers' mess. Sasha eavesdropped on their conversation as she supervised the kitchen cleanup.

Eichmann was responsible for the current logistics of deporting the hundreds of thousands of Jews out of Hungary and into Auschwitz, while Hoess, who had been the camp's commander from May of 1940 to November of 1943, had been ordered to return to the camp to oversee the massive extermination of the Hungarians.

Frank was charged with squelching partisan attempts to disrupt the railways as the Jews were being transported through Poland. And Reichsfuehrer Himmler, the commander of the SS and the Gestapo, was also the orchestrator of the "Final Solution."

These were four of the most diabolical and powerful of Hitler's henchmen. They were speaking anxiously about the Jews; tension filled the air. Hoess swung his leg under the table incessantly. Himmler rapped his pen on the table, while Frank's upper lip twitched nervously. Eichmann was perspiring so profusely one could see rings of moisture under the arms of his uniform.

Himmler was clearly in charge; he asked Hoess for alternatives to speed up the extermination process. Thousands of Jews were arriving now every day, and the gas chambers and crematories, even working at peak performance, were not keeping up. "We must accelerate the process," Himmler insisted, his eyes so wide with excitement that they appeared larger than his wire-rimmed glasses. "When we evacuate this hole, we can't allow any witnesses to remain."

Hoess, clearly annoyed by Himmler's command, countered, "How do we do that? Even if we shoot them as they come off the train, we have no way to dispose of the bodies. And the crematories are working at full capacity."

Frank, a lawyer by training, had always been uncomfortable with Himmler's *Endlosung*—wholesale murder without a legal basis for action. Under his jurisdiction in Poland, Frank had found rooted somewhere in law justification for deportations or executions of individuals, even though most of these actions were taken against unwanted populations and for no cause. But this, Himmler's "Final Solution," was mass murder. Frank spoke up now. "We need time to formulate a justification for this, and we need to predate it to the opening of the camp so that—"

"*Scheiße!* We have no time for formulating!" Himmler responded, banging his fist on the table. Frank glanced nervously at the others, looking for support, but neither Eichmann nor Hoess spoke. Himmler then demanded the four proceed with a plan for completing his "Final Solution."

Several minutes later, while Sasha was directing the floor sweepers, she heard the word, *Zigeuner*. Gypsies. Abruptly, she stopped talking and turned to fold napkins near the door where she could better hear the conversation. Hoess was confirming something that had just been decided: On August 1, less than three months away, all Gypsies in the camp would be exterminated. Sasha's head reeled. There were still thousands of Gypsies at Auschwitz. All would be killed. She had to get this information to the camp's underground and to the Gypsy camp. The Gypsies had to be prepared, but she couldn't leak the news too soon or it would get back to camp officers. News had a way of spreading like lightning at Auschwitz.

Sasha was still trying to grasp this horrible news when she and the other interpreters were called into the officers' mess hall.

"The Allies will soon surrender," Hoess explained to the group. "The war will be over and Germany will be victorious. Your job as *Dolmetscherinnen* is to tell the prisoners to prepare for evacuation. Tell them that the Germans are soon to triumph, and all the prisoners will be released."

Hoess directed his next order directly to Sasha. "We know that some of the Gypsies have been gathering weapons. Tell them to give them up to the kapos; anyone who does not comply will be shot."

Sasha stood straight and tall with the other interpreters, simply nodding her head that she understood and would comply with the orders. But inside she was thinking, "Trickery. Cold-blooded Nazi trickery. No one will be released. They will lull the Gypsies into a sense of security, take their weapons, and then move in and liquidate the entire complex."

Emil Dep stood outside his barracks and threw down a shot of vodka he had traded for drugs. He was incensed that he had been denied membership in the underground, and he was sure it was Sasha who had foiled his request; the whore he had once imagined taking for his wife. That was until the day she had humiliated him in front of his own father and his clan.

He and Sasha had been fifteen years old when the Vesh boys, a local Polish gang, had surrounded the Keldari camp early one morning, armed with pistols and rifles, riding tall on their horses. They had demanded money and jewelry. Emil thought them the most glamorous of all bandits in Poland. More than anything in the world he had wanted to ride away with them, he remembered. He was tired of being the son of the Shero Rom, always expected to live up to his high standards, never having fun, always having to think first of the clan.

Mar Dep was away from the camp, and so Emil was free to do as he pleased. He offered Leo Vesh, the gang leader, three of the best horses belonging to the clan if they would take him into the gang. But the bitch Sasha had come after him, screaming, "Traitor, dirty traitor," and kicked him in the balls. As Emil fell writhing to the ground, the Vesh bandits had laughed uproariously and rode away.

"Now she shames me again," Emil said to himself. "She hates the Gypsy life. She wouldn't have run off with a Gadjo if she gave a damn about the clan, and now she sleeps with Nazi pigs. The Keldari are stupid to trust her. She knows where the Gypsies are hiding the weapons and gunpowder, and yet my own father won't even tell *me*. Me, the *kapo* of the camp. But I'll fix that; I'll get even with her, and this time it will be for good."

A few nights later, deep in the darkness, a Nazi guard entered the female Gypsy barracks and shone his light from bunk to bunk, his boot heels clinking against the cold concrete floor.

"Karmazin? Where is Sasha Lacatus Karmazin?" he barked.

The words struck fear in Sasha's heart as she woke up with a start. She knew it was only a matter of time until she would be killed now that her pregnancy was becoming more and more apparent, but she never expected it to happen like this, roused from her bed in the dead of night and taken out to be shot. She had expected to be sent to the gas chambers along with the thousands of others who were now dying every day.

The woman in the adjacent bunk motioned for Sasha to slide over and hide in her bunk, beneath the thin burlap blanket, but Sasha refused the kind offer, knowing that would only result in two deaths instead of one.

"Here, Sir. I am Sasha Lacatus Karmazin," Sasha whispered, voice quivering as she rose to her elbows.

The guard stopped in front of her and motioned with his flashlight for her to climb down from the bunk. Her expanded midsection made her clumsy and slow, and when she didn't move quickly enough the guard grabbed her arm and yanked her from the bunk, slamming her hip to the hard earthen floor. She wanted to cry out in pain and wasn't sure why she didn't. After all, if she were about to be killed, why would it matter whether they took her out and shot her or if the guard simply put a bullet in her head right here? Still, she remained silent as the guard pulled her to her feet and marched her out of the bunker and into the cold moonlit night.

But Sasha was surprised when, instead of being taken to the electrified fence where many executions took place, she was marched to Klinsmann's office, where he was waiting for her in the dark. "Thank you," Klinsmann said to the guard as he grabbed Sasha from him. "I will take care of this prisoner myself."

Sasha nearly fainted. The child kicked inside her, and tears filled her eyes. She did not want to bring a child into this world. Not this world. The guard left and Sasha stood, barefoot and freezing in the same clothes she had worn to work the day before, watching Klinsmann as he organized his briefcase and tidied his desk. What was he doing? She couldn't fathom. Why didn't he just take her out and kill her as he had implied? What possible business could he have to do first?

During this time, a good ten minutes that seemed to last for hours, Klinsmann said nothing and showed no emotion. He did not seem angry, or nervous, or upset, or pleased. He seemed like an ordinary bureaucrat, clearing his desk in preparation for the following day. Sasha's knees ached, her back hurt, she needed to urinate, but she didn't dare say a word. She tried to clear her head of all negative thoughts, deciding that if she were to die now, she wanted to go to the Lord with her arms and heart open wide. *At least this will be over,* she thought, and a strange kind of peace came over her. She always knew that someday her suffering, her incarceration, would end. It had to; nothing lasts forever. Of course, she had hoped it would end with liberation, but now, standing in this cold, drafty little office with a bowl of yesterday's fruit and a stack of perfectly-aligned papers on the desk, she realized that freedom was freedom, and if she were executed she would not have to suffer this life, this Auschwitz life, one more day. Death might be good if one welcomed it. "Let me welcome it," she prayed.

Klinsmann grunted something inaudible when he finished at his desk, then grabbed his pistol and shoved it into the leather bag at his side. Still not looking at Sasha, he grabbed her by the upper arm and led her out the back door of the office and into a dark alleyway between two buildings. An SS car was parked very close to the back door and Klinsmann, after checking that no one was around, opened the trunk of the car and motioned for Sasha to get in.

At first she was dumbfounded, unable to move. Why did he want her there? What kind of a sick joke was this? He reached into his bag, pulled out the pistol, and pointed it at her. "Get inside. Now," he ordered.

Sasha did as he told her, struggling to bend at the waist. She barely fit in the trunk. Lying on her side with her legs bent backward behind her and her arms at her sides, she placed her hands on her abdomen. Klinsmann threw an old flannel horse blanket on top of Sasha and warned, "Do not make a sound. If you do, I will kill you." He touched his gun for emphasis and then pulled the blanket over Sasha's head.

Sasha cowered, terrified, as the door closed and the engine started. Klinsmann drove slowly through the concentration camp. Sasha knew the layout well enough to picture precisely the route they were traveling, past the administration building, the officers' mess hall and the canteen. She held her breath. For a few horrible moments she feared that she was being taken to Dr. Mengele's lab, where torturous and often fatal experiments regularly took place. She feared that her unborn baby would be ripped alive from her womb and she would bleed to death. In that moment she wished she had chosen suicide instead, and wondered if she could suffocate herself in the trunk.

She breathed a sigh of relief when she knew they were past the lab. Traveling further still, they reached what she knew must be the gate at the front entrance, below the chilling entry motto, Arbeit Macht Frei.

The car stopped and boot steps approached. From the trunk Sasha could hear Klinsmann talking to the guard manning the gate. It was a cool and quiet night, windless and with little late-night activity, so she could hear almost everything. High above she knew guards filled the watchtowers, rifles poised at their sides.

"You've been working late, Lieutenant? Going into town?"

"Yes. A great deal of paperwork related to next week's transport from Galicia; I need a break," Klinsmann replied.

It was well known in the camp that the SS often visited Krakow late at night for after-hours activities at Nazi-controlled taverns and clubs.

"You'll be back early in the morning, then?"

"Absolutely," Klinsmann answered. If he were nervous, his voice did not betray it. Of course, the young guard at the gate wouldn't dare to check the trunk of his older, superior officer. As Sasha heard the gate close behind the car, she realized that she was outside of Auschwitz. Her heart leapt with excitement, but she knew enough not to hope. Where could they possibly be going?

As the car moved out onto the open road, Sasha, not knowing what was ahead, tried to get some sleep. But the ride was cold and bumpy, and the cramps in her abdomen, which had been going on all day, became stronger and more frequent. Suddenly she felt something tearing inside her and then a surge of liquid wetted her skirt. The sensation was familiar. Her water had broken! She was going into labor. She couldn't have the baby here. She began pounding on the trunk above her head.

"Help, help!" she screamed. "I need help," she called out in German. She felt the car slow down, pull to the side of the road and stop. At that moment she let out a great wail of pain.

Klinsmann approached the trunk barking out orders, but when he opened the trunk he stepped back in shock.

Sasha, her arms now free, reached down under her skirt between her legs trying to feel the baby's head. She couldn't feel it yet, but when she brought her arm out into the bright moonlight, she saw that not only was her hand covered in thick, dark blood, but so were her torso, her legs, her dress, and the blanket.

"Lieutenant Klinsmann," she whimpered as another contraction seized her, "you must help me. Please. You did not take me from Auschwitz to kill me. You are a good man. You wanted to save me. And the child. Now please, help me out of this trunk. I will tell you how to deliver this baby. Please."

Klinsmann looked horrified. He opened his mouth but could not speak. Shaking his head, he slammed the trunk closed, returned to the driver's seat, and started up the car.

Sasha's faint glimmer of hope died quickly. For a moment she had believed that both she and the child might survive, but now she wondered if Klinsmann planned to drive around until both she and the child were dead, then dump their bodies by the side of the road. The contractions were getting closer together, and she wondered what she would do when the baby emerged. There was barely room for her to breathe; how would the child get air? She had no way to tie off the umbilical cord. And what if she did not stop bleeding once the baby was out?

It must have been two or three hours after they left Auschwitz that the car slowed down and Sasha guessed that they were near a town. The baby's head still hadn't emerged, although the painful contractions continued. Sasha was weak and trembling, overwhelmed with thirst. The stench of blood and urine overwhelmed her. She wanted to be strong, wanted to do whatever she could to save herself and her child, but she had lost so much blood she felt as if the very life force were seeping out of her.

At last the car stopped. The driver's door opened and Sasha heard Klinsmann's footsteps, moving not toward the trunk but away, in the other direction. After a few seconds he was gone, and Sasha heard nothing but some distant birdsong and a slight breeze. She guessed it was around four in the morning. Was Klinsmann just going to leave the car here with both her and her unborn baby still inside? Should she try to get out? She doubted she could open the heavy trunk, and even if she did, she was a Gypsy woman, a Gypsy woman in labor and tattooed with a concentration camp ID number. No ordinary Polish citizen would help her. In her mind she could see every door slamming in her face.

A few seconds later she heard footsteps again, approaching on what sounded like a gravel drive. There were two, maybe three people. Suddenly the trunk popped open and in the slight light of very early morning Sasha could make out the silhouettes of three figures, Klinsmann and two others. The shortest figure, which appeared to be a woman, leaned over the trunk and gasped when she saw Sasha covered with blood.

"Dirk, we must get her out now," the woman ordered in Polish as she reached out and grabbed her husband's arm.

"Yes, yes, Gerta," the man named Dirk responded. The man appeared to be about sixty. He spoke in Polish, but with a noticeable German accent and he spoke perfect German to Klinsmann. And once, no, twice, Sasha heard Klinsmann call the man to whom he bore a strong physical resemblance, "Uncle." Sasha surmised that Dirk was indeed Klinsmann's uncle, a German man who had married the Polish woman and who lived with her here in the countryside. There was a strong minority of Germans in Poland, particularly near Lodz, who had settled in that area two or three generations earlier. They had come when times were good in Poland, and many had stayed and married locals. But the wars with Germany had been particularly hard on these Slav and German intermarriages.

Klinsmann grunted an acknowledgement, then he and the man named Dirk reached in and lifted Sasha out of the trunk. Dirk and Klinsmann were both large, strong men, and Sasha, even in labor, weighed little more than one hundred pounds, so it took only a few seconds to release her. The men carried Sasha up the long gravel driveway and into what looked like an old stone farmhouse surrounded by several small and shabby wooden outbuildings.

Sasha was weak and dizzy, moving in and out of consciousness as the pains tore through her body, but she struggled to comprehend what was going on. Klinsmann had brought Sasha to his aunt and uncle's farm? Did that mean that he wanted to save her and the child? Sasha could not believe it. Klinsmann, whom she despised, had risked everything, even his life, to make this late-night journey.

Gerta directed Dirk and Klinsmann to place Sasha on a bed situated in the back room. The farmhouse was very small, consisting of just three rooms: a sitting room in front, a dirt-floor kitchen, and a small bedroom to the kitchen's side.

Gerta, who seemed to be in charge, ordered Dirk to boil some water and Klinsmann to fetch clean towels. Gerta tried to soothe Sasha, motioning for her to lie back on the bed. "I … I speak Polish," Sasha panted, struggling to catch her breath. "I am from Warsaw."

"So?" Gerta raised her eyebrows in surprise. "What is your name, child?"

"I am Sasha. Sasha Karmazin." Sasha did not want to give Gerta her Gypsy name, Lacatus. A good Polish Catholic woman would not touch a Gypsy's blood or skin. But then Gerta would have noticed the tattoo on Sasha's arm by now. If she understood what the Z stood for, she chose to ignore it.

"When is your child due?" Gerta asked, positioning a pillow behind Sasha's back.

"I am not certain," Sasha replied. "Not yet … I know this is too early. I can't be nine months along."

"Some babies are anxious, eh? This one will come soon." Gerta gave Sasha some water and tried to get her to swallow some thin soup.

Klinsmann, after gathering some towels and brusquely handing them to Gerta, said something to Dirk that Sasha couldn't hear. Then he left the room without looking at her, walked out to the car, and drove away. Sasha couldn't imagine where he would be going, but something told her that he would never come back, at least not while she was there, and she would never see him again. She imagined he didn't want to see the baby that his violence had created.

Sasha was relieved, even as a million questions ran through her mind. What did these two peasants think? They must have realized that their nephew was the father of Sasha's soon-to-be-born child. They must have known that Sasha was a Gypsy who had been imprisoned in a concentration camp. Gerta and Dirk's lives were now in more danger than they had been. Obviously, this was not something that concerned Klinsmann.

Sasha also had questions about the war, about politics, and about the outside world. She had been imprisoned for over a year. She did occasionally catch snippets of news. Klinsmann had a radio in his office, but the Nazi station played only Wagner music and propaganda messages. She had caught sight of Klinsmann's newspaper once or twice, but it was a Nazi paper, with enlarged pictures of Hitler and news about great battle victories on all fronts.

Sasha tried to keep her mind focused and alert, but it was difficult. She was exhausted and in extreme pain. Gerta helped her sit up, helped her roll to her side, helped her brace her back against the strong wooden headboard, but nothing helped; nothing seemed to relieve her discomfort. By seven o'clock that evening Sasha had been in labor for close to nineteen hours, and progress seemed to have ground to a halt. The contractions still came, but intense pushing yielded few results. The baby had yet to emerge and Sasha's bleeding, which had slowed to a trickle earlier, became heavy again. "You must get the midwife," Gerta told Dirk.

"But … but we can't," he argued fearfully. "It's too risky to leave the farm."

"This woman will die, and the baby too," Gerta insisted. "We must try to help."

Finally Dirk left in the old truck that was parked beside the barn, just as the sun was going down. "There, there," Gerta soothed. "Just try to stay calm. Save your strength for when you need to push."

As Sasha tried to relax, Gerta took an old cloth and tore it into strips, then wet one of the strips and used it to blot up some of Sasha's blood. She took Sasha's arm and tied the strip of fabric around her forearm, making certain that the stain of blood completely covered the small dark numbers and the tattoo would appear as nothing more than a wound that had been bandaged. Then Gerta took one of her own scarves from the dresser drawer and tied it around Sasha's head, covering her telltale shaved scalp with its uneven black stubble.

Sasha didn't know how to thank this kind stranger who was risking her life to help her. "Do you have any children?" Sasha asked.

Gerta shook her head. "No. Not anymore. We had two daughters; one died at six months old, the other at two. That's a long time ago now."

"I have two sons," Sasha offered. "The older boy is seventeen." Sasha caught herself, realizing that a year had passed. "Actually, he is eighteen now and my younger son is seventeen. I did not expect to have another child at my age."

Gerta shook her head. "Nor in this way, I am sure. Where are your boys?" Gerta asked, preparing a cool rag for Sasha's head.

"I don't know." Sasha winced as another contraction moved through her body. "I haven't seen them in nearly a year. I pray they are somewhere safe."

"This war," Gerta said, angrily shaking her head. "It has destroyed so many lives; so many innocent lives. Damn the filthy Jews! If it weren't for them, this whole thing wouldn't have happened."

Sasha was shocked but said nothing. *Why would this woman who hates Jews treat a Gypsy with kindness?* she wondered.

About forty-five minutes later Dirk returned with Paula, the midwife, a stout older woman with a round face and thick, strong hands. She seemed shocked when she entered the room, her eyes growing wide at the sight of the dark-skinned, emaciated woman with the huge eyes and the scarf tied tightly around her head, struggling through a difficult labor. Once Paula got over her shock she went to work quickly, pulling up Sasha's skirt and assessing the situation.

"How long has she been in labor?" Paula asked.

"It must be nearly twenty hours now," Gerta replied.

"Is this her first child?"

"No, her third," Gerta answered, holding the oil lamp high over Paula's shoulder so she could get a better look.

"How much blood has she lost?" Paula inquired.

Gerta squinted. "It must be a great deal. She's very weak."

The midwife felt Sasha's forehead with the back of her hand. "She's burning up with fever," she said. "Infection has already set in." The midwife slid her hands into Sasha's birth canal, causing Sasha to flinch. "The baby is breech. We will have to take the baby."

"No!" Sasha screamed. "Please, not that."

"It's all right, dear," Paula said, patting Sasha's hand. "I have done this many times before. I'll give you ether so you will sleep and not feel a thing. When you wake the baby will be here."

Sasha was frantic. "No please, let me stay awake. I can handle the pain."

Gerta gently squeezed Sasha's hand. "It will be fine. I know you are frightened, but you will be all right."

The midwife heated the ether and dripped it over the mask she placed on Sasha's face. Sasha felt the pain retreat as she entered the slow, drowsy, soft, and comforting embrace of sleep. She felt warm all over. The candles flickering on the table seemed to invite her in, and the down-filled mattress and wooden frame bed felt huge and softly luxurious beneath her. She felt a tear trickle down her cheek as her breath came slower and deeper.

"Just relax," Paula instructed, and Sasha couldn't help but relax. Faces turned to watercolor, while sounds dropped to a murmur and a hush. Gerta's gentle hand blotted Sasha's face with a cloth.

Once Sasha was unconscious Paula went to work, pulling back the sheets, the blanket, and Sasha's skirt to reveal the bloody belly. Her tools sufficiently cleaned in boiling water and alcohol, she traced a knife line from the navel downward and broke the skin. Now, having a guideline to follow, she used a bigger tool to cut through the skin, letting loose a terrible smell. "It's the infection," Paula said darkly. "It's much worse than I thought."

The midwife worked diligently, finally reaching the baby, a tiny boy who couldn't have weighed more than three or four pounds. His arms and legs were thin as twigs. Too weak to cry, he gurgled his first few breaths. The women wrapped him in a towel and Dirk sat with the baby by the fire. "He's a handsome little lad," Dirk said, coaxing the baby to grab his little finger.

"The mother won't survive, will she?" Gerta said sadly as she watched Paula sew up the incision.

"No," Paula replied, "and the child is early and very small. I expect soon you will bury him with his mother."

CHAPTER EIGHT

Paris, France
July 1985

"There were fifty of us, members of five or six extended families—mothers, fathers, brothers, sisters, cousins—hiding together in an abandoned barn on the outskirts of Szentgal, about seventy-five miles southwest of Budapest."

The man's voice was thin and crackling with age, but he spoke clearly and with strength behind his words.

"It was November of 1942, and we had managed to survive there for several weeks, drinking melted snow and eating seed potatoes and scrub grass. Then the Arrow Cross soldiers—Hungary's equivalent of the Gestapo—found us and marched us on foot through the freezing snow to the Csillag prison in Komarom. My mother and my sister died during the march. They were exhausted, cold, and starving, and I could do nothing to save them; most of the rest died later at Csillag. I believe that I, Karoly Fojn, am the only one of my family who survived the Porraimos."

Beth Karmazin hit Stop, then Rewind, on her portable tape recorder and listened to the last chilling sentence again.

"I believe that I, Karoly Fojn, am the only one of my family who survived the Porraimos."

In her many years advocating for Gypsy causes, Beth had listened to, recorded, and transcribed many Holocaust survivors' testimonies, but each one still held the power to stir her soul and touch her heart. As she rewound the tape and listened to Karoly's statement once more, she remembered sitting across from him in his cramped garret, mesmerized by his pale green eyes set like fiery gemstones in his deeply lined face.

Beth stopped her tape recorder, sighed, and looked out her narrow hotel window to Boulevard St. Michel two stories below. She longed to be down there mingling with the students and artists, or window shopping with the tourists and stopping for a *café au lait* and a *pain au chocolat*, instead of being cooped up in this tiny room with no air conditioning and the dank bathroom with its broken toilet down the hall.

Beth had three weeks until the deadline came due for the article she was writing on Gypsy Holocaust survivors who had settled in France, but as she read over her jumbled pages of notes, the words she was looking for just wouldn't come. She grabbed another cigarette, an unfiltered French Gauloise, and leaned back in her chair, balancing her bare feet on the narrow brick windowsill and letting the slight breeze through the thin lace curtains cool her skin. Unbidden thoughts about where she was in her life rose to the top of Beth's consciousness. She was now thirty; it had been eight years since she graduated from the University of Nebraska with a bachelor's degree in journalism and communication, and it had been six years since she had earned her master's degree.

Although she had never wavered in her commitment to Gypsy advocacy and the fight for civil liberties, Beth's career path had led her to work first at jobs in public relations and later in management of nonprofit professional associations in Atlanta, Washington DC, San Francisco, and now in Chicago, where she was the director of the International Sugar Growers' Alliance. She had been promoted often, with regular salary increases, but still her compensation was less than inspiring. What held her captive to the job was her generous vacation schedule, which allowed her to spend a significant amount of time traveling and doing volunteer work for Gypsy advocacy groups. It was that very commitment that had brought her here to Paris, where she was researching and writing an article for a Gypsy history publication in Toronto. She had four weeks to do the story and enjoy Paris.

Despite all of Beth's career changes, the one constant in her life had been her ten-year relationship with Andy Weinberg. When Beth and Andy started dating in college both families had had "issues" with the fact that Andy was Jewish and Beth was Catholic, but the families had since gotten over that and were now actually more scandalized that after ten years together, Beth and Andy still hadn't made it down the aisle. The couple had often discussed marriage, but the time was never right. First there was college and then grad school and law school to finish. Then Beth wanted to establish her career, and for the next several years they had to cope with the strain of a long-distance relationship.

But now Beth knew that, at age thirty, she was running out of excuses. For the past two years she and Andy had been sharing a condo on Lake Shore Drive in Chicago. Andy, at age thirty-two, was on the verge of making partner at the law firm of Isenman, Daniels, and Duke. He longed to have children and a nice home in the suburbs. He argued, maybe rightly, that he had been patient with Beth long enough, and the time had come to settle down.

Beth loved Andy; yet, she had to admit, sometimes she felt that their lives were moving in different directions. She had stayed true to her counterculture, liberal, ever-questioning-the-establishment roots, while Andy had grown increasingly conservative. And Beth was afraid that money was now beginning to drive a wedge between them. Her relatively modest salary meant she continued to live frugally, scrimping and saving as much as possible. Meanwhile, Andy's financial success, along with the expectations of his colleagues and clients, allowed him to indulge in the finer things in life: the best restaurants, good champagne and caviar, imported cheeses, five-star hotels, and expensive cars. Andy wasn't wasteful or extravagant; he never forgot his humble roots, but he was enjoying what he had worked so hard to earn. Beth worried that Andy's newfound materialism could eventually conflict with her distaste for displays of affluence.

Beth dropped her feet to the floor, sat forward, and rubbed her eyes. The sting of the strong French cigarette burned her throat and tightened her chest. "Stuff it," she said, closing her notebook and stretching her arms high over her head. "Come on, Paris, infuse me with some literary inspiration from the streets where Hemingway and Fitzgerald and Balzac walked."

A long sojourn through the Latin Quarter, a stroll through Luxembourg Gardens, and a light dinner with a glass of Burgundy helped to lift Beth's tense and fretful mood. She slept well that night and woke early, catching the Metro to the offices of the CIT—*the Comite International Tzigane*—the International Committee for Gypsies, a worldwide organization headquartered in Paris. Beth had an 8:30 AM meeting with Joanne Magirs, the head of the Paris office, whom Beth had known quite well since they first met five years earlier at a conference at the Roma Community and Advocacy Centre in Toronto. Beth was hoping that Joanne could provide her with some demographics on Gypsies living in France.

Joanne welcomed Beth into her modest office in the Marais area within the Third Arrondissement of Paris, an eclectic and diverse neighborhood of boutiques, bakeries, small art galleries, and museums. The inhabitants of the Marais were a melting pot of French and outsiders: North African Muslims, Asians, and Orthodox Jews. To Beth this district seemed the perfect spot for a Gypsy organization.

Beth and Joanne drank strong coffee and chatted as old friends, gossiping about colleagues in the tightly-knit Gypsy community of staff and volunteers. Like Beth, Joanne was part Gypsy. Her grandfather had been a full-blooded *Sinti*, a German Gypsy, who managed to escape to Canada before the Nazis rose to power. Unlike Beth, Joanne's Gypsy heritage was not visible in her short, curly blond hair, freckled complexion and round blue eyes. At thirty-five, Joanne was five years older than Beth, and Beth had always admired Joanne's energy, sense of humor, and commitment to the Gypsy cause.

As the two women talked, Beth glanced at the bookshelves behind Joanne's head. There, among a number of historical and Holocaust books, Beth noticed the spine of Dr. Peter Mavik's book, *The Porraimos: Gypsy Genocide in World War II*, which had been published in 1977. Even after eight years, seeing the book made Beth's blood boil. She shuddered to think that between those pages lay the accusation that her grandmother had collaborated with the Nazis at Auschwitz. Beth's encounter with Mavik in his office in the summer of 1976 had not been enough to stop him from publishing his lies.

"I see you're noticing my favorite book," Joanne remarked sarcastically, turning in her seat and following Beth's gaze to the spot in the bookcase. "I've found a number of untruths in it; the man must have been desperate to publish. Of course, we must keep everything here that is written on the subject of Gypsies, good and bad. I hear that Mavik is planning to publish a second edition of the book sometime in the next few years."

Beth looked down at her black coffee and twisted the mug between her palms. "I've heard that as well," Beth replied, nodding her head. "Hopefully I'll have enough proof by then to pressure him to retract the things he wrote about my grandmother. If I have to, I'll threaten legal action."

"You know," Joanne said with a twinkle in her eye, "if you worked for CIT here in Paris, you'd have close contact with the Gypsy community throughout Europe, and you'd have a better chance of finding out what happened to your grandmother and clearing her name."

"Maybe so, but that's not going to happen. I have a job back in Chicago with an adequate salary and lots of great benefits."

Joanne leaned forward, pressing her elbows on her desk. "Beth, we've got a job opening up here next month and you'd be perfect for it. I've put in your name." Joanne contained her excitement beneath a professional smile, while Beth nearly spilled her coffee as she precariously lowered her cup to the desk.

"What are you talking about?" she asked.

"Our current press officer and director of publications is retiring due to ill health. You'd be the perfect replacement and the CIT chairman has said he will accept my recommendation. What do you say?"

"I … I don't know what to say," Beth stuttered.

"Say you'll consider it!" Joanne replied. "I can arrange an interview for you for the end of the week, before you fly back to Chicago."

Beth's head spun. Had she really just been offered a job at the Comite International Tzigane? In Paris? This was an incredible opportunity, but for once in her life she wondered if she was really up to the challenge.

"Surely there is someone more qualified," Beth said finally. "Someone who has lived here in Europe. Hell, I've only got street French and college German."

"Come on, you're perfect for the job," Joanne replied. "I've already contacted the Roma Community and Advocacy Centre in Toronto and gotten a reference. They say your volunteer work has been exemplary. And obviously you have the educational credentials—degrees in journalism and communication and plenty of PR experience. Now, the salary is not great, but there are a number of perquisites, including living in the most beautiful city in the world. This is the opportunity of a lifetime. You won't regret it."

"I need some time to take this all in," Beth said softly, draining the last of the coffee and hoping the lukewarm liquid would give her some courage.

"Of course. I understand." Joanne smiled. "Look, Beth, you're coming back tomorrow to get those demographics from the Lyon office anyway. Sleep on it tonight and let me know what you think tomorrow. If you're interested, the job is yours."

Beth returned to her hotel, still in a daze. The tree-lined avenues and broad boulevards that she had gazed upon as a tourist just a few hours earlier were now her potential home. Not only could she be living in Paris, but she could be doing the work she had waited her whole life to do. But what about Andy? There was a chance he could find a job in Paris; after all, many American and multinational companies had offices here, and they all needed attorneys. But would he move here? For her? Just for a couple of years?

Beth woke late that night alone in her hotel room. At first she was frightened and confused, not understanding the dark and strange shapes surrounding her. Then her eyes adjusted and she realized she was looking at nothing more threatening than her sprung-open suitcase and a summer sundress hanging over the door. She got up, fumbled for a cigarette, and sat on the bed thinking about Andy. She missed having his arms around her holding her close in the darkness. She missed feeling his hands smoothing her hair. She had to turn down the job. She had to tell Joanne no. There would be other chances to help the Gypsies. She needed to go home to Chicago, to the life she had built there with Andy.

After a few more restless, nearly sleepless, hours, Beth rose, dressed quickly and made her way across the River Seine from the Latin Quarter to the Marais in a warm summer rain that left the streets clean and glossy.

As she strolled down Rue des Rosiers toward the offices of the CIT, she was shocked to see swastikas and anti-Semitic graffiti spray-painted on a synagogue, a Jewish bakery, and Titelbaum's Watch Repair. By the time Beth reached the building housing the CIT offices she was enraged by what she had seen. She hiked up the stairs two at a time, anxious to talk to Joanne, but as she reached the third floor and turned the corner, she saw down the hallway that something had been spray-painted on the frosted glass door to the CIT offices. Beth ran down the hallway and stopped in her tracks when the word became legible: ZIGEUNERUNRAT—German for "Gypsy filth."

When Joanne opened the door, Beth, still breathless, had only one question for her: "When do I start?"

Beth left the meeting with Joanne feeling both nervous and excited. She had had every intention of turning the job down, but when she saw the racist graffiti, the anti-Gypsy slur, something inside of her snapped and her mind was made up—she had to take the job. There was still a lot of paperwork to complete, of course, but Joanne seemed certain that Beth's application would be approved.

As the sun emerged from the clouds, Beth strolled the Parisian streets feeling less like a tourist and more like a native, returning home after a long time away. "This is the art gallery I will pass each day on my way to work," she thought. "This is the street vendor who will sell me roasted chestnuts at Christmastime." Then her thoughts turned to Andy. "It won't be forever," she told herself. "After a couple of years in Paris I can move back to the United States and resume my career there. Andy will understand; he'll know that this is my dream come true. In two years I'll only be thirty-two, still young enough for marriage and children. Andy has always been so supportive. Why would he stop now?"

Rather than phone Andy and tell him of her decision, Beth decided to wait until the end of the week, when he would arrive in Paris in person to spend the second week of Beth's working vacation with her. They had big plans to tour the Louvre, the Eiffel Tower, and Notre Dame.

Beth was filled with nerves as she waited for Andy's taxi to arrive. She had moved her luggage from the ramshackle Latin Quarter hotel to the Hotel Crillon at Andy's insistence, and was waiting in the opulent lobby, surrounded by Louis XVI furniture, overhead chandeliers, and elaborate floral arrangements that spilled petals to the red-carpeted floor.

Beth saw him through the revolving glass door as he stepped from his cab, looking elegant in a cream-colored summer weight linen suit with powder blue shirt and yellow tie. She had always teased him about dressing so formally when he was on vacation, but he always said, "You never know where or when you'll run into a client. It's about image."

Beth ran down the front steps and into Andy's waiting arms. He embraced her tightly and lifted her clear off the ground, even though she was nearly as tall as he was.

"God, I missed you," she said, filling her lungs with the smell of him, his brisk aftershave, the feel of his smooth skin. Somehow, in typical Andy fashion, either during or after the nine-hour flight from Chicago, he had found time to shave.

They were planning to go immediately to dinner, but when they got up to their room on the eleventh floor to drop off Andy's luggage, the spirit overtook them, and they made love on top of the king-sized bed. Even though it had only been ten days, Beth hadn't truly realized how much she had missed Andy until afterwards, when she lay back naked, relaxing in his arms. She had forgotten, even though she kept his photo in her wallet, how handsome he was with his short, perfectly clipped dark hair, his wire-rimmed glasses, and his evenly-tanned skin. Always so skinny in his twenties, he had filled out as he had matured, becoming more fit and muscular.

"I missed you so much, Gypsy girl," he sighed. "Chicago just ain't the same place without you."

"It was worse for me," Beth insisted, rising to an elbow and tracing her fingers on his chest. "Can you imagine the agony of being in Paris, the city of lovers, the city of light, knowing that my man is thousands of miles away from me? It was pure torture."

"Well, at least you had a productive week," Andy said. "Didn't you? You said on the phone that you got some great quotes for your article."

Beth froze. "Let's not talk about that now," she whispered, hiding her nerves. "Pleasure first, business later." She began kissing him, moving down one side and the other of his neck. Andy reached for the phone, dialed, and changed their dinner reservations for later. When they seemed to have exhausted every lovemaking possibility, they dressed and grabbed a cab to the Le Grand Vefour, a French cuisine restaurant located beneath the arches of the Palais Royal. They had finished their entrées and were sharing what remained of a bottle of Chateauneuf-du-Pape and listening to the violinist in the background, when Andy commented, "I can tell you're going to miss this place, you've got that dreamy look in your eye."

"Andy, there's something important I've got to tell you. I've been offered a job here in Paris. At the Gypsy center, working as the press liaison and information officer."

Andy smiled and sipped his wine. "Wow! That's pretty exciting. How did they react when you turned them down?"

"I didn't. Andy, I took the job." Beth's voice was barely a whisper.

Andy nearly choked as he set down his glass and pressed his napkin to his lip. "What? Are you kidding? You aren't serious."

Beth fumbled nervously with her silverware. "It'll only be for a year or two," she argued. "Then I'll move back to Chicago and we'll pick up where we left off. This is the chance of a lifetime."

Andy shook his head slowly, with a look of profound sadness. "It's not enough that you said yes to the job. It's that you never even asked me. You don't need my permission, of course. But you never even asked my opinion. You never asked what I thought. After ten years, I'd like to think my opinion counted for something."

"It does." Beth reached across the table and clasped Andy's hand, which was oddly cold to the touch. "It counts for everything. We can make this work; if any couple can, it's us. Look, we've had a long-distance relationship before. When you were in Chicago and I was in San Francisco, we had most of a continent between us and we made it work. So, now, instead of a continent, we'll have an ocean. But we can do it."

"I think not." Andy very quietly dabbed his lips and neatly folded his napkin beside his plate. "I've waited long enough. Long enough for you to be my wife; long enough for you to have our children. I've spent the last ten years of my life waiting for you to 'find' yourself. I'm finished, Beth. I'm used up. This is over."

Andy stood slowly, and carefully pushed his chair back to the table. His face showed little emotion save for a tightening around his lips and a furrow above his eyebrows. He took two steps, then turned back to Beth, reached into his jacket pocket, and pulled out a small velvet-covered box, which he tossed onto the table.

"I was going to give this to you," he said evenly as Beth opened the hinged box to reveal a dazzling diamond engagement ring, which sparkled and glittered in the light. "Tonight. After dinner, as we walked hand in hand along the banks of the Seine. I was going to ask you to marry me; to become my wife. I suppose I should thank you for sparing me the embarrassment of having you say no."

Beth was too shocked, too frightened to cry. She felt as if she were sitting on the top of a roller coaster, about to watch her entire life plunge out of control. Her heart was pounding and her throat so dry she couldn't speak.

Andy began to walk away with slow, even, measured steps, heading toward the front of the restaurant.

"Wait!" Beth called after him, rising from her chair and nearly tipping the table in her haste. "Please wait. Andy, the answer is yes. I will marry you. I'll turn the job down; I'll come home with you. Andy, please. You mean everything to me."

A million thoughts and emotions ran through Beth's mind. She did love Andy, and at that moment the job in Paris seemed unimportant in comparison.

She reached Andy quickly and grabbed him by the arm, but he pulled away. "Andy, please," she begged. "At least let's talk. Let's sit down, finish our dinner, and discuss this like rational human beings. Let's not decide anything tonight. Let's just talk and see what tomorrow brings. I love you."

Andy shook his head, and Beth barely recognized the flat, empty expression in his blue eyes, unblinking behind his wire-rimmed glasses. "No, Beth. I'm done talking. I'm done with everything. I'm done with you. Just let me go and get on with my life."

"Andy?" Beth stood, too stunned to move, as she watched him walk past the other diners, out of the restaurant, down the steps, and out of her life. "Andy?" she asked again, realizing that he was no longer there to hear her.

CHAPTER NINE

Auschwitz, Poland
Summer 1944

After Sasha was removed from Auschwitz, rumors began to circulate among the prisoners about what had happened to her. One of the most outrageous claims was that she had been secretly gathering magic herbs from the camp's grounds and she had used them to cast a spell that allowed her to disappear like a ghost into thin air. Others claimed she had bribed a guard with sexual favors and he had helped her to escape out of the back gate late at night. Still others argued that Sasha was pregnant with Hans Frank's child, and that Frank had arranged for her safe passage to Switzerland, where he would keep her as a mistress and join her after the war. The more time passed, the more elaborate and outlandish the stories and conjectures about Sasha's fate became.

The female prisoners who had been in the barracks the night the guard took Sasha away were surprisingly quiet. They had all agreed to tell no one what they had seen, not even if other Nazi guards questioned them about it. They feared that saying anything, even telling the truth, could get them killed. They were, after all, supposed to have been sleeping when Sasha disappeared.

Stefan, Sasha's brother, grieved; he had absolutely no clue as to Sasha's fate, and not only did he have no idea what had happened to Sasha, he knew nothing about the fate of his other sister, Melina. Before Sasha's disappearance Stefan had been moved from the Gypsy camp to another barracks on the far northern edge of the concentration camp, where he was grouped with several hundred relatively young and healthy men, mostly Jewish. These men had been placed on a new work detail and given the backbreaking task of moving large stones from one area of the camp to another. The heavy stones had to be lifted individually by hand into wheelbarrows and then transported to the new location. Stefan's job was to move the wheelbarrow when it became full.

While this was tortuous work, Stefan was grateful for the assignment. Since the Nazis had made Emil Dep a *kapo* at the Gypsy camp, life had been even more difficult for the Gypsies. His father, Mar Dep, was sick with typhus and unable to assert authority over the Keldari. Emil, greedy and without principle, took more than his fair share of the food and medicine and sold the rations to the Jews and Poles on the Auschwitz black market. And often he turned over the sick or the frail to the Nazi selection, hoping to earn their favor.

Stefan hoped that by being useful, his life might continue. He had stayed remarkably strong through his imprisonment, even though he was thin, often dehydrated, and the work was exhausting. Every day a handful of men, and on the worst days a dozen or more, died at the work site, particularly as the summer sun reached its zenith and the temperatures soared to 100 degrees.

When the men fell, they were carted off and their bodies thrown into a nearby ditch that had been dug specifically for this purpose. When the stench from the ditch became unbearable, the Nazis threw in buckets of gasoline and set the rotting corpses on fire, burning them down to ash. Days on the work site were as long as twelve to fourteen hours, with sometimes only a cup or two of brackish water to drink and a brief thirty-minute lunch break, during which they were served only bread and a cup of cabbage soup.

On the morning of July 21, 1944, Stefan Lacatus woke before dawn to the sound of rapid and continuous gunfire from the Black Wall, better know as the "killing wall." He knew instantly that many prisoners were being executed. Something was happening; there was a strange sensation in the air. The execution of prisoners was common, but this many, this early in the day, and this quickly, could only mean that the Nazis were in a hurry and a major change was taking place.

Stefan lay back in his wooden bunk, wondering. Could it be that the Allied forces were advancing and the war would soon be over? In that case, the Nazis might kill every last prisoner, to complete the "Final Solution" before their own most-certain deaths. Or had the Axis nations finally been victorious and the Nazis simply decided the worn-out and mostly sick prisoners were of no further use to them?

Whatever will be, will be. *Bibaxt*, Stefan told himself, rolling over and closing his eyes, desperate for a few more moments of sleep and trying to ignore the rats that darted over his bare feet. There was no use in speculating. Just take it minute by minute, hour by hour, day by day. Stay strong. Survive.

Two hours later, as Stefan and his fellow workers marched to their work site, they passed the killing wall. Blood was spattered in all directions, creeping like an enormous crimson spider web. Kapos were gathering dead bodies, tossing them into wagons and taking them away toward the crematoria. Even after having witnessed so much death, Stefan covered his mouth with his hand and swallowed hard to fight off the bile and vomit. An aura of increasing evil and impending doom permeated the air.

When Stefan and the other men reached the work site, they were surprised to see Standartenfuehrer Friedrich Swartz there. Once all the prisoners were assembled in even rows, Swartz called them to attention and made an announcement.

"There has been a change of plans," the colonel announced in German, then waited for the *Dolmetscherinnen*, two young Polish interpreters, to translate his words into Polish, Rumanian, and Czech.

"You will not work on the building site today. Today you will be transported to Buchenwald, a work camp east of here. You are very, very lucky men." Swartz clicked his heels and made a half-turn on the wooden podium. "Once you have completed six months of work there, you will be given your release papers and set free."

It took several minutes for this news to filter through the crowd as the translations were made, and more and more of the men understood what had been said. The crowd's low whisper rose to excited chatter, until Swartz shouted angrily, *"Ruhe! Ruhe!"* an order to silence; a command they all understood.

"You will leave immediately. The transport waits at the front gate. Anyone who does not proceed immediately to the train will be shot on sight. Herr Obersturmbannfuehrer Schlegel will lead you there."

As the Polish, Rumanian, and Czech translations were transmitted, the men turned in place and saw Lieutenant Colonel Schlegel waiting at the back, which was now the front, of the group, ready to lead the way. As Swartz gave the order, Schlegel offered a salute and began marching back through the camp, past the killing wall, where bodies were still being picked up and tossed aside like garbage.

As the men marched, a tall man just behind Stefan tripped and fell out of formation. Before he could get back in line, a guard grabbed him and shot him between the eyes. Stefan did not blink and did not look back. He just continued marching, keeping steady steps and counting out the footfalls beneath his breath.

When the men reached the train they were herded into cattle cars, just like the ones that had brought most of them to Auschwitz. In addition to Stefan and the other men from his work detail, most of whom were placed in the same car, there were hundreds and hundreds of other prisoners, mostly younger, healthier men being loaded into other cattle cars in the long train line. Stefan figured there must be at least one thousand prisoners filling the train. Now his joy at leaving Auschwitz alive was tempered by the fear of what horrors might lay ahead.

Once Stefan was forced into his cattle car, he struggled to breathe in the dark, dusty, and unbearably hot environment. Limbs pressed against limbs, and already several men had urinated and vomited, adding to the horrific stench of filth and sweat. The men were stacked almost three high, and fought each other for space, pushing the smaller and weaker men to the dusty floor of the car.

The train pulled away from the gate and the prisoners tried to get comfortable. Several people began to talk, at last free of Nazi supervision. Mostly they compared horror stories, and asked for news about missing family members, members who had arrived at Auschwitz together but had been placed in different barracks. Some men sobbed, others wailed as they learned of loved ones' deaths.

The prisoners positioned closest to Stefan were debating whether to believe the Nazis' promise that they would be released after six months at the new work camp. Some argued that the fact that the train was full mostly of younger, healthier men suggested that the story might be true. But others argued that the Nazis likely planned to kill all the men at once, making it easier to then liquidate the elderly, the weak, the women, and the children left behind at Auschwitz.

About an hour into their journey, Stefan, who was near the front of the cattle car, noticed that the lock on the door hadn't been completely secured. In their haste to lock up the prisoners the Nazis had closed the lock but hadn't pushed the padlock's pin in all the way. Stefan slipped his hand through the slight crack in the door and demonstrated. "Look here," he said to the other men. "I can move the lock up and down on the bolt. If

I were to push it all the way out, the lock, and then the door, would swing open."

"We could escape by jumping from the train," someone said excitedly.

"You must be joking," another man replied. "At this speed, we would be killed on impact."

"And we have no idea what we might be jumping into," someone else argued. "We could be on a bridge, or suspended over a river."

"Do you notice how sometimes the train slows a bit?" someone posed. "That must be when we are passing through a town. If we wait until the train slows after nightfall, we can jump then."

"But we might reach our destination before night falls," another man argued. "We have no idea as to the length of this journey."

"I agree it's risky to wait; it's risky to jump at all. But I cannot believe either option is riskier than facing whatever awaits us at the end of this journey," one man argued. "The Germans will not set us free after six months, of that I am certain. Why would they release us when they can kill us just as easily, once we have outlived our usefulness?"

There was one man on the train, Reuven Greenblatt, who had worked as a civil engineer before the war and had a degree in cartography. He was also a private pilot who had flown small planes all over Europe. "I know the location of Auschwitz and the geography of Poland and Germany," Reuven said softly. "Let me show you."

The men around him moved back, pressing their backs against the car's walls, creating an open space. Reuven used a small twig to draw a makeshift map with the dirt, dust, and sand on the floor. Meanwhile, another man bent back one of the loose wooden slats in the train's door, to allow in as much sunlight as possible.

Reuven traced a roughly four-sided shape with the twig. "Imagine this is Poland," he said. "Here is Warsaw." He pointed to a spot in the middle-right of the shape. "That is where I was taken into custody and placed on a train such as this one, to be transported to Auschwitz. I could not see outside to gauge where we were going, but I felt the train travel due south, then slightly west, for approximately two-hundred-and-fifty kilometers. That would have put us around Krakow, and, indeed, the train slowed considerably at that point, leading me to believe we were passing through Krakow's central station. I have been at that station many times, before the war. From Krakow it was a short journey, about fifty kilometers due west, to Auschwitz."

The men considered the dirt-and-sand map. "Now, when we left Auschwitz, we headed northwest, toward Wroclaw," Reuven continued. "There is a major railway line heading that direction. From Wroclaw we headed due west; if this is correct, we will cross the border into Germany soon. From there, who knows where we are heading?"

Reuven, who was kneeling, sat back on his heels and looked up into the other men's expectant faces. "What is this 'Buchenwald' that the swine colonel was talking about?" he asked. "I know of no such town. Once we reach our destination, we will have no chance for escape. I say we move, as soon as the sun goes down and the train slows. Fellows, it is our only hope."

The men argued for a while, debating the merits of staying on the train versus leaving. Stefan said very little, allowing the other men to debate, but secretly he had already decided that he would leave, and he hoped that only a few others would join him. Clearly, there would not be time for every man in the cattle car to jump to freedom, and the more men who jumped the greater the risk of discovery by the Nazis who manned the front of the train.

When the sun was down the men steadied themselves, bracing the muscles in their legs. There was no way to predict when the train would slow, and once it slowed they wouldn't have time to react, so they had to be ready to push open the door and jump at a moment's notice. Along with Stefan, six other men decided to risk the jump—Janko Hatvan, Reuven

Greenblatt, Meir Amin, Pavel Hrodotsky, Vaclav Kaminsky, and Binyamin Geldbart.

"Good luck," said the men who had decided to stay behind. "If you survive and we don't, please tell the world about us. Don't let them forget. Tell the whole world what happened at Auschwitz."

"The same is true for you," said Meir, a young man with intense dark eyes. "If you survive and we don't, please tell the world about the horror."

Suddenly, without warning, the train began to slow. "Now!" Binyamin yelled. "Now! Now! Now!" Stefan reached through the gap in the door, found the padlock with his hands, and forced it open. The lock shuddered and flew off and the heavy wooden doors swung open with an enormous whoooosh of air.

"Go! Go! Go!" Meir shouted. One, two, three, four, five, six—the men jumped from the roaring train and tumbled hard on the ground, landing on their hands and knees. The train barreled past and the men huddled together, linking their arms and bowing their heads.

Once the train had passed, the men looked around at their surroundings. They were fortunate that the nearly full moon gave them good visibility. They had landed in what looked like a typical small Middle European town with a town square bordered by an onion-domed church and a town hall. The train station was very small, consisting of three intersecting rail lines, a two-windowed ticket booth beneath a clock, a glassed-in waiting room, and a length of canopy that overhung approximately twenty yards of the tracks.

The rest of the town, the houses and businesses, seemed to be located to the south of the station, while to the north was the ridge of what appeared to be a dense evergreen forest. "There—the trees—that direction," Stefan panted, struggling for breath. "Safer there than here."

The men had only taken a few steps forward when suddenly another train appeared on the horizon, chugging down another track. The train was still quite a distance away but the noise of its approach shook the wooden platform and the tiny station. Suddenly, a guard who had been asleep slumped inside the ticket booth jerked awake. As his eyes opened, he saw the dark huddle of the six men just over the tracks. He jumped up, grabbed his rifle, and ran from the booth.

"Go!" Stefan shouted to the others. "Just run!" All six took off running toward the woods.

In a moment the guard was behind them, yelling, "Halt! Halt!" Suddenly a shot rang out, slicing the bark off a tree just ahead. Another shot rang out; a man screamed and then fell. It was Meir. Binyamin turned to help him, but Pavel grabbed Binyamin by the shoulder and pulled him away. "No, we must go. You can't help him now," Pavel argued before another shot hit him square in the throat.

Additional shots ricocheted against the trees as Stefan, with Janko at his side, closed in on the deepest part of the forest. Suddenly Janko screamed and fell to the ground. Stefan stopped and went back to him.

"I've been shot," Janko panted. "Go. Leave me here. Save yourself," he argued. Stefan looked around. There was no sign of the guard. He looked down and quickly determined that Janko had been shot in the arm. The arm was bleeding profusely, but Stefan didn't think the wound would be fatal.

"Come on," Stefan said, grabbing the uninjured arm and helping Janko to his feet. "You'll be all right. Let's go."

After walking for more than an hour, Stefan and Janko came across what looked like an abandoned farm with a rundown farmhouse and a large stone barn a good distance from the house. Stefan bid Janko to wait in the woods while he checked that the barn was empty. Janko was weak and exhausted from the loss of blood, and he sat with his back against a tree trunk, struggling for breath.

Meir and Pavel were dead; Stefan didn't know what had happened to the others, whether they had escaped to other parts of the woods, or if the guard's bullets had brought them down as well. Now Janko was pale and shaking. Stefan knew full well that he might be the only survivor of the escape.

Stefan entered the barn carefully. There were no cows, horses, or other livestock, but there were several bales of hay and some bags of feed. A number of cats stalked the corners of the barn. Stefan looked to the farmhouse. It was empty; there didn't appear to be even a candle or fire lit inside. Still, it was too dangerous to venture over there tonight. He decided to go back the next day and if the house was empty, see if there was anything there that could be salvaged.

Stefan returned to the tree and found Janko unconscious. "Wake up, please wake up," Stefan pleaded, shaking Janko's uninjured arm. Janko roused, and Stefan led him slowly to the barn, where they collapsed on bales of hay and both fell into a deep sleep.

In his dream Stefan was running from the Nazis and their vicious Alsatian dogs, which nipped at his heels, snarling and tearing flesh from his limbs. Blood began to spurt from his mangled arms and legs, covering his whole body in hot sticky fluid as he cried out in pain. Stefan woke with a start in the darkened barn and for a moment had no idea where he was or what was happening.

Slowly his eyes adjusted. It was early morning and sunlight had begun to enter the barn through the broken glass windows. He was not at Auschwitz anymore. He had escaped; that much was not a dream. He looked over at Janko. At first he feared the man had passed away in the night, but as Stefan looked closer he could see the man's chest rise and fall.

Janko was a tall man, in his mid-to late-thirties, but he looked closer to sixty. He had fair skin and what looked like a shadow of blond hair. His naturally deep-set eyes were sunken from emaciation; the paper-thin lids barely closed and the translucent skin was stretched to nearly breaking across his cheeks and nose. He had large open sores on his neck and forearms, and

Stefan feared the man would die before he ever woke again. If that were to happen, Stefan didn't know what he would do with the body, or what words he would say for a Jewish soul.

Seeing that Janko was still asleep, Stefan left the barn to explore his surroundings. After checking that no one was around, he walked to the farmhouse and entered. The house was empty, stripped nearly bare, and it appeared that no one had been here for months, perhaps longer. One of the few things that remained was a framed photograph of Adolf Hitler on a wooden shelf. This confirmed what Stefan suspected; they were over the border and inside Germany. They had waited too long to jump from the train.

Stefan took whatever he could, which was really just some old women's clothing and some dried and yellowed newspapers, which he wasn't able to read. They could use the papers for bedding and use the clothing to bandage Janko's wounds.

There was a well with a pump behind the house, and Stefan nearly whooped with joy when he saw it. He feared the well might be dry, and that could be why the inhabitants had abandoned the house. Stefan grabbed the pump's handle and began pumping furiously. At first just stale air emerged, but finally, after he had pumped a good ten minutes without a break, a trickle of dark, iron-smelling water dripped out. Inspired, Stefan pumped harder and faster, until the water ran clear, clean, and cold in a steady stream. Stefan cupped his hands beneath the flow, brought the liquid to his lips, and drank and drank. He drank until his stomach distended and he felt painful pangs of gas.

He waited for the pain to pass and then he drank some more, drinking until he felt he couldn't hold another drop. When he was full, he removed his black-and-white striped cap and filled it with water, then soaked some of the clothing he'd taken and tied the soaking items in a ball.

When Stefan returned to the barn Janko was semiconscious and moaning. Stefan took Janko by the shoulders, and, trying to avoid the injured arm, moved him into a sitting position against the bale of hay. Janko's head tipped backward and his jaw fell open. The cap that Stefan had filled with water was now empty, but still dripping with liquid. Stefan held the cap over Janko's mouth and twisted it, dribbling the water over his lips. The cap, and therefore the water, was filthy, but Janko drank eagerly. The water seemed to help Janko regain full consciousness, and his eyes focused clearly as Stefan continued squeezing water into Janko's withered mouth.

"Why do you help me?" Janko asked wearily. "I am a Jew."

"And I am a Gypsy." Stefan felt the man's forehead with the back of his hand. "We are brothers in our suffering."

Janko's eyelids flicked and he swallowed hard. Stefan understood. Janko was disgusted, physically repulsed, by the realization that he had been touched by, fed by, and tended by the hands of an "unclean" Gypsy. Fury rose inside of Stefan and he contemplated smothering Janko, or at least leaving him alone and allowing him to die. Even here the two men were not free from the same kind of fear and hatred that had created the horror of the Third Reich and the horror of Auschwitz. But just as quickly as Stefan's fury had come, it passed, and something new filled Stefan's heart. "Forgive," Stefan told himself. "Forgive this man for his ignorance. Break the cycle of hatred that has kept us all in chains."

"What did you say your name was?" Janko asked.

"Stefan Lacatus," Stefan replied.

"Lacatus?" Janko's eyes widened. "Did you have a sister named Melina Lacatus?"

"Two sisters," Stefan replied. "Melina and Sasha. Both were also at Auschwitz, but Sasha's married name was Karmazin. I don't know if they live or …" Stefan tried to banish the dark thoughts. What chance was there that his sisters had survived? If they hadn't escaped, and there were no women on the transport to Buchenwald, what chance would they have? It was clear that all the Gypsies at Auschwitz had been marked for extermination.

"Sasha Karmazin?" Janko squinted. "Was she a Dolmetscherin?"

"Yes." Stefan's mind flashed back to the day he had arrived on the transport from Mielno and saw Sasha on the platform, translating for the Nazis.

"I knew of her," Janko said. "It was common knowledge in our barracks that she was Hans Frank's woman and she was carrying his child. He spirited her away in the middle of the night to Switzerland, where he will meet her when the war is over."

Stefan's fury ignited once again, but alongside his fury was a small glimmer of hope. *If Sasha is alive and safe, then nothing else matters. I would rather have her alive, no matter the circumstances, than in an unmarked grave among the millions of others.*

Stefan walked to Janko and grabbed the frail man by his shirt, squeezing so tightly Janko fought to breathe. "If you ever say anything like that about my sister again, I will kill you without a second thought. My sister would not sleep with a Nazi swine, no matter what." Stefan released the man's shirt, and Janko fell back heavily against the bale of hay.

"I'm sorry," Janko whispered. "It was only a rumor." He paused. "What do we do now?"

"We wait," Stefan replied. "What else is there to do? We can gather food—plants and berries—from the woods. We have water. Even as the seasons change there will be warmth here in the straw and protection from the elements."

"How long will we wait?" Janko's pale eyes watered.

"Until the war is over," Stefan replied.

"That could be years," Janko argued. "How will we know when the war is over?"

"We'll know," Stefan replied. "We will know."

As Stefan and Janko waited at the deserted farmstead in eastern Germany, Stefan had no way of knowing what was taking place at Auschwitz. The Nazis had transported the younger, healthier Gypsies to other camps—

the men to Buchenwald and the women to Ravensbruck—where they would again work for the Nazi war machine, this time in the armament factories, until ultimately it was their time for the gas chambers.

However, the Nazis mistakenly believed that sending away the stronger men and women from Auschwitz would make the task of eradicating the remaining Gypsy women and children effortless. But the Gypsies heard that something was going on. Although they would never know who it was, it was Sasha who had passed the word through the Auschwitz underground that the Gypsy camp was soon to be liquidated, and that word was passed on to the Gypsy leaders in the camp.

The remaining Gypsies were determined to fight for themselves. On August 1, 1944, when at three in the afternoon the Nazis once again began the process of "liquidating" the Gypsy camp at Auschwitz, the Gypsies staged a revolt. As the guards tried to force them into lorries that would take them to the gas chambers, they fought back, using strips of stolen sheet metal, razors that they had sharpened into knives, and clubs that they had fashioned from torn pieces of wood. They fought valiantly even with their bare fists, punching, beating, and kicking the guards. The Nazis responded to the revolt by mowing down the resistance with machine guns. By seven in the evening, four hours after the revolt had begun, the Nazis had retaken control of the Gypsy camp and resumed herding the surviving Gypsies onto trucks, barrack by barrack. The trucks then began the short journey to the gas chambers and from there to the crematoria.

By the early morning hours of August 2, 1944, the liquidation of the Gypsy camp was complete. The last of the Gypsies at Auschwitz, numbering between three and four thousand, had been killed and cremated in one mass action, bringing the total number of Gypsies killed at the Auschwitz concentration camp to twenty-three thousand. In the Gypsy world, the night of this slaughter would be forever known as *Zigeunernacht*.

CHAPTER TEN

Grandview, Nebraska
May 1944 – April 1945

Lillian Olson watched as Karl Karmazin, her eighteen-year-old foster son, tall and blond with strong, broad shoulders and suntanned skin, adjusted his mortarboard in front of the bedroom mirror and fidgeted with the gold tassel. He was draped in a long, but not quite long enough, black graduation gown that ended above his ankles, skirting his canvas sneakers. His face was serious, his brow furrowed and nose wrinkled, as he moved the tassel this way and that.

"Here, let me give you a hand with that," Lillian offered helpfully, striding toward him. He turned to face her as she stood on her tiptoes and straightened his cap. She had just come from the kitchen and there was a smell of shortening on Lillian's hands and fine flour dusted her blond eyebrows and lashes, giving her an almost ghostly look. Such closeness to his foster mother made Karl ache, made him miss his real mother, Sasha, whom he had not seen in over a year and whom he now feared he might never see again.

Lillian squinted, licked her fingertip, and wiped a smudge of dirt from Karl's cheek, the cheek with the fading scar inflicted by a Nazi's rifle butt. Karl flinched like a child as Lillian touched his skin. Teasingly, she said, "you'll never be too big for me to fuss over."

After a brief embrace, she held him at arm's length and looked him over from head to toe. "You look perfect," she pronounced. "Now, let's get a move on, or we'll be late for the graduation ceremony."

As Lillian turned to walk away, Karl took her hand and awkwardly cleared his throat. "Aunt Lillian," he said, "I just want to thank you for everything."

As the boys and their foster parents had gotten to know one another, the Olsons had not pressed the boys to call them Mother and Father, or Mom and Dad. They knew that would be painful for boys whose real parents' whereabouts were unknown. But calling them Mr. and Mrs. Olson was too formal, while Kermit and Lillian was too casual. So they settled on Aunt Lillian and Uncle Kermit—names that offered respect and familiarity, but didn't intrude on the titles Mama and Papa, which were reserved for their birth parents.

Lillian and her husband Kermit had been unable to have children of their own, so they were especially thrilled when they applied, and were approved, to become foster parents to two Polish boys, Karl and Dimitri Karmazin, who were refugees from the war in Europe. The boys had left Warsaw in the spring of 1943 after spending several weeks hiding in a warehouse on the outskirts of the city. Their uncle had secured them tickets on a train to Gdansk and from there passage on a ship to Sweden and then on to England. Eventually the boys were sponsored by the Polish-American Alliance in New York and arrangements were made to bring them to the United States, where they arrived in July 1943.

When the boys arrived in New York they were told they were being sent to work on a farm in Nebraska. They knew nothing about Nebraska, but they steeled themselves for working long hours in dirty conditions, sleeping in a barn with little to eat and little protection from the elements. "We'll be no better off than unpaid servants," Karl grimly told Dimitri.

"Unpaid servants are slaves," Dimitri responded flatly.

Having such low expectations, Karl and Dimitri were surprised when they arrived in the small town of Grandview, Nebraska to find a shy, kindly-looking couple in their late forties waiting to greet them. The Olsons welcomed them politely and offered them a single small, but cozy, bedroom to share, complete with homemade quilts and clean, starched, ironed sheets that were changed weekly, without fail. Although the boys were expected to help on the farm with chores in the barn and the fall corn harvest, they were relieved to find they only had a few hours of work a day, and when school started, only two hours of chores per day. And they were never asked to do anything dangerous.

Communication was difficult at first; the boys spoke only the broken English they had learned from the BBC, and there was no one in Grandview who spoke Polish. However, the one medium that quickly united the Olsons and their foster sons was food. Lillian Olson was a good cook, and she took tremendous pride in feeding her "boys." And Karl and Dimitri, who had nearly starved the six months before they reached Nebraska, and indeed hadn't eaten properly since the war had begun several years earlier, wolfed down everything that Lillian placed in front of them. They came to love real buttermilk and homemade cheese, pancakes, bacon, and sausage drowning in maple syrup, something they had never tasted before. On Sundays the family feasted on thick slabs of ham and hot baking powder biscuits slathered with gravy.

Fall came quickly and the boys were introduced to the joys of apple cider, acorn squash, corn on the cob, and Lillian's wonderful pumpkin pie, peach cobbler, chocolate cake, and blueberry muffins. In the first six months on the farm Dimitri grew two inches and gained nearly twenty pounds. Karl, meanwhile, grew nearly three inches, to six-foot-three, and had gained almost thirty pounds.

The Olsons were not emotionally expressive, but they had quiet ways of showing concern and respect, as they gradually brought the boys into their lives. Although staunch Lutherans themselves, the Olsons understood that the boys had been raised Catholic. Every Sunday they dropped Karl and Dimitri off at Grandview's single Catholic church, St. Agnes's, before continuing on to their own Gethsemane Lutheran on the other side of town.

Neither boy was particularly religious; after what they had experienced during the occupation, God seemed a distant partner, but they took comfort in listening to the familiar Latin Mass.

School was, of course, difficult for the boys at first. When they arrived in Grandview Karl was seventeen and Dimitri was sixteen. Based on their ages, Karl was placed in the senior class and Dimitri in the junior class. They did well in math but struggled with English, history, and social studies. Every night after chores and supper, while Kermit listened to the farm report in the living room, Lillian worked with the boys at the kitchen table on their English, using children's reading and spelling books from the library. The stories about ponies and princesses and ice skates and fairy tales were silly, but the boys made great progress.

By Christmas, the end of their first semester in an American high school, both boys were able to converse in English. By the time the school year ended in June, Karl had earned enough credits to graduate and Dimitri had been promoted to twelfth grade.

In the weeks before Karl's high school graduation, Lillian and Kermit spoke to the boys about their futures. The Olsons explained that they would prefer to adopt the boys and become their legal parents, but since Karl was already eighteen and Dimitri only one year younger, by the time the paperwork was complete, there would be little point in it.

"But you are our family. You will always have a home here with us," they explained. Kermit expressed hope that Karl would attend the community college in Lincoln to study agriculture and take over the farm someday. Dimitri seemed to have a mind for business. The Olsons hoped he would go to the university and study economics and commerce, then perhaps return to Grandview to open a business. The Olsons, who had missed out on being parents until later in life, held high hopes that there would be many grandchildren to bring them joy in their old age.

The Olsons were filled with pride as they watched Karl stride across the gymnasium stage and accept his diploma. He shook hands with the principal and turned to face the crowd and smiled as cameras flashed and clicked away. Lillian thought to herself what amazing progress Karl had made—in the span of nine months he had gone from being a withdrawn and defensive boy who spoke no English to a strong and even-tempered young man who expressed himself articulately.

After the graduation ceremony was over, the Olsons hosted a modest party at their house, which had been decorated with tissue paper streamers, helium balloons, and a large hand-lettered congratulatory sign. The backyard had been transformed into a party area with a large picnic table holding fruit punch in a huge glass bowl. Meanwhile, Kermit stood at the grill cooking burgers, hot dogs, and corn on the cob. Dozens of guests had been invited, including neighbors, extended family, and friends from school.

Both boys had become quite popular. As their English improved, so did their standing with their classmates. Dimitri was well-liked for his quick intelligence, his sense of humor, and his willingness to help others. Karl was especially popular with the girls, who liked his tall blond good looks and his success on the basketball and baseball teams. He had even found an American girlfriend of Spanish-Irish descent: Margaret Sullivan, a bubbly cheerleader with dark curly hair, blue eyes, and alabaster skin.

The party was well underway when Karl, to everyone's surprise, called the party together and asked for their attention. Once everyone was silent, Karl cleared his throat. Redness colored his cheeks and threw his subtle scar into high relief.

"Thank you all for coming to my party," he began. Although his English was close to perfect now, he still had a pronounced Polish accent and when he was nervous, such as now, the accent increased and he struggled to find the right words. "I have an announcement to make."

Whatever chatter there had been disappeared now, as all eyes riveted on Karl. "But first, I want to thank my foster parents, Aunt Lillian and Uncle Kermit, for welcoming my brother and me into their homes and into their hearts. They have given us more than we could ever have dreamed of. I truly do not know what would have become of us had it not been for their generosity. I also want to thank the town of Grandview and everyone here for making us feel so welcome." He took a deep breath. "And, of course, I must thank this wonderful country, for everything it has given to me and Dimitri. I intend to pay back my debt, so I am enlisting in the U.S. Army."

The gathered group was confused, not sure what this meant. Kermit and Lillian had always talked of the boys going to college. Lillian spoke first. "Karl, by the time you finish college the war will surely be over," she said.

Karl shook his head. "No, I have already enlisted in the Army. Today."

Several people whooped and rushed forward to congratulate Karl and clap him on the back, while Lillian's face fell and she fought back tears. "But … but you aren't even an American citizen," she argued. "And you're only eighteen. You're not old enough to vote, even if you were a citizen, which you aren't!" Flustered, she turned to her husband beside her. "Kermit, explain to Karl why this isn't possible. He can't join the army."

Karl untangled himself from the congratulatory crowd and came closer to his foster parents. "The recruitment officer said it was okay. I don't need to be a citizen, and at eighteen I can sign for myself." He looked down, and his lip trembled slightly. "Please be happy for me," he whispered. "I am going to fight for America."

Kermit, in a rare show of emotion, grabbed Karl's right hand and shook it, then slapped the boy on the back. "We are happy for you, son! I am so proud of you, my boy. There is no greater honor than to fight for one's country."

Dimitri could hardly speak. He was happy and sad at the same time; he had never been without his big brother. "When do you leave?" he asked when he finally found his voice.

Karl took a deep breath and released it, relieved that his big news was out. "I start training next week," he replied. "At Fort Bliss, Texas. After six weeks I'll be shipped out."

"Where will you go?" Karl's girlfriend Margaret asked, like Lillian, trying to hide her shock and disappointment that Karl would be leaving.

"I don't know," Karl admitted. "That's up to the army. I could end up in the Pacific, or Europe, or maybe the Mediterranean. It is my deepest hope that I'll be sent to Poland."

As more people crowded around Karl, listening to details of his impending departure, Lillian quietly excused herself and went to her bedroom, sat down on her neatly made bed and sobbed.

Later that night Dimitri and Karl lay in their beds in the room they shared. The lights were off, the windows were open, and a warm prairie breeze moved through the humid room as mosquitoes buzzed around the screen. In the distance, huge windmills twirled and turned, while weathervanes pointed toward the north.

"Karl, are you afraid?" Dimitri asked at last, his voice sounding small in the darkness.

"A little."

"Karl, there might not even be a war for you to fight," Dimitri offered. "It is said an invasion is planned soon for the continent and the Allies will be victorious."

"True," Karl agreed. "But I don't think it will be over so quickly. Hitler won't quit until the entire continent is in flames."

"Will you search for Mama and Papa?" Dimitri asked softly.

"If I am sent to Poland, yes," Karl answered. "I'll go to Warsaw and find Papa and if Mama is not there, I will help him find her."

"Do you think she's still …?" Dimitri whispered.

"I have to believe she is," Karl answered. "Otherwise …" His voice cracked. "Otherwise, I could not bear it. Dimitri, I must see Mama and Papa again. I must." His voice took on urgency. "Lillian and Kermit are wonderful, and I appreciate everything they have done for us. But they did not give birth to us; they did not raise us from children. In my dream, I find Mama and Papa and bring them home with me here to Nebraska, and they buy a little house in town, and we can all live here together. Stupid, huh?"

Dimitri had tears in his eyes. "No, Karl, it is not stupid. But my dream is a little different. I miss Warsaw. Do you think our friends from school are still there? Sometimes I want to play soccer, not baseball. And I want to walk through Stare Miesto; I want something more than the smell of dirt, the buzz of mosquitoes, and cow dung in my nose. Rather than white bread and mayonnaise, I want rye bread and kielbasa and pierogies." Dimitri paused, seemingly surprised by his own outburst. "When you see Mama and Papa, tell them I love them," he said softly.

"Dimitri, I will. I promise."

The week following Karl's graduation passed quickly. There was so much to do: shopping for Karl, buying him clothing and luggage, and visits to all the friends and neighbors to say good-bye.

On the day of Karl's departure, Kermit, Lillian, and Dimitri drove him to Lincoln, where he would pick up the train to Fort Bliss. As they waited in the station's lobby, Lillian gave Karl a sack lunch complete with a lettuce, mayonnaise, and roast chicken sandwich, an apple, a bottle of grape Ne-Hi, and some homemade oatmeal cookies.

Then, while Lillian stuffed clean handkerchiefs into Karl's tan duffel bag, Dimitri presented Karl his going-away gift, two new Superman comic books that Dimitri knew Karl would love; Karl read comic books incessantly to help him learn English. Then Kermit gave Karl his gift, a compact shaving kit designed for travel, with a horsehair brush, powdered soap, and a non-breakable metal cover that served as a mirror. Karl's fair complexion had just begun to sprout facial hair and he was pleased to receive such a useful gift.

Finally, Lillian gave Karl her gift, the small leather-bound Bible that had been given to her by her father on her wedding day. "I know it's a Protestant Bible. I wasn't sure what words to change to make it Catholic, but the Lord will know."

Suddenly the waiting room shook, and they all looked up to see the train pulling into the station. Karl quickly slipped his gifts into his duffel bag, and Dimitri and Kermit helped him gather his things.

"Send us a postcard when you get there," Lillian pleaded. "Just let us know you've arrived in one piece."

"I will. Take care. Good-bye," Karl said, climbing the steps to the train. "Good-bye for now. I'll be home soon, before you know it."

As Karl moved through the train cars looking for his reserved seat, he glanced through the windows and watched as his new family followed his progress down the platform. He stopped once, bent down, and waved. They waved back. He blinked hard, grateful that they could not see his tears.

As the train pulled out of the station Karl took stock. A number of other enlistees were already on the train, which had originated in Chicago and made a stop in Des Moines before Lincoln. From Lincoln, the train would stop in Oklahoma City before arriving in Fort Bliss the following morning. Some of the other young men on the train were soldiers on leave between tours of duty and they had a noticeable swagger in their step as they moved confidently from train car to train car. Still others were fellow enlistees, the youngest of whom looked no more than sixteen. A few complained of homesickness already. Karl kept his cool, feeling his chest brim with unmistakable excitement. But when Karl arrived at Fort Bliss, he learned he would not be doing his basic training there. Instead, he would be sent directly to England to prepare for the invasion of the European continent.

Although an American assault on the European continent was anticipated, the massive invasion of Normandy on June 6, 1944, surprised the world. Even Private Karl Karmazin, now into pre-invasion training in Staffordshire, England, was unaware when and where the invasion would take place, but he knew he wanted to be there, and the sooner the better. He wanted to kill Nazis.

On July 18, Karl's 687th Field Artillery Battalion shipped out to Utah Beach on the northern coast of France, where they attached to the 90th Infantry Division, U.S. First Army, VIII Corps, and entered the battle. Over months of grueling fighting, the Americans liberated Paris and pushed the Germans out of France. Karl thought surely things would end here; he had seen enough of dying by now on both sides. Many of the Nazis he had come to kill turned out to be young men and boys like the American soldiers, just trying to survive. Karl would never forget the first German soldier he saw dead on the battlefield, a boy no more than fifteen, with his eyes staring up at the sky and a cross and a photograph of his mother clutched in his hand. Karl wanted it all to be done with, but it would not be soon. A determined and fanatical Adolf Hitler would not give up. The war was far from over.

On December 16, 1944, Karl's battalion faced the Germans again, this time in the bloodiest fight of the war, the Battle of the Bulge, a massive battle along an eighty-five-mile stretch from southern Belgium into Luxembourg. It was a costly victory for the Allies, leaving seventy-six thousand American soldiers dead, wounded, or captured. Karl survived and was promoted to the rank of Corporal, First Class.

In March, General Patton's massive coalition of infantry, artillery, and armored tanks crossed the Rhine and eventually pushed the Germans deep into the heart of their own country. It was April, and the war in Europe was effectively over, yet Karl was about to witness human suffering far worse that anything he had seen in his childhood in occupied Poland or more recently on the bloody battlefields of Western Europe.

On April 11, 1945, Karl's battalion pushed through the gates of the Buchenwald concentration camp. The soldiers had been told that conditions would be grim, and the task dangerous, as the Nazi guards would fight to the last man to keep control of the camp. But nothing could have prepared the American soldiers for what they encountered. As they rolled through the gates of the camp they were met by a sickly crowd of Russians, Poles, Jews, and Gypsies. Nearly all the SS guards had deserted the complex several days before, leaving twenty-one thousand prisoners behind who were now guarded by other inmates trying to maintain control of the chaos and anarchy left behind.

The stench of death and decay permeated the air. American soldiers in jeeps skirted the barbed wire perimeter of the camp and moved through the interior. They were stunned. Dead bodies were everywhere: mass graves, and living skeletons, bags of bones that miraculously moved and even spoke. People so thin, blood beat visibly beneath their transparent skin.

Men, women, and children, their heads shaved, dressed in garish striped prison garb and covered in filth and excrement, walked aimlessly and stared at the new intruders. Some people, still alive, were too weak and emaciated to stand. Dead bodies filled large open pits and wagons. Many of the living begged to be put out of their misery.

Buchenwald had not been established as an extermination camp; there were no gas chambers, but mass killings took place regularly here and thousands died as victims of grotesque medical experiments. What one sick mind didn't think of, another did. The Americans learned the women of the Third Reich could be as diabolical as the men. Ilse Koch, the beautiful German wife of Buchenwald's camp commander often rode her horse through the camp wielding her riding crop and beating any prisoner who dared to look at her. She earned her infamous name as the Bitch of

Buchenwald by specially selecting prisoners with interesting tattoos, then having their skin stripped and made into decorative accessories; lampshades, billfolds, and books.

The soldiers, many as young as Karl, became mentally distraught and physically sick at the inhumanity they witnessed. Some fainted; many vomited or openly wept at evidence of cannibalism or rats gnawing on dead bodies. The soldiers had come expecting to be liberators of thousands of war prisoners well enough to celebrate the end of their incarceration; instead they were witnesses to torture and genocide, and people too sick to appreciate their newfound freedom. The soldiers walked in shock and disbelief around dead bodies, uncremated because coal had been in short supply.

Although Karl's battalion hadn't been sent to Europe to manage the liberation of a concentration camp the size of a small city, they got the assignment. Karl's war-torn battalion was temporarily relieved of combat duty and given responsibility for managing food services at Buchenwald. The GIs couldn't find wheat flour or yeast anywhere in the camp, so they devised unleavened oat bread that they baked, dried, and gave to the prisoners in the form of small crackers. They shared cigarettes with the smokers and taught them how to play poker. And, in anger and disgust, the American soldiers rounded up German civilians in nearby villages and marched them through the camp to witness the atrocities that had happened under their noses. What did they think had been happening inside this massive camp?

Karl could not believe his eyes as he walked through the camp. War was cruel, violent, random, shocking. He had witnessed all that and more on the battlefields of Western Europe; his own first sergeant had been the victim of a direct hit by a grenade that tore him to pieces. But what he saw here was different; hundreds of thousands were dead, but there had been no battle. This was evil incarnate; this was hell on earth. And now Karl knew why the Americans had entered the war and why they had to win it.

When some of the prisoners were well enough to speak of what had happened to them, the Americans began asking questions. Karl knew by now that he would never fight the war in Poland. There had been a deal made among the Allies that would require the Russians to drive the Germans out of Poland and in return they would be given Poland for reconstruction. But Karl was still desperate to know what had happened to his mother and father and what was happening in Warsaw.

Most of the Gypsy men who had been transferred from Auschwitz to Buchenwald were still afraid of authority—anyone in a uniform—and they refused to speak. But Karl eventually found a man named Fritz who had been a violinist at Auschwitz in the camp orchestra. He told Karl he had been transferred to Buchenwald by train in July of 1944. He tried but couldn't remember Sasha Karmazin.

"I was one of the lucky ones," he explained. "I was selected with the other healthy Gypsy men to be transferred here before the Gypsy camp was to be liquidated."

"Liquidated? What do you mean, 'liquidated?'" Karl asked anxiously.

"All remaining Gypsies were to be exterminated in August 1944. The Polish prisoners who were transferred here from Auschwitz in October confirmed to me that this happened."

Karl rushed to the next barracks, where many of the Polish prisoners were assigned. He found the healthiest of the bunch and pulled him from his bunk. "Tell me what you know of the Gypsy liquidation at Auschwitz," he pleaded.

The prisoner, who had been resting, was wide-eyed and fearful now. He stammered, "The liquidation?"

"Yes, the Gypsy liquidation."

"All gone: men, women, and children. Gassed. The Gypsy camp was gone in August, before I was deported to this place."

Karl stared at the man, tying to absorb this news. Then he pulled the man closer, holding tightly to the front of his shirt. "And Warsaw, what do you know of Warsaw?"

The prisoner's eyes were pleading, and Karl loosened his grip, chastising himself for being so rough with a war victim.

"The city is rubble; nothing is left. The Poles rebelled in August last year and the Germans retaliated, razing and burning the city. Those who survived were executed on the street. Luckily I was outside the city when the battle began; the Germans had sent me to the country to pick up produce. I escaped with my wagon, but was captured several days after the battle was over and sent to Auschwitz."

Filled with grief, Karl ran from the barracks, tears trailing down his cheeks. He found a large boulder outside an empty barracks in a quiet corner of the camp and sat down. His hands shook so violently he had to press his elbows to his chest to light a cigarette. He drew in a deep breath and let the mentholated smoke fill his lungs. He blew out the breath and closed his eyes. But nothing would block out the devastating news he had just heard about his mother and father. For the first time in months he cried, and when there were no more tears to cry, he made a solemn vow to himself. "When this war is over, I will never set foot on this continent again. There is nothing here for me. As long as I live I will never return."

CHAPTER ELEVEN

Spring 1986

"I now pronounce you husband and wife. You may kiss the bride." As the deep-voiced priest said the words, Beth's eyes filled with tears, and her bridesmaid's bouquet trembled in her hands. She couldn't help but think about Andy, who had tried to propose to her nine months earlier in Paris.

"This could be *my* wedding," she thought, blinking quickly. "I could be the one kissing my new husband right now and would be starting a new life together that included a real home and children. But I took the job in Paris instead."

Ellen looked beautiful in her long white dress and matching veil. And Beth finally decided she liked her new brother-in-law, Bob, although at times he appeared a bit stuffy and tedious. Beth smiled and tried to be supportive as Mr. and Mrs. Robert Kramer turned to face their guests assembled row after row in the stiff wooden pews of St. Stephen's Catholic Church in Grandview, Nebraska. Still, Beth couldn't ignore the ache in her heart as she thought about Andy. Where was he now? What was he doing? Had he met someone else? She hadn't spoken to him or received so much as a note or a phone call since that fateful night in Paris when they split up so abruptly and he left her standing outside Le Grand Vefour. And her love life had been painfully barren since Andy had walked away that night.

"It's foolish to think about that now," Beth chided herself, staring down at her flowers. "I made a choice and I'm doing work that I love. This is my fate: *Baxt*, as the Gypsies say."

Ellen and Bob's grand wedding was followed by an even grander reception at the Grandview Knights of Columbus lodge. Beth played the part of dutiful older sister and bridesmaid: greeting guests, hugging maiden aunts, kissing babies, and answering question after question about what it was "really like" to live in Paris. The only moment in which her mask slipped came as her father and her sister took the honorary first dance across the smooth wooden floor.

Late that night, after all the guests had gone home or back to their hotels, after shoes had been removed and ties loosened, Beth and her father sat in the den at home, talking. Beth was drinking a Portuguese sherry, while Karl drank his usual Kentucky bourbon on the rocks. The lights were low, and father and daughter were relaxed, as comfortable as two old soldiers who had been through a battle together and come out safely on the other side.

"It was a beautiful wedding," Beth said, massaging her tired feet. "And a beautiful day. You and Mom did an amazing job with everything."

"I hope it was beautiful. It cost me as much as a new truck." Karl chuckled, swirling his drink in his hand. "You know, we really miss you here, Beth. Seeing you once or twice a year just isn't enough."

"Paris is fantastic," Beth replied. "Dad, I'm doing the most fulfilling work of my life. I am helping people who really need help; if you haven't noticed, not very many people are interested in taking up the gauntlet for the Gypsies. And I'm working my butt off to get the Gypsies the compensation they deserve for their losses, same as the Jews. I know I had good jobs when I was in the States and I miss you and Mom terribly, but I love my work."

"I know you do." Karl's face darkened, and he looked down at his hands, folding them awkwardly in his lap.

"Dad? What is it?" Beth asked. "What's wrong?"

Karl looked uncertain, then stood and went to his desk, opening a drawer and sliding out a letter. "You might like to read this." He handed the letter to Beth. "It came several days ago and I haven't had time to respond. It's from my old friend Feliks Lubonski in Warsaw." Feliks was a childhood friend of Karl's who had tracked Karl down in Nebraska through the Polish-American Alliance after the war.

Beth held the letter up to the light. "There's no censorship stamp on this."

Karl nodded. "Feliks is in an unrestricted category when it comes to mail, a perk he received from the Polish government some years ago for his dedication to his people."

Beth pulled the letter from the envelope. Karl had acquainted Beth with Feliks's history years earlier. Feliks's family had escaped to Denmark before the war and returned in 1945, only to be caught soon behind what would later become the Iron Curtain. After earning a PhD in architecture from the University of Warsaw, Feliks became a professor and learned to live within the Communist system, even how to take advantage of it. Eventually, he was appointed to the commission on rebuilding the war-ravaged country.

Dearest Karl,

I hope this letter finds you well. How nice it would be if we could spend some time together before we are too old to remember why it was a good idea. I have been granted a permit that allows me to bring in specialists from the West to work on restoration projects in Stare Miesto. With your knowledge of that part of the city and experience in the electrical business, I am sure I can secure you a temporary visa to visit.

Please think over my proposal and let me know your answer.

Fondly,
Feliks

Beth folded the letter and sat back in her chair. "What an opportunity! So when are you going?"

"I'm not," Karl said emphatically. "I have no intention of going back to Warsaw. Not ever. There is nothing left there for me."

Beth was shocked. "I can't believe you would turn this down," she argued. "It's a perfect chance to visit Feliks. Dimitri and Matthew can watch the business while you're gone, and Mom has plenty to keep her busy here."

Karl shook his head, eyes darkening. "Under no circumstances will I ever set foot in Europe again, and I don't want to discuss it any further."

Beth's forehead furrowed. "Dad, how would you feel if I went in your place?"

Karl looked surprised. "Why would you want to go to Warsaw?"

"To see where you and Dimitri and Grandma and Grandpa lived," Beth replied. "To see if I can find out anything more about what happened to Grandma Sasha. A visa to Eastern Europe is not easy to come by. I'd hate to lose this opportunity."

Karl slowly poured himself another shot of bourbon, and then stroked his chin. "You'll find nothing, but if it will make you happy, I guess I don't see any harm in you going in my place if Feliks can change the paperwork."

Beth knew she had to move quickly. The day after Ellen's wedding she contacted an old friend at the University of Nebraska and had him send a telex to Feliks, crossing her fingers as she exaggerated her abilities in restoration.

Dear Feliks—my father is unable to accept your invitation to Poland—I would like to come in his place—I have a background in site restoration and have studied pre-war Warsaw—please respond.

Best regards—Beth Karmazin

Two days later Beth received a telex back from Feliks, letting her know that she had been approved to work as a consultant on the project. She could pick up her visa on the way back through Paris, and Feliks would meet her at the Warsaw airport.

Beth, energized beyond belief, called Joanne at the CIT office in Paris and asked to take the remaining two weeks of her vacation for that year. Then she spent the next few days boning up on her conversational Polish, her knowledge of history, and a basic overview of historical site restoration. She knew she was taking a big risk in pretending to have a background in a subject she actually knew little about, but her passion to see Poland drove her forward. The night before she left Nebraska she had her Uncle Dimitri draw her a map of Old Town from memory, the Old Town he remembered, and detailed plans of the family apartment, the watch repair shop, and other key locales.

Throughout the process of Beth's preparations, Karl stood back, seeming uneasy. Beth was hurt that he wasn't more enthusiastic, but she knew she couldn't focus on that now.

The day that Beth's mother was to take her to the Lincoln airport, Karl asked her to stop by his office. Beth's heart was pounding as the door closed behind her. She couldn't imagine what her father wanted to talk to her about, since they had said their good-byes that morning at home. "What's wrong, Dad?" she asked.

Karl gently placed his hands on Beth's shoulders and looked her straight in the eyes. Beth held his gaze.

"I'm worried about you. I don't need to remind you that during the war in Poland most of the Polish Gypsies were exterminated by the Nazis. The

Polish people did not try to stop this from happening. The Poles have never accepted the Gypsies. In fact, in that part of the world it was once believed that Gypsies descended from a sexual encounter between a Gypsy woman and Satan. I doubt forty years have changed people's attitudes much. Watch your back, Beth."

Less than a week later, Beth found herself sitting aboard a Russian Aeroflot airplane, preparing to land at Okecie Airport after a short flight from Paris. She fidgeted with her hair, longing for a cigarette but not wanting to suffocate in the already smoke-filled cabin, or break her record of having gone nearly four months now without a cigarette.

As she peered out the small round window on the inside seat, Warsaw came into view in brief, tantalizing glimpses between the clouds. Warsaw looked nothing like Paris, or even like Lincoln or Omaha, for that matter. Warsaw's topography was drab: concrete buildings and shadowy streets with tiny, boxy cars lining up at streetlights and overpasses. Beth felt a wave of sadness, trying to picture the elegant old European capital that Uncle Dimitri had so lovingly described to her.

After the flight landed and the passengers disembarked, Beth had no trouble spotting Feliks waiting for her at the gate. He had quite accurately described himself as a tall man with graying hair, a long thin face, and a neatly-groomed, narrow gray mustache. His quick smile and warm handshake made Beth feel immediately comfortable, despite the armed and grim-faced Communist guards posted at every corner.

When Beth's luggage arrived, she and Feliks moved quickly through the security points and out to the parking lot with no one questioning Beth's mini cassette recorder, which she had worried might be confiscated by the nervous authorities. They arrived at Feliks's two-bedroom, one-bathroom flat and he gave Beth a quick orientation, explaining that he had been unexpectedly assigned to a project in Budapest and needed to catch the midnight train.

"I'm sorry, but I won't be back until Thursday," he explained. "I'll leave you the manual regarding the work we are doing in the Old Town and when I return we can review your comments and observations. And remember, the Communist government has forced the Gypsies to assimilate; their children have to go to school and the adults have to work like everyone else. But ordinary Poles still haven't accepted them. Be careful."

The next morning Beth was up early and eager to go. The Old Town was just blocks from Feliks's flat and she walked there in a matter of minutes, passing by beautiful Lazienki Park, a place where her father had told her that he and Dimitri had played as children. Her intention was to find the site of the watch shop first and see what might remain there from Karl and Dimitri's childhood. But as she strode down Mokotow Street, a narrow side street no wider than an alley and inlaid with cobblestones, she was shocked to see a sign marking Broza Sklep Meisny. Beth stopped dead in her tracks, her mind reeling. She looked at the sign again: Broza Sklep Meisny. The Broza family butcher shop. This was the very shop that had been owned by Klaus Broza, the man whom Mavik had implied had turned Sasha over to the Gestapo. *How could this shop still be here after all these years?* Beth wondered. The government had recently allowed privatization of many of the small businesses in the Old Town, but Klaus Broza, if he were still alive, couldn't possibly be in charge. Could it be his son or nephew or grandson who now ran the place?

Beth strode up to the modest little shop, pulled open the glass door, and stepped inside. The shop was nearly empty, and the meat displayed in the cases consisted of small, sinewy roasts and rough-cut briskets marbled with ashy-looking fat. The prices were high and the quality and quantity uniformly poor. Beth realized that only the Communist Party bosses in Poland were likely to be eating good cuts of meat on a regular basis.

The few other patrons stepped aside and the man behind the counter, a tall, heavyset man about forty with a florid complexion and an auburn mustache, smiled at Beth. "Can I help you?" he asked in Polish.

"I'm afraid my Polish is not very good," Beth stammered. "I am from the United States and I am doing some family research."

"Ah wonderful! A chance for me to practice my English then." He turned to the back room and shouted in Polish, "Lech! Come out front please, and man the counter for a while. I have a guest from the United States."

A skinny red-haired boy, looking no more than seventeen, skulked out from the back room and listlessly adjusted his grease-stained apron, double-tying it over his narrow hips. Meanwhile, the older man washed his hands and came out from behind the counter. "Hello, my American friend! My name is Cy Broza. Welcome to our shop."

Beth took his outstretched hand and shook it, hoping Cy couldn't feel the nervous sweat on her palm.

"My name is Beth Karmazin. I come from Nebraska, in the United States, but my father and uncle, Karl and Dimitri Karmazin, were born here in Warsaw. Very near to here, in fact."

If Cy Broza recognized the name Karmazin, his face did not reveal it. "So many of us have relatives in the States," he said wistfully. "Unfortunately, we have no contact with them, due to East-West politics."

"Are you related to Klaus Broza, the man who owned this shop in the nineteen-forties?" Beth asked carefully.

Cy led Beth to a small table at the front of the shop and motioned for Beth to sit down, which she did.

"Of course I am. I am Klaus's grandson. Klaus bequeathed this shop to my father, Sygmund. Of course, private ownership meant nothing in Poland until the rules were changed and Papa was able to buy it back from the government. Unfortunately, my father died of cancer six years ago, and the shop has belonged to me since then." Cy looked away sadly.

"Did your father or your grandfather ever mention the name Karmazin—Sasha Karmazin, or Henryk Karmazin?" Beth asked.

Cy shook his head. "Not that I recall." He paused to stroke his mustache. "Why don't we ask my grandfather?"

Beth was stunned. "Ask your grandfather?"

"Yes."

"You mean he's still alive?" Beth nearly choked. She had assumed that Klaus Broza was long dead, and nothing Cy had said so far had changed that impression. Until now.

"Yes, he is still alive. At eighty-five years old he is declining, with poor eyesight and unsteady limbs. But his mind is still sharp and lively. Do you want to see him? He is upstairs."

For a moment Beth panicked, not sure what to say or do. The man who could answer her serious and long-held questions was under this very roof. But she felt overwhelmed and woefully unprepared. She didn't even have her mini-cassette recorder with her to record his comments, she thought ruefully.

"Miss Karmazin?" Cy looked quizzical. "My grandfather?"

"Y … yes. Yes, I would like to meet him," Beth stammered, feeling the blood rush to her face. "I apologize for losing my composure. I didn't think anyone from my family's past would still be …" she hesitated to say *alive*, "… accessible. This is quite a surprise."

"My grandfather doesn't speak English. Do you speak any German, by chance? Otherwise I can translate the Polish for you."

"I took several years of German, so we should be able to communicate," Beth replied.

Cy led Beth upstairs to a cramped but clean and neatly kept sitting room and directed her to a stiff wingback chair. Lace doilies adorned the tabletops, and the curtain appeared handmade. The wooden floor was shining and freshly waxed. A collection of black-and-white family photos was arranged on the mantel above the fireplace. Beth swallowed hard, trying to calm her nerves. She could hear Cy in a room down the hall, talking in Polish, alternately sounding kind and cajoling.

A few minutes later, a tall, thin man with a full head of thick, tousled white hair entered the room. He walked with a cane, and his pale blue eyes had a distant, vacant expression. He was nicely dressed in an Oxford shirt, dark pants, and a beige cardigan sweater. Beth's immediate thought was that he looked nothing like a retired butcher who had spent decades in cold storage rooms, lifting and cutting large slabs of animal flesh with his bare hands. Instead, he looked like a teacher or a writer; perhaps an academic of some kind.

Klaus seemed to stumble for a moment, and Cy was quick to steady his grandfather's arm. "This way, Grandpapa," he said in Polish, leading the old man to the sofa across from Beth. "You have a visitor today. A young lady all the way from the States! Her name is Beth Karmazin. Her family used to live here in Old Town."

At the mention of the name Karmazin Klaus nearly tripped and let out a groan that seemed to come from his soul. He turned as if he intended to return to his own quarters, but Cy held him gently in place. "Grandpapa? Are you all right?" he asked.

Looking stricken, the old man slowly lowered himself to the sofa. His hands shook visibly as he laid his cane aside and attempted to straighten his sweater.

"So many years," he said in a hoarse whisper. "So many years I have waited, wondering when someone would come and expect me to answer for Sasha Karmazin. But you are not the first. One day a few years back, a man came to see me. He said he was a professor from the United States, working on a book about the war years in Poland. He thought I could help, and I agreed to do so. But it seemed he was only interested in information about Sasha. He wanted to know about her contacts with the Nazis. I told him I didn't know that she had contact with the damn Nazis, except for one day when I saw her with Hans Frank in the town square. And now you are here," Klaus said with a heavy sigh.

Cy suddenly seemed alarmed, and put a comforting hand on Klaus' shoulder as he looked Beth straight in the eye. "Miss Karmazin, maybe this isn't the best time to talk. Perhaps if you come back—"

"No," Klaus interrupted, composing himself. "I have carried this burden long enough. The time has come for the truth."

Klaus seemed to be waiting for Beth to take the initiative, so she did. "Why did you do it? Why did you turn Sasha over to the Gestapo?" she asked harshly. "You had to know that would be a death sentence."

Klaus looked down at his folded hands, then back up, his eyes full of sorrow. Beth wanted to look away, but she couldn't. She had to look in his eyes, and she had to listen to him very carefully to understand what motivated this man to betray his friend and countryman.

"So, you want to know the story? Okay, I will tell you. My oldest son, Bolek, was sixteen years old at the time, and he was very ill with pneumonia. Penicillin could be had on the black market, but it cost a fortune; far more than my wife and I could pay. But the Nazis, yes, the Nazis were clever. They knew how to prey on those of us who were poor and desperate. They were offering two hundred *zloti* to anyone who revealed the whereabouts of a Gypsy. They paid even more for a Jew. Do you have any children?" Klaus whispered.

"No," Beth replied.

"Then you can't possibly understand the choice I faced. My son was dying. He needed medicine. With that money … it was enough for the penicillin. A few doses would save his life." Klaus swallowed hard, fighting back tears. "The truth is, I didn't even know for sure Sasha *was* a Gypsy. I thought perhaps if I turned her in, the Gestapo would take her into custody, ask a few questions, and then Henryk would come with her birth certificate and other papers and get her released. I actually thought Henryk and I would look back and laugh about it over a drink someday. Can you imagine that?"

Klaus paused and rubbed his hands over his eyes and up through his hair, while Beth stared at him, stunned by his story.

"So you sold out Sasha, your friend's wife, for money," Beth said evenly. "Are you aware that Sasha was sent to Auschwitz and died there?" Beth asked.

Klaus nodded. "Yes. Everyone knew. But, you see, I didn't report Sasha to the Gestapo. Yes, I thought about it very hard, but I couldn't do it. We Poles are loyal to the end. I couldn't betray my old friend Henryk."

For a moment Beth could think of nothing to say. Finally she found her voice. "But your son … you said he was dying, and so how …?"

"How did I get the money for the penicillin? I went to Henryk, my good friend. I knew if he had the money, he would give it to me. Unfortunately, he was broke too, but he gave me the best watch he owned, and I was able to sell it. That's where I got the money for the drug." Beth choked back tears. This is not what she had expected to hear. Since Karl had first told her about Klaus she had thought of him as a greedy, licentious man who took advantage of the venalities of war, accepting bribes and betraying friends. Now she didn't know what to think.

"It doesn't make sense. Why didn't Henryk protect you from the rumors? Surely he could have saved you from such condemnation."

"After Sasha was taken away and his boys escaped the city, Henryk lived in another world. No one could talk to him. He isolated himself in his bedroom and died alone, only three months later, of a broken heart."

Klaus Broza began to weep, his frail body wracked with sobs as his breathing became labored.

"Miss Karmazin," Cy said, "you have upset my grandfather greatly. I ask that you please leave us now."

Beth was stunned. She rose slowly from her chair and took a CIT business card from her purse. Placing it on the small coffee table, her voice shaky, she said, "Let me know if there is something I can do for you."

The day after the staggering meeting with Klaus Broza, Beth went to the building that had been her family's watch repair shop and home, which was located on Zoshka Street. Before he had left for Hungary, Feliks had told Beth that the shop was now a *kawiarnia*, a café, owned by Thomas Piast. It was another private business that the government had allowed in the restored area of Old Town, just a block off the main square on a street parallel to Broza's butcher shop.

As Beth approached she noticed a welcome sign hung on the door and flower boxes filled with red geraniums adorning the windows. She peered through the glass. There were only five or six tables—all full. People were drinking coffee and having lunch in the pleasant, friendly environment.

Hoping the man behind the counter would understand her prickly Polish, Beth asked to speak to the owner. The clerk tilted his head and looked at her quizzically, a shock of dark hair falling down over his forehead. "It's my accent," she thought, "or maybe I didn't put the words together right."

She tried again—this time in English. Still the same puzzled look. Finally she tried German, hoping it wouldn't offend him. "I am visiting from America," she explained. "My grandfather had a watch shop in this building from 1924 to 1943. Do you mind if I stay and have coffee?"

The man smiled thinly and extended his arm over the counter, responding in German. "*Ich bin* Thomas Piast. This is my café. Was your grandfather Henryk Karmazin?"

She was surprised to hear the name spoken so quickly. "Yes, I am Beth Karmazin. You know the story?"

"I'm sure not all of it. History here has been told in bits and pieces, and there have been many distortions over the years." Thomas sighed. "I suppose you would like to see the upstairs. By the grace of Mother Mary, this building was not destroyed by the war. Only one wall had to be rebuilt. My wife is away but my son, Aleksander, can take you up. I must stay with my customers."

It didn't seem right to Beth that she should need permission to view the property that rightfully belonged to her father and Dimitri, but she was grateful that the offer had been extended. Thomas Piast summoned his son from the kitchen.

"This is Aleksander," Thomas said proudly as the boy emerged. "He doesn't speak German, but he is pretty good at English. The children are learning it in school now. I'm sure you will get along."

Beth introduced herself to the curly-haired, green-eyed boy, who appeared to be about seventeen. He looked at Beth suspiciously, but then, following instructions from his father, turned and led her up the wooden staircase.

"Is this the main stairway to the upper floor?" Beth asked.

"I would think so; it is the only stairway to the upper floor."

Beth wasn't sure whether this was Aleksander's attempt at humor or a smart-aleck response from a teenager who would rather be doing something else with his afternoon. At any rate, she chose to ignore it.

The steps were narrow and steep; she counted thirteen. At the top of the stairs and through a door only a few inches taller than Beth was the living room. A boxy-looking modern sofa, two worn armchairs, and a coffee table filled the small space. Then through a set of wide French doors was a larger and more elegant dining room, where it was obvious that the Piast family spent most of their family time. Boxes of yarn, a pipe, a model car, and newspapers lay on the table. Beth could immediately picture her father and Dimitri playing games on a table in this room, while Henryk sat smoking in his easy chair and Sasha painted in the corner, near the window, where the light was good.

The first room down the hall was the "adult bedroom," as Aleksander put it. He seemed uneasy when Beth walked past him and into the center of the room; the room that had belonged to Sasha and Henryk. Dimitri had described to Beth a room with several family photographs on the bureau and a crystal chandelier above the bed. But now the room was drab and nondescript, smelling of soiled sheets and stale cigarettes.

Aleksander was anxious to move on; perhaps he was too young or too simple, or both, to understand why Beth would want to linger a moment. He took a step back toward the door. Beth followed his lead to the room that had been Karl and Dimitri's and now belonged to Aleksander. The walls were a mustard color. Dark wooden crown molding covered two of the four walls, leaving the room with an unfinished look. A bookcase stood in the small alcove where Karl had studied at his desk, taking advantage of the light from a dormer window above. The bed against the far wall was in the same place as Karl's had been. It was a quaint and cozy room, the kind of room Beth could imagine her father growing up in.

Then they moved again to the hallway. Alexander was talking, but Beth wasn't taking it in; her mind was spinning with thoughts and images of her lost family.

"Miss Karmazin?"

"Oh yes, yes. Excuse me. Jet lag, you know."

Reluctantly Beth followed Alexander back down the steps. Thomas Piast came out of the kitchen to say good-bye and Beth asked if she could take a few photos.

Thomas looked around the café furtively, as if the secret police might be lurking in a corner waiting for him to make a wrong move. "Yes, I suppose that is all right," he said. "But I would ask you not to take any photographs outside the building."

"My grandmother, Sasha Karmazin, was taken away by the Nazis from this very place and later died at Auschwitz," she explained. "I'm trying to fill in some missing pieces from her life. There is so much we just don't know."

Thomas thoughtfully stroked his chin. "There is a woman who worked as a clerk at the Gestapo station during the war," he said. "She is old now, long past retirement age, but the government has allowed her to continue working. She still has a good memory; perhaps she will know something about your grandmother. Her name is Pauline Myszkow and she works at the State Central Library."

Beth was surprised by this tidbit; surprised and pleased. She hadn't thought anyone in a Communist country would be so forthcoming. She thanked Thomas profusely as he scribbled the directions to the library on a small piece of paper.

Feeling renewed energy, Beth rushed on foot to the library and was surprised to find Pauline working in a small back office. She looked to be in her mid-seventies and wore thick bifocal glasses and large, old-fashioned hearing aids in both ears. Pauline explained that it was her job to make sure that the government rules of strict censorship were followed explicitly; her large desk was covered in two-foot stacks of books, documents, magazines, and official-looking dossiers.

Thomas had been right: Pauline's mind was clear and her memory exceptionally sharp. She remembered Henryk, Sasha, and both of their sons as an outgoing and well-liked family. She described Sasha as a strong-minded but compassionate woman who taught her children good manners. "They attended Mass as a family every Sunday. The youngsters were boys, mind you, full of mischief, but they always obeyed their parents."

Beth smiled, and then posed her next question delicately.

"Were you working at the Gestapo office on the day that Sasha was deported?"

Pauline lowered her voice and her eyes darted around the room, as though the Gestapo were still lurking somewhere nearby. "You understand that I never wanted to work for the Gestapo," she whispered. "I had no choice. I despised the work, but it was the job the government gave me."

Beth nodded. "I understand," she said, hoping to encourage the woman to open up.

"It was a busy day when your grandmother was brought in. The local Gestapo was under pressure to clean up the city, get the rest of the Jews and the Gypsies transported. Some didn't even get registered. But your grandmother was registered; I remember that. I remember it because the Nazis asked why this obviously Gypsy-looking woman had a Polish last name. I tried to help your grandmother; I told the Nazis there were many dark-skinned Poles with ancestry from Bohemia. Still the Nazis were convinced she was a Gypsy." Pauline paused, shaking her head at the memory.

"She was kept in a cell at the police station for several days, in solitary confinement, I think. The Gestapo were pressuring her to reveal the names of her fellow Gypsies in Warsaw, but she refused. The Gestapo simply could not break her; she had a will of steel. After a few days they opened her cell and loaded her onto a train for the next transport."

"To Auschwitz?"

"To Auschwitz."

Beth shivered. "And then no one ever heard of Sasha again." Beth's voice was flat, drained of emotion. This trip to Poland had taken more out of her than she could have imagined.

"That's not entirely true," Pauline said. "We did get a report that mentioned her name; it was a little more than a year later. Hans Frank had been to Auschwitz on one of his unofficial visits and he was unable to find Sasha. He was angry. I don't know why this was so important to him, but he insisted that the administration office in Auschwitz investigate her disappearance and send him a report, even though he had no real authority over Auschwitz. A report followed soon, signed by an SS Lieutenant that said Sasha had been transferred to another concentration camp along with a number of other Gypsy women. But I don't remember which one."

"What?" Beth was shocked by Pauline's revelation.

"Yes, I remember, because I recall thinking after I saw the name Sasha Karmazin, *if she is still alive, there is a chance she will come home to her family after the war.* But alas, she never did come back, as far as I am aware. And anyway, by then Henryk was dead and her sons sent away. A sad, sad story." Pauline rocked back and forth, shaking her head.

"Do you remember the name of the concentration camp where Sasha was transferred to from Auschwitz?"

"Not offhand I don't. But I could try to look it up for you." Pauline lifted a thin index finger and pointed at the shelves and shelves of dusty old books and ledgers surrounding her desk. "Our records here are very good, and most survived the war because the Gestapo locked them up in the station in a fireproof safe and that is where we found them after the Nazis burned the city and retreated. I imagine I can find the record of your grandmother's transport here. I have some free time after work tonight; I can come back after supper and do some searching."

"I don't know what to say," Beth admitted. "I hate to ask you for this favor, but I would do absolutely anything to find out more about my grandmother. As a family we always assumed she died at Auschwitz, but there is a professor in America who wrote a book ten years ago claiming that my grandmother collaborated with the Nazis. Anything you can find for me will be very helpful."

Pauline smiled serenely. "It is my pleasure to help. I might not uncover much beyond a date and location of transport …"

"That's fine," Beth reassured her. "Any tiny scrap of information you can uncover will be a great help."

"Very well, then. Why don't you return here tomorrow at noon?" Beth was nearly walking on air as she thanked Pauline and left her to her work.

The rest of the day and evening passed in a blur. Beth knew she should be continuing her research, given that she only had six days to spend in Poland, but she was too excited to think.

The next morning Beth woke early, before five o'clock, and tossed and turned, counting the interminable hours until it would be time to go to the library. She decided at last to get dressed and do some research at some of the lesser-known historical sites of Warsaw, documenting her notes in a way that she hoped would impress Feliks, at least enough that he wouldn't regret having obtained a visa for her.

At a quarter to twelve, Beth worked her way back to the state library and mounted the wide concrete steps with a mixture of excitement and trepidation. She walked past the large front desk to the smaller reference desk in back, behind which lay Pauline's office. Standing at the reference desk she noticed that Pauline's office was dark and the door was closed. Perhaps she'd had to step out for moment. Then again, Beth was a few minutes early for their meeting. Beth caught the attention of the young blond woman manning the reference desk.

"Excuse me, I'm looking for Pauline Myszkow. My name is Beth Karmazin and I'm to meet with Pauline at noon," Beth said in her best Polish.

The woman looked confused. "There's no one here by that name," she said slowly.

Beth realized her accent must be way off, so she tried again, speaking very carefully. "Pauline Myszkow. I spoke to her here just yesterday." Beth took a pencil and a piece of scrap paper from the reference desk and carefully wrote out the name in clear block letters. "Pauline Myszkow," she reiterated.

The blond woman would not look Beth in the eye as she replied. "I'm sorry. There is no one here by that name. There never has been, as far as I know."

Beth began to panic. "But that office," she said, pointing to the darkened room behind the woman. "Whose office is that?"

The woman turned and looked where Beth was pointing. "That office belongs to Magdalena Gnojewski, our archivist. She is off sick today. If you'd like to talk to her, she'll be back tomorrow." A strange red blush was working its way up the young woman's neck.

A cold chill ran down Beth's spine and something told her to get out of the library as quickly as possible. She felt as if a million eyes were watching her from the stacks of books, and the walls seemed to be closing in on her.

"Thank you," she mumbled to the woman. "I must be mistaken."

Beth hurried out of the library and into the streets of central Warsaw, where a slight rain had begun to fall. She was only half a block from the central train station, so she ducked in and found a pay phone with a Warsaw phone book in a cubbyhole beneath it. She leafed through the pages quickly until she found the listing for Myszkow, Pauline. Fumbling for some coins, she put the money in the slot and, fingers shaking, dialed the number. There was a mechanical click, then silence. Clearly the line was dead and the number disconnected.

Beth was still in shock as she worked her way slowly through the rain-slick streets back to Feliks's flat. She was about a half block away when she saw a piece of cardboard tacked to the building's front door. She ran the last few steps, until the words came clearly into view. "Gypsy Go Home!" it said in English.

Beth grabbed the note and crushed it in her hands, dropping it to the ground. "The sons of bitches!" she said aloud. "The sons of bitches." Then she sank to the steps, put her face in her hands, and wept.

CHAPTER TWELVE

Czechoslovakia
April 1988

Beth glanced up from her desk and looked at the photograph she had taken of the Piast family inside the home of Thomas Piast in Warsaw's Old Town, the home that had belonged to Beth's father and grandparents so many decades earlier. In the photo Thomas was smiling broadly, his arm around the shoulder of his sulking teenage son, Aleksander. Beth sighed. It had been two years since her trip to Warsaw, and she had uncovered precious little more about Sasha during that time.

Beth had been in touch with Feliks many times since her visit, and although he was always very kind and helpful, he hadn't been able to uncover the truth about Pauline Myszkow's mysterious disappearance, or the information Pauline may have had about Sasha's eventual fate. The official word was that although Pauline had worked at the Central Library in Warsaw, she "retired" to the Carpathian Mountains in 1986.

Beth's mind wandered. She glanced at the other photos tacked haphazardly to the corkboard above her desk. She smiled at the recent photo of her nephew, Ellen's first baby, six-month-old Jack, and the new engagement photo of her youngest sister, Lilly. At thirty-three years old, Beth knew that she had a lot of life ahead of her, but at times she feared it was passing her by. She'd dated several men recently and had had one serious six-month relationship with a handsome Italian man named Marco who was living in Paris. But now she was single again. She hadn't heard anything from Andy, but an old friend from Chicago had written that he was dating a Jewish girl and it looked pretty serious.

Beth's phone rang, and she jumped in her chair. She was grateful for the nudge back into reality.

"Bonjour, CIT. Beth Karmazin."

"Hey, Beth, glad I caught ya. Got a sec?" The breathless voice belonged to Julianna Duvalier, a friend and colleague of Beth's who was in Prague, working on a documentary film that was being funded by a German public television network. The film traced the history of the Sinti, the German Gypsies, who had been caught behind the Iron Curtain after World War II. "Sure, what's up?" Beth asked with a smile. Julianna's infectious energy and enthusiasm never failed to cheer Beth up.

"How soon can you get here to Prague?"

Beth was dumbfounded. "What? To Prague? Why? Is something wrong?"

"No, I think something is very, very right. Beth, hold on to your hat—I think I've found your Aunt Melina living here in Prague. I can't be sure, of course, but the details jive with everything you've told me."

Beth was speechless. Could this be the break she was looking for? "This is incredible," Beth sputtered. "Tell me you're not kidding."

Julianna took a deep breath. "When I was doing some interviews for the film yesterday, I met a young Gypsy man named Jan Kraus. Turns out he is a Czech Gypsy, so I can't use him in the film, but as we were talking he mentioned that his uncle had married a Polish Gypsy woman named Melina Lacatus Brzezinska who had survived Auschwitz and Ravensbruck. She belonged to the Keldari clan, which was encamped in eastern Poland at the time she and her husband, her two children, and her brother Stefan were deported. She found when she arrived that her sister Sasha was also a prisoner at the camp. During the selection process Melina was separated from her husband and her children, and she never saw them again. Afterwards she married Jan Kraus's uncle and has been living in Prague ever since. Beth, the details are too close. She is your aunt."

"Oh, my God," Beth said. "I can't believe it. Can you arrange a visa for me to come to Prague?"

"It shouldn't be a problem," Julianna replied. "But Beth, you need to hurry and get here as quickly as possible. Apparently Melina is very frail and failing quickly."

"Okay." Beth flipped through her desk calendar. "I've got some vacation days coming; I can leave soon. Do whatever you have to do to get me that visa."

"Will do. I'm on it. Give me a couple days. And Beth, when I call, have your suitcase packed, okay? And bring me a bottle of good French wine."

"Of course," Beth replied before saying good-bye.

Like Feliks in Warsaw, Julianna had an instinct for working the Byzantine systems behind the Iron Curtain. However, the current Communist Czech government had recently taken a hard-line approach with the West. The only reason Czechoslovakia's first secretary had agreed to the German television station doing the documentary was his eagerness to show off his government's apparent commitment to improving the lives of the Gypsy population.

Only three days later, Beth flew from Paris to Prague and was met at the airport by a government escort, Commissar Josef Capek. Unfortunately, Julianna would not be able to accompany Beth during her time in Prague. Julianna and the film crew, on a very tight schedule and even tighter budget, had already moved on to filming in East Germany. But Julianna had arranged for Beth to be escorted by Commissar Capek. Beth did not speak any Czech, nor did Capek speak any English. But Capek spoke excellent French, and Beth, after two years living in Paris, was nearly fluent, so they used French as their lingua franca.

Capek was a rather blank-faced man, wearing a black suit, the jacket dated by narrow lapels, and the buttons strained by his heavy girth. Julianna had advised Beth to be nice to him; he was the best the government had to offer. A small tip now and then, Julianna had said, would loosen him up, although he would insist he did not take bribes. But tips were different; they were tokens of appreciation.

Julianna had recommended the Hotel Europa because of its proximity to the world-famous Wenceslas Square. The hotel had once been very fashionable, built near the turn of the century. Except for the obvious neglect, Beth thought it still had the possibility of being grand.

After Beth registered and dropped off her luggage, Capek suggested they have a drink at the bar in the lobby. Capek quickly chugged down a glass of beer, which Beth assumed would go on her expense account. She was quite sure that his account wouldn't allow for such indulgences; he wasn't high enough up the party ladder. Before leaving he said, "I will pick you up tomorrow morning at eight-thirty for your meeting. I've never been to the area, but I know that the dark ones live near the aluminum factory where most of them work. I'm sure I will be able to find it."

The dark ones. Beth shivered and crushed her urge to put Capek in his place. No matter how the Czech government wanted to present it, the "dark ones" were still victims of discrimination. But bigot or not, the truth was that she needed Capek a lot more than he needed her.

"The dark ones," Beth repeated. "So that's what the Gypsies are called now?" Beth had hidden her own Gypsy heritage for this trip, lightening her dark, shoulder-length hair and wearing beige-toned makeup. Today she even chose a traditional look in clothing, a navy blue cardigan sweater and a pair of khaki slacks and loafers.

"Yes, but in line with the government's policy on deracination, the Gypsies soon will be completely assimilated into the mainstream population. It will be as if 'Gypsies' never existed."

Beth held her tongue, ignoring her true thoughts. "Goodnight, Commissar," she said as pleasantly as possible, slipping some cash into his hand. "I will see you tomorrow morning."

"At eight-thirty sharp," Capek said, bowing slightly and clutching the currency in his chubby fist.

The next morning Capek and Beth headed away from the town center and toward the industrial outskirts, where Julianna had arranged for Beth to meet with Jan Kraus, and from there, to meet Melina. Capek knew nothing of the true nature of Beth's activities; he was merely serving as an escort and interpreter, if needed. Although Beth occasionally caught Capek looking at her strangely, Beth had no intention of telling him that she was part Gypsy.

The smell of Capek's cigar smoke in the tight confines of the car was nauseating, but Beth didn't want to start the day off by offending him, so she told him she was warm and asked if she could roll down the window. Fortunately, the weather was clear and crisp. The sun shone brightly over the Vltava River, and the air was still. As the tiny box-shaped car crossed the Charles Bridge, Beth spotted the monolithic Prague Castle rising above the west bank of the Vltava. Prague had not been as shattered by World War II as Warsaw and some other European capitals had been. Though blanketed with layers of grime, decay, and industrial pollution, the city beneath was teeming with charming Old World baroque edifices.

At a small sidewalk café in the suburbs of Prague, and with the aluminum factory looming in the distance, Beth and Capek met Jan Kraus, the Czech Gypsy whose step-aunt was Melina. In a strange way Beth and Jan were related, Beth realized, as she shook the man's hand. Melina was Beth's great-aunt by blood, and Melina was Jan's aunt by marriage.

Jan was a husky man of medium height. He had a typical olive-toned Roma complexion, curly black hair, and piercing pale blue eyes that stood out in contrast to his darker face. Although not conventionally handsome, he had the kind of face that was hard to look away from.

Fortunately, Jan spoke fluent English, and, even more fortunately, Capek understood almost none, so Beth and Jan could speak without restriction, as long as it appeared to Capek that they were only discussing business. Beth began by asking questions about Jan's job, his work as a poet, and the general conditions at the Gypsy settlement. Finally, when she felt he was honest, direct, and could be trusted, she broached the subject of Melina.

"Tell me about your Aunt Melina," she said.

"Of her early life, I know very little. She rarely speaks of it, you see. She married my uncle, Mikhail Brzezinska, in 1949, just a few years after the war. He was a widower with two young children, and she had lost her first husband and children at Auschwitz. It was a marriage of convenience, more than anything else. My uncle needed a wife for his children, and Aunt Melina needed a husband to take care of her. I wish I could say it was a happy union."

"There were problems?" Beth asked carefully.

"Oh, they were always kind and civil to one another. They rarely argued or quarreled. But both had suffered so much, you see … so much pain and loss. People did not talk of such things in those days. There was no 'therapy'; they had no way to lament the pain; no place to put their sorrow. They were told to move on as if nothing had happened. But Aunt Melina often wakes up screaming in the middle of the night, reliving the horrors of Auschwitz. One time I found her sleepwalking in the kitchen, scrubbing her arms at the sink until they were bruised black and blue. She was trying to wash off the blood of a dead child she'd been forced to carry and throw into an open grave."

Jan shuddered at the memory, and Beth swallowed her tears. Ever since Julianna had informed her of the possibility that Melina had survived the war, Beth had rejoiced. But now the thought occurred to her that life after

Auschwitz might have been no life at all. "Those bastard Nazis," Beth thought. "The people they didn't murder physically, they killed in spirit."

"Is Melina bedridden?" Beth asked.

"Yes," Jan replied, nodding sadly. "She is eighty-six years old and very frail. Her bones are brittle and her memory is spotty. Sometimes she remembers everything and is as sharp as a tack; other times she is lost so far in the past, no one can reach her. When I bring you to her, I can't promise she'll be able to tell you much."

"I understand," Beth said. "Just to see her will be a blessing. Anything beyond that will be a gift." Beth looked down and continued speaking in English. "But my friend here beside me, he can not know the true nature of my visit. He needs to believe that Melina is just someone who I am interviewing for the documentary film project."

Jan's eyelids flitted toward Capek, then he quickly looked away. "Understood," he said evenly. "I will do whatever I can to help."

Beth nodded and pulled an American fifty-dollar bill from her briefcase and placed it in front of Capek. "Perhaps you can help me," Beth said in French. "This man tells me there is someone, a very old woman, I need to interview. She lives in a tenement not far from here. Can you take me there?"

"It is not on our agenda," Capek replied, stubbing out his stinky cigarette.

Beth withdrew another fifty and placed it on top of the first. "I am sure our visit will be brief," she said evenly.

The commissar's eyes darted around the small café. Then, apparently convinced that no one was watching, he slipped the money under the table and into his pocket. "We should leave now," he said, face expressionless, eyes blank, "before our change of itinerary is … noticed by an interested party."

When they arrived at the Gypsy settlement, Capek parked on a side street, away from traffic and prying eyes. Capek, Jan, and Beth walked several blocks along back alleyways to the concrete block tenement building, the smell of garbage permeating the stale, smoky air. Smiling children, filthy, and some toothless, played in a vacant lot, pushing wheels with sticks and kicking half-inflated footballs to one another. A number of teens preened on the street corners, boys with slick black hair and girls with short skirts and fishnet stockings engaged in an elaborate dance of attract and repel. It was two-thirty in the afternoon, and Beth wondered why the children or teens weren't in school. Perhaps the Communist government was not as good as it claimed to be at taming the Gypsies.

It was a long, dark, and somewhat ominous hike up to the fourth floor of the concrete block tenement building. The elevator, of course, was broken, and the cobwebs around the door suggested it had been that way for months or even years.

When they reached the apartment, Unit 407, with the plain black number stenciled on the metal door, Beth paid Capek another "tip" to wait outside. She was very clear about not having him in the room while she spoke to Melina, regardless of how much he would or would not be able to understand.

Jan knocked on the door, then led Beth inside, where several young children played on the floor, supervised by a bored-looking woman in a colored headscarf. Another woman, about thirty, and livelier-looking with round dark eyes and long wavy hair, came out of a back room and into the small front living area. Upon seeing Jan she rushed toward him and into his arms, planting a passionate kiss on his lips. He responded with a huge bear hug that lifted her off her feet.

"Ah, this is my wife, Antonia. The best cook in all of Prague," Jan said, playfully patting Antonia's behind. Antonia blushed. "Antonia, this is Beth Karmazin, from America. She is here to see Aunt Melina."

Antonia spoke only Czech, and Beth spoke none, so they could only communicate through facial expressions and gestures. Beth was nervous but felt somewhat comforted by Antonia's kind and steady demeanor. Antonia led Beth through the drafty, narrow flat, past a series of closed doors and two little boys playing with wooden blocks on the uncarpeted floor. As they passed, one of the boys glanced up at Beth and waved. "Peter," Antonia said, and Beth realized that the boy was Jan and Antonia's son.

As Beth and Antonia entered the shadowy room, Beth could see Melina's frail, tiny form lying beneath a patchwork quilt adorned with small stitched bluebonnets and cornflowers. Her head was propped up with a large feather pillow against a worn horse saddle, and her long white hair had been pulled to one side and secured with a ribbon. Beth did not immediately see any physical resemblance between Melina and herself or any member of her family, but she knew that advanced age and years of sorrow had altered Melina's features beyond recognition.

As she stepped closer Beth noticed the cross around Melina's neck and it took her breath away. The cross was identical to the one that Karl had given Beth on the day of her high school graduation, the cross that the Nazis had torn from Sasha's neck as they dragged her away from her family and home. That cross was still around Beth's neck and her hands flew to it immediately, as if to remind herself it was still there and hadn't been magically transported to the woman lying in front of her.

Antonia stepped to the bed, took Melina's hand, and sat beside her, speaking softly in Czech. Melina had obviously become fluent in the language after her marriage to her second husband. Beth heard her name, "Beth Karmazin," mixed into the long stretches of Czech. Antonia was gentle and patient, continuing to stroke the woman's hand and repeating a few key words until the old woman seemed to understand.

Melina sighed, looked up, and squinted. "Do you speak Polish?" she asked Beth in Polish.

"Yes," Beth replied. "A little."

Melina beckoned Beth closer and motioned for her to sit on the bed beside her, which Beth did. "Antonia says you are the daughter of my nephew, Karl, the son of my sister, Sasha."

"Yes, I am. Karl came to America in 1943, when he was seventeen. He married an American woman, Margaret, and had three daughters. I am the eldest. My name is Elizabeth Ann Karmazin. Your sister Sasha was my grandmother." Beth leaned forward and pulled the cross from beneath the collar of her sweater. "My father gave me this cross. It belonged to Sasha. See, it looks just like yours."

Melina's gnarled old fingers touched her own cross, and her eyes, clouded with cataracts, filled with tears. "Oh my goodness, oh my goodness," she sobbed, so wracked for breath Beth feared she might stop breathing. "I never thought … after so many years … any of my family would come back to me. Lean close to the light, child. Let me see you clearly."

Beth shifted to her left so the lamp on the nightstand illuminated her face.

"Oh yes, I see it so clearly now," Melina said, catching her breath. "You look so much like her. Your hair, your eyes, even the bridge of your nose. You are the image of Sasha; Sasha before she was sent to Auschwitz."

"I know this is painful," Beth said, stroking Melina's hand, afraid that even her gentle touch might injure the woman. "I need to know what happened to Sasha. Did she die at Auschwitz? Or was she sent to another camp? Or was she somehow spirited away from the camp by someone on the inside? There are so many stories about what really happened to Sasha."

Melina sighed, her tiny chest barely lifting the quilt. "I don't know for certain," she replied. "I don't believe she died at Auschwitz. A few days before the Gypsy camp at Auschwitz was liquidated on August 1, 1944, many of the able-bodied and relatively healthy Gypsies were transported to other camps. I was on the only transport of female Gypsies out of Auschwitz, to Ravensbruck. The healthy Gypsy men were sent to Buchenwald. Sasha was not on my transport." Melina's eyes, which must have been a deep hazel color when she was younger, grew wide and opaque, drifting into the past.

"How do you know she hadn't already been killed at that point?" Beth asked as gently as possible.

"It's possible, but I do not think so," Melina said. "There were women in the barracks who saw Sasha being taken away by a guard one night, about three months before the Gypsy liquidation."

Beth tried not to gasp. "Did you ever speak to these women directly?"

"For a long time none of them would speak of that night, but finally they did. They swore on their lives it was the truth, and I believed them. After all, they had no reason to lie."

"Do you remember their names?" Beth was frantic. "Did any of those women survive the war?"

Melina's translucent eyelids began to flutter. "Oh, child. It's so long ago. I don't remember names. It would be better if you spoke to Stefan. He might remember more than I do."

Beth was torn between her desperate need to know more and her reluctance to press the sickly old woman, who had already told her more than she had hoped for.

"Stefan? Your brother? Is he still alive?"

"I don't know whether he still lives. But I know for a fact that he survived the war. I heard from him, once. In 1948. He managed to track me down; he was in Germany and I was in Prague. He found my name on the Red Cross's list of displaced persons. We exchanged letters. He promised we would meet up. But then I never heard from him again. Everything from the West became strictly censored here."

Now Beth's mind was really racing. "Do you remember the name of the town in Germany where Stefan was living?" Beth asked.

Melina sighed, slipping into sleep.

"Melina? It's Beth. Can you hear me?"

"What?" Melina asked sleepily.

"The name of the town where Stefan was?"

"Something like 'Bensheim,' I believe. At least that is where the mail came from." Beth turned as she heard the door behind her softly open and close. It was Antonia carrying a mug of something resembling black tea. She offered it to Beth, indicating that it had been made with boiling water. Beth nodded gratefully, taking the mug and sipping the lukewarm, tar-flavored liquid. She was relieved when Antonia left the room and she was able to step to the window and, after checking that all was clear below, pour the tea quickly over the windowsill.

When Beth returned to Melina's bedside she saw that the old Gypsy woman was deeply asleep, her pale, drawn lips moving steadily in and out with her breath. Beth hated to wake her when she was resting so peacefully. But Beth knew that she would probably never see this woman, perhaps the only living link to Sasha, ever again. She couldn't leave without a final word.

"Melina?" Beth asked, gently shaking the woman's shoulder, which felt thin and bony beneath her hand.

"Yes?"

"Thank you. Thank you so much." Beth leaned closer and kissed the woman on the forehead.

"Elizabeth?"

Beth was surprised the woman remembered her name. "Yes, I'm here."

"Please find Stefan, and let him know that I survived. Survived Auschwitz, survived Ravensbruck, and survived everything that happened afterwards. Those bastard Nazis couldn't kill my strong old Gypsy soul. Find Stefan for me and tell him."

Beth smiled through her tears. "I will do that," she promised, squeezing the woman's hand and straightening the blanket beneath her chin. "I will definitely do that."

As Beth headed back to the hotel with Capek at the wheel, her mind churned over what she had learned. There were women in the barracks at Auschwitz who had seen Sasha taken away by a guard. Might those women still be alive? Might Beth be able to track them down? More importantly, Stefan had survived the war and had apparently registered as a displaced person with the Red Cross in Germany. Those records should still be traceable. Would Stefan still be alive? If so, he'd be in his eighties.

As they crossed the bridge over the Charles River and back into Prague proper, Beth reached into her purse and took out her pocket dayplanner. She had already used up all her vacation days for the year, and it was only April. Her boss had been very generous about letting her take extra time off to pursue new leads, most of them worthless, as to Sasha's fate. But if Stefan were still alive, time would be short. Beth made a decision.

The next day Beth phoned Joanne, her boss at CIT, and gave her the news. "I have to leave the job."

"What? You've only been here two years and things are going so well."

I know, but I've reached the make-or-break point. This could be my last chance to find out what happened to my grandmother."

"What is it, Beth? I know she was your grandmother, but …"

"I don't expect you to understand, Joanne. This is something I just have to do. Maybe it's the Gypsy in my soul."

CHAPTER THIRTEEN

Heidelberg, West Germany
1988

As Beth cleaned out the desk in her Paris office, the enormity of what she was doing hit her squarely in the chest. Her hands began to shake, and she had to take a deep breath to still her queasiness. Joanne and her other colleagues at CIT had been supportive and understanding when she told them she was leaving, but the board was clearly disgruntled by her abrupt decision to quit the job. Beth felt guilty leaving on such short notice, and to pursue what could only be seen as a selfish goal, but she could not be persuaded to stay. It was now or never; time was moving on and the people who might have the answers to what happened to Sasha were growing old and dying.

Beth's task was overwhelming. She only had a few thousand dollars to fund her journey, and she couldn't afford to be out of work for more than a month or perhaps two at the very most. She had undoubtedly burned her bridges here in Paris, and her visa would only extend for six months beyond her last date of employment. When the six months were up she would have no choice but to return to the States with no job, no money, no man in her life, and most likely not even a letter of recommendation to accompany her resume. And the end of six months might find her with no more information about her grandmother, Sasha, than the little she had right now.

She took a deep breath, stood, and began removing photos and other personal items from the corkboard above her desk. "Maybe this is for the best," she told herself. "If I fail, I fail. But at least I can get on with my life knowing I tried."

Beth's first action after leaving her job was to contact the Red Cross in Germany and find out what information they had on Stefan Lacatus. The Red Cross records on displaced persons after the war were surprisingly detailed, and Beth soon learned that a Stefan Lacatus, a Polish Gypsy born near Warsaw, had been a prisoner at Auschwitz and had escaped from a train bound for Buchenwald in 1944. After spending nine months hiding at an abandoned farmstead with another escapee, he had been found by Allied forces and was sent to a displaced persons camp at Bensheim, Germany. He was released from Bensheim in 1946 when the camp became designated exclusively for Jews. He tried to return to Poland but was sent back at the border because he had no proof of Polish citizenship. Then, on the return journey, he was robbed of his DP card and jailed in Munich until his records could be located in Bensheim and a new card issued. Eventually he found a few surviving members of the Keldari clan in Germany and was last seen at a Gypsy settlement near Heidelberg.

Beth called the Zentralrat center for Sinti and Roma in Heidelberg, to follow up on the information she received from the Red Cross. The CIT were encouraging Gypsies to register with the Zentralrat. It gave them a legal address, even though the Zentralrat was not a government entity. Most Gypsies were afraid to register with local government bureaus, for reasons that were understandable. Although the Zentralrat did not have any records on a Stefan Lacatus, the head of the agency said that Beth would likely have more luck tracking him down if she came to Heidelberg and inquired about him in person.

As Beth thumbed through the train schedule from Paris to Heidelberg she contemplated what Stefan had been through. It disgusted her to think that he had been jailed by the Germans, the very people who should have offered him comfort and support after the war. It was a known fact that the Jewish refugees were treated better than the Gypsy survivors were. When the Jews showed their tattoos they were given immediate upgraded refugee status. Many refugees complained that this was because the Jews were considered more intelligent and better educated than the non-Jewish refugees. Others felt it might have been based on guilt, a German reaction to the magnitude of the Jews' losses.

Disembarking at Heidelberg's main train station would have put Beth closer to her hotel, but after sitting for so many hours she welcomed the chance to stretch her legs. She jumped off the train at the east end of the old city of Heidelberg, the Altstadt, leaving herself a mile walk to the Europa Hotel. She pulled her small overnight bag behind her, which was easy enough save for a few short stretches of cobblestone, where she had no choice but to lift and carry the case or risk losing the wheels.

Beth walked along the Neckar River, a tributary of the Rhine. The day was warm and she was glad she had pulled her hair up in a ponytail that morning and dressed lightly. Europeans were taking advantage of the beautiful weather. Several groups of picnickers sunbathed along the riverbank, while tourists and workers on lunch breaks soaked up the sun at sidewalk cafes. At the Karl Theodore Bridge Beth turned and headed back into the city. The baroque architecture of the old buildings, the flowers everywhere, and the twisting roads and alleys exuded a romanticism that fired Beth's passion.

After passing the university, a school well-known in the world for its focus on science and medicine, Beth stepped on to the Hauptstrasse, the "pedestrian only" main street of the Old Town. Several women pushing large, elaborately decorated baby carriages crossed her path, chatting with one another and cooing at their little ones. Students were lined up at the snack shops. Beth enjoyed the city's relaxed ambience, even as she nervously pondered actually meeting her great-uncle, Stefan.

After registering at the hotel and dropping off her luggage, Beth headed toward the Zentralrat office, just a few blocks from her hotel. A lively woman with a round face and kind brown eyes met her at the door. *"Willkommen,"* she said, taking Beth's jacket from her arm and hanging it on an iron tree stand in the corner. Then in English she continued, "You must be the American lady who phoned, Beth Karmazin."

"Yes," Beth replied, reaching out to shake the woman's hand.

"My name is Vali Schmidt, and I am the director here. I believe you are looking for someone."

Beth was relieved the woman spoke English. Beth's German was rusty. Since she had been living in Paris, she had focused primarily on her French. "I am looking for my great-uncle, a Polish Gypsy, Stefan Lacatus. He escaped from a transport train from Auschwitz to Buchenwald, and later ended up at the displaced person's camp at Bensheim."

"Ah, yes." Vali smiled. "You told me a bit of the story over the phone. Quite an amazing tale of survival." Suddenly her face turned serious. "I only wish we had more such stories." She paused. "We couldn't find your great-uncle in our computer database, but not all the old records have yet been typed into the system. It's painstaking work, as you might imagine. We'll try the written logs."

Working through the unentered logs was slow and tedious work. Many of the records were handwritten in the old-fashioned German script, while others had become damp or faded with age, making them difficult to decipher. Not only that, but because Gypsies were so frequently on the move, three or four addresses were often recorded for the same person.

When they had finished one log book, Vali would say brightly, "Okay, let's try the next one. We're sure to find him in there."

By eight o'clock that evening Beth was stiff and tired with her eyes burning and her shoulders aching. She was tempted to call it quits for the day, but Vali's enthusiasm pushed her forward. A few minutes later their persistence was rewarded when Vali suddenly shrieked in delight, "Got it!"

Beth looked over Vali's shoulder. There, in a shaky hand, someone had written, "Stefan Lacatus. Born, 1906, outside Warsaw. Arrived from Bensheim, 6 October, 1948. Relocated to Schwetzingen, 12 December, 1949."

"He was definitely here, no doubt about that," Vali said with a tired smile.

"What, or where, is Schwetzingen?" Beth asked.

"It's a suburb outside of Heidelberg. Many Gypsies settled there after the war. It's the closest thing they have to a permanent community in this part of Germany," Vali explained.

"I don't suppose there's much chance that he'd still be there after all these years," Beth said wearily.

"Perhaps not, but there's a good chance that someone there will know where he is, if he is still alive. There are many older Gypsies there who have been there since the war ended. Tomorrow morning we'll go and see for ourselves."

The next morning Vali picked Beth up at seven-thirty sharp in her army-green Volkswagen van, and they headed for Schwetzingen, a small town seventeen miles west of Heidelberg. The town had once been the summer residence of the Palatine Electors, southwest Germany's old royalty, but was now better known for the wonderful white asparagus farms surrounding the village. As they drove, Vali explained to Beth that the Poles who lived in the Sinti settlement had not registered with the German authorities or the Zentralat. Vali had tried to warn them that they could be jailed or deported, but they hadn't listened.

"You know how Gypsies are," she said with an exasperated sigh, shaking her head. Suddenly she remembered to whom she was talking, and she bit her tongue, blushing. "Sorry," she mumbled.

"That's okay," Beth said evenly, trying to picture Vali saying something along the lines of, "You know how Jews are." That would never happen. It disturbed Beth to find that prejudice could live within even the most fair-minded individual.

As they approached the outskirts of the town Beth could see the Gypsy settlement that consisted of a dozen or so low-rent apartment buildings, three vans, an old school bus, and two traditional Gypsy wagons, all of which appeared to be inhabited. Outside on the grass, near a picnic table, stood two women cooking something that smelled of curry in a large pot connected to an extension cord that ran through an open window into one of the apartments. A group of men dressed in white shirts and dark suits with shiny buttons and old-fashioned tailoring stood outside the school bus chewing tobacco or smoking and engaged in an animated conversation. A few less-energetic fellows sat on wooden planks balanced between tree stumps playing cards on a folding table.

Vali pulled off the road and parked, and she and Beth left the car and approached the men on foot. Suddenly the door to the apartment building opened, and out bustled a tall man with dark, handsome features. He rushed toward Vali and greeted her warmly, giving her a kiss on the cheek. "Beth, this is Marcel," Vali said, introducing the man. He smiled flirtatiously at Beth and winked, but quickly became sober as he turned back to Vali.

"Is there trouble?" he asked her in German.

Vali shook her head. "Oh *nein, nein.* My friend from America here is looking for her great-uncle."

Marcel turned back to Beth and gave her a long, lascivious look that began at the top of her head and descended slowly to her feet, stopping to linger lovingly at all the predictable places. "So? You are one of us?" he asked, his dark eyes slicing through her like lasers.

Beth tried to hide her discomfort. Marcel could be very helpful, and his knowing about her Gypsy heritage would likely be an advantage.

"Yes," she replied. "My grandmother, Sasha Lacatus Karmazin, was a full-blooded Gypsy. Stefan, the man whom I'm looking for, is her brother."

Marcel stroked his darkly-stubbled chin. "I'm not familiar with that name."

"He was here in 1949; he came here from the camp at Bensheim," Vali said helpfully.

"Let me go ask the elders," Marcel said. "They know more about the history of this place than I do. There are a few here who have been around since that time."

Beth and Vali sat and waited on a picnic bench while Marcel made his inquiries among the neighboring apartments. About twenty minutes later he returned, his black eyes dancing.

"It seems that today is your lucky day," he said. "There is a man from Warsaw who has lived in this settlement since the late nineteen-forties. For protection he took his wife's name when he married her. Polish Roma are not well accepted among the Germans or the Sinti Gypsies. Anyway, this man now calls himself Stefan Nordquist and he lives on the fourth floor of that building over there." He gestured over his shoulder.

A flight of butterflies surged through Beth's stomach. "Is he home now? May we speak to him?"

"He isn't home, but you may be able to speak to him if you go to the city jail. Lans, over there, just came back from town, and he said he saw the *polizei* questioning Stefan out on the highway south of the village."

Beth was shocked at how nonchalant Marcel sounded. Her great-uncle was in his eighties; why hadn't Lans stopped to help him?

Vali looked deeply concerned as well. "The police? Why?" she asked.

"It seems Stefan and another man from the settlement, Markus, were bringing one of our wagons back from a Gypsy settlement near Frankfurt; someone had borrowed it for a few weeks to live in until they could find an apartment. Apparently, one of the wheels came off the wagon, and as Stefan and Markus were fixing it, the police came by and started to harass them."

Without wasting a moment, Vali hurried toward the van and motioned for Beth to follow her. The two women hopped in and sped off toward the highway in full search-and-rescue mode. Just a few kilometers down the road they spotted a horse and wagon beside a police car. Two men in uniforms were handcuffing the white-haired men, who offered little resistance.

Vali pulled off the road, screeching to a halt and sending dust flying onto the policemen's uniforms and the apprehended men's dark trousers. The officers looked at the women disapprovingly as Beth and Vali jumped from the car but Vali offered no apology.

"What are you doing with these men?" she asked breathlessly.

"They are being charged with camping on the side of the road and lack of proper identification. And, this is a police matter that has absolutely nothing to do with you," the taller officer said gruffly.

"Wrong, sir, it has everything to do with me," Vali said evenly, her breath now under control. "These two men have appointments to register with the Zentralat tomorrow," she lied, handing the officer her business card and her driver's license. "My name is Vali Schmidt. I am the director of the Zentralat and I have several witnesses who will attest to the fact that these men were tending to a broken wheel, not camping."

The younger police officer pursed his thin lips dismissively. "And how do you think a judge will respond to the testimony of a Gypsy?"

Now it was Beth's turn. She pulled out her CIT card, which hadn't expired yet, and handed it to the older officer. "Unless you want this injustice reported to the chancellor and your photo plastered all over the papers tomorrow, I suggest you release these men. We will see that they are properly registered." Beth spoke in English, hoping the police officers would understand her words.

The older man seemed to understand both the words Beth spoke and the significance of her ID card. "Let them go," he said in German to the younger officer.

"But, Captain—"

"I said, let them go, Sergeant."

The sergeant uncuffed the elderly Gypsy men while the captain furiously scribbled on a pad. "I am issuing them warning tickets. See that they are both registered before the end of this week, or else. They may not be so lucky next time." He paused. "And get this wagon off the road. It's a hazard to other drivers."

The police left, and Vali and Beth helped Stefan and Markus repair the wheel and push the wagon back onto the road. Beth decided to wait to tell Stefan who she was until they were back at the settlement and things had settled down. Both men tried to act unruffled by the situation, but Beth could see how pale their faces were and how shaky their hands. They had been through a frightening and unsettling experience that might well have ended with them both locked up, or worse.

When they reached the Gypsy settlement, Stefan took the horse and wagon to a communal barn on the edge of the settlement and then returned to meet Beth and Vali in the parking lot in front of his apartment building.

Beth used the opportunity to get a better look at Stefan. He was in his early eighties but remarkably spry. He could pass for early seventies; perhaps even younger. He was a tall man with a thin build, a still-full head of white hair, and a neatly trimmed white mustache and beard. His eyes were hazel and still bright, his cheekbones high and smooth.

"Now, ladies, would you like to join me for some tea?" he asked with a smile, bowing dramatically and indicating the door to the building.

Beth could wait no longer. "I don't know how to say this, so I'm just going to say it," she blurted out. "My name is Beth Karmazin. My grandmother was Sasha Lacatus Karmazin, and I believe that you may be her brother, Stefan Lacatus."

What shocked Beth most was Stefan's utter and complete lack of shock at her words. His eyes filled with tears, and a slow, sweet smile spread across his face. "I know who you are," he whispered. "I knew the minute you stepped out of the Volkswagen. My darling Sasha; you are too young to be her daughter, so I thought you must be her granddaughter. You are her spitting image. My eyes may be old and bleary, but the heart never loses its sight. I would have known you anywhere."

Stefan opened his arms and Beth went to him and embraced him tightly. Then, pulling away, she asked, "Why didn't you say something earlier?"

"In front of the Germans?" Stefan mingled a chuckle with his tears. "The less those Krauts know the better. Safer for all of us."

Vali too, strong and Teutonic though she was, had been reduced to tears by the touching scene of reconciliation. She wiped her face with her sleeve. "Come now," she said huskily. "Let's go upstairs. I think we all could use some tea."

The three made their way upstairs and soon found themselves sitting inside Apartment 12 at Stefan's kitchen table.

"I have another surprise for you," Beth said softly, her mind and heart still spinning. "Your sister, Melina, is still alive. I met her recently in Prague. She is frail and bedridden and her mind is ..." Beth searched for the right word. "Unpredictable. Sometimes she remembers everything; other times, not so much."

Stefan took a deep breath and sighed. "Ah, my dear Melina. Who would have believed that a brother and sister, both Gypsies, would survive Auschwitz? It was our great good luck indeed. *Baxt.*"

"She said that you and she were in touch after the war, and then something happened. She was expecting you to visit her, but then she didn't hear from you again," Beth said carefully.

"Yes, a great shame. When I was robbed of my DP card and jailed in Munich I lost touch with the outside world. By the time I was released from custody the Iron Curtain had descended on Eastern Europe, and there was no way for someone like me, in the West, to contact someone on the other side in Czechoslovakia. We couldn't telephone, we couldn't write, we couldn't travel to one another …" his voice trailed off as his eyes again filled with tears. "But I never stopped thinking about her. I never stopped praying for her, hoping that she was well. And now you bring me this wonderful news—Melina lives! Tell me, how has her life been?"

Beth blanched. She didn't want to lie to her great-uncle, but she feared the truth about how Melina had suffered would break his heart. "She has had some struggles," Beth explained. "As I'm certain every Auschwitz survivor has. She lost her first family, but she remarried, raised stepchildren, and has had a quiet life in Prague. And she never stopped thinking about you too."

"Ah, my dear. You spare your old uncle's feelings. You show tender concern for my heart." Stefan smiled. "We have all had our struggles, haven't we?"

"Yes. But you'll be happy to know that Melina is comfortable and being very well cared for," Beth added, grateful to be able to speak the truth.

"When she was young, Melina dreamed of going on the Gypsy pilgrimage to Lourdes, France. I wonder if she ever got there," Stefan said wistfully, looking to the south as though he could see the holy place where over the years hundreds of thousands had journeyed to worship at the shrine of the Black Madonna.

Abruptly, Vali excused herself, saying she needed to get back to her office but that she would come back to pick Beth up later that night. After saying good-bye to Vali, Beth told Stefan everything she could remember about Melina, also telling him everything she knew of Sasha, and of Karl and Henryk and Dimitri, and all the family Stefan didn't even know he had in America.

Overcome by emotion, Stefan held his head in his hands and wept. When he raised his head again, his wife, Christine, a tall, thin, Swedish woman with long graying blond hair, came to comfort him, stroking his back and murmuring in his ear. "This is wonderful news," she whispered. "You have found your sister alive in Czechoslovakia, and you have a new family in America too. We should be celebrating."

With that Christine put a white cloth on the kitchen table, and Stefan filled three glasses from a bottle of Trollinger wine, which he explained was a favorite from a nearby vineyard in the Neckar Valley. As Beth swirled her wine, she noticed a wedding photograph of Stefan and Christine on the bookshelf behind Stefan, and as Beth squinted for a closer look she was surprised to see two worn leather volumes of *Mein Kampf* to the left of the portrait. Stefan turned and followed Beth's gaze to the books.

"The words of a madman," he said.

"You've read them?" Beth asked, surprised.

Stefan nodded. "Oh yes. Christine is a schoolteacher. She taught me to read, and those were my first real books. I wanted to read them. We must try to understand the minds of evil men if we are to defend ourselves against them."

"How true," Beth mused. She took a slow sip of wine from her glass. "I know this is painful, but can you tell me about how you came to be at Auschwitz?"

"Ah … Auschwitz. I knew the conversation would turn to that forsaken place eventually." Stefan's eyes darkened.

Beth now wished she hadn't asked, but she had to know about Sasha. Maybe this just wasn't the time. "Perhaps we should wait ... I didn't mean to upset you."

Stefan shook his head. "No, it is all right. I survived that hell on earth. Speaking about it will never compare to actually having lived it." He paused, collecting his thoughts.

"One afternoon, I was chopping wood in the camp when a friend from another clan rode in and he warned me that the Nazis were deporting Gypsies, even in Warsaw now. 'You and Melina must flee,' my friend said. 'Take your families and go as far as you can to the south. Leave now and do not look back.' Unfortunately, I did not believe him. 'How do you know?' I asked. He wouldn't tell me. I thought he was overreacting to silly street gossip. Besides, there was nowhere to go south. Every European country to the south was under German control. There was no way through to the west, and the Russians were to the east, and even though the Russians were now on the side of the Allies, we feared them more than the Germans. We could only go deeper into the woods, but the Nazis would find us there.

"Eventually the Nazis did come to our campsite, but they were not hostile. They told us we were Aryans, like the Germans, not racially impure like the Jews. The Nazis said they needed our help at a labor camp making weapons for German soldiers to fend off the Russians threatening the Eastern Front. The Lord knows we did not want the Russians to take Poland. Also, many Roma had fought for the German Army in the First World War, and many Gypsy men had been conscripted by the Germans into this war. We could not believe the Nazis would turn against us when our own men had fought for them. We didn't know that as the Germans were speaking to us, they were pulling our men from their units at the Eastern Front and sending them to concentration camps, even those who had earned medals for heroic action."

Stefan stopped and took a long drink of wine, then wiped his lips on his sleeve. "The day we were taken was a beautiful spring morning. Our parents had died several months before when a flu epidemic came through the Ukraine and eastern Poland, so it was just me and Melina and our families, along with the rest of the Keldari clan. I remember it well—the women had been cooking; the smell of coriander and cumin filled the camp. Our cousin, Anna, had picked flowers that morning and put them in a vase of water on the table next to the stove. After lunch, the men began to break camp and the women, with children tugging at their aprons, began to pack for the journey, knowing only that we all would be going somewhere by train. But halfway through our preparations, the German officer in charge of the move came to the camp and ordered us to leave everything. He said it wasn't safe to stay at our camp any longer; the soldiers would bring everything later. The Shero Rom, Mar Dep, the King of the Gypsies, and other leaders protested, but the soldier in charge refused to listen. And what did we know? How could anyone imagine what awaited us at Auschwitz?

"When we approached Auschwitz-Birkenau and saw the barbed wire we realized we had been tricked. We were not at a labor camp; we were at a very large prison. Then came the second shock—when we arrived on the dock Sasha was there, translating for the Nazis. Sasha! My sister Sasha! I could not believe my eyes. I hadn't seen her for years. After she married Henryk our father forbade us to visit her. We did sneak out to see her occasionally, but at that point I hadn't seen her for about five years. I was glad she was alive, of course, but so, so sorry to know she was at Auschwitz."

Stefan sighed. "'You must cooperate,' Sasha was saying to the Gypsies, who by now were fighting and screaming at the soldiers. 'You will receive better treatment and you will be freed as soon as the war is over.' Melina and I wanted to believe her. Mar Dep, the Shero Rom of the Keldari, wasn't so sure, but he ordered the Gypsies to stop resisting. Emil Dep, the King's son, had fire in his eyes. He was an evil young man, and he despised Sasha. She was the only Gypsy woman who had ever dared to confront him.

"Incarceration, as you can imagine, was the worst nightmare imaginable for the Gypsies. We needed open air and sky and the freedom to move about. The Nazis didn't put us to work helping to make equipment, as they had promised. We would learn too late that they didn't consider Gypsies to be trainable. They did not even consider us to be human."

"Did you ever get the chance to speak to Sasha privately while you were at Auschwitz?" Beth asked.

Stefan shook his head. "No. Never. Sasha didn't live at the Birkenau Zigeunerlager, the Gypsy camp, at that point. She had been moved to the main camp where the other interpreters and essential workers were imprisoned. But she came to Birkenau often to interpret and she always brought a hopeful message that things would change for the better. But eventually we knew that something terrible was happening. Stories passed through the complex that the Jews were being exterminated by the tens of thousands. If this were true, it didn't make sense that the Nazis would allow the Gypsies to survive the war to tell this story. It soon became clear to us that we were also destined to be victims of Himmler's *Endlosung*, the "Final Solution." The Gypsies, as a people, were marked for extermination. From then on it would only be a matter of time. If I hadn't been placed on the transport to Buchenwald with the other healthy younger men, I no doubt would have been killed on the night of the Ziguenernacht, along with thousands of others."

Stefan sighed sadly as Beth looked away. The sun had begun to go down while Stefan had been talking and now the room was dense with creeping shadows. "What about Sasha?" Beth asked carefully. "Do you have any idea what happened to her?"

"No, not for certain. There was a story that circulated in the Auschwitz underground that Sasha was taken to a farm outside of the village of Oswiecim where both she and the baby died shortly after Sasha gave birth. A local midwife passed word that they were buried there."

"Is that what you believe?" Beth asked, disillusioned at yet another story lacking hard evidence.

"I don't know; it sounds very suspicious to me. But I don't believe Sasha survived the war. Afterwards, I searched and searched until I found Melina. The Red Cross was very helpful. Gypsies who wanted to be found had a number of options after the war to reconnect with their kin and clan. Sasha never registered anywhere."

CHAPTER FOURTEEN

Auschwitz, Poland
1988

After a tasty traditional Gypsy dinner with Stefan and Christine, Vali picked up Beth and drove her back to town in the green VW van. Vali suggested a chat, so they stopped in the Altstadt for a beer at *Der Rote Ochse*, the Red Ox, a traditional German pub near the university. There were a number of students in the front area, so they found a quiet spot to sit in the back of the room. Beth appreciated having the chance to "debrief" with Vali and share the myriad of thoughts and emotions that fought for her attention. It was wonderful to have found Stefan and made such a strong emotional connection with him, but Beth also felt a huge loss, a void she'd never experienced before. She mourned now the years she might have had with Stefan. She thought of her Great Uncle John Sullivan back in Grandview and how much fun she had had with him over the years. She especially remembered the time when she was a kid and he gave her several sips of his ale at the annual family picnic. They both got tipsy and in trouble with her parents. How sad that she would never have memories of childhood years with Stefan, and that her father had missed the benefit of knowing his uncle.

By the time Beth entered the Hotel Europa's dark, quiet lobby she was feeling the effects of the alcohol and she was drained, and exhausted, wanting nothing so much as a good night's sleep. She didn't even bother to look around the lobby as she made her way to the front desk. After picking up her key she headed for the stairs.

"Good evening, Miss Karmazin," a deep male voice called out in English.

Beth gasped and stumbled, reaching out to grab the rail of the banister. The voice sounded familiar, but Beth knew she had to be dreaming. Frightened, and cursing herself for not being more observant, she clutched her room key, pointed tip outward, between her knuckles and spun around. "Yes?" she said, trying to sound confident and strong as she prepared to defend herself.

"Please, Ma'am, don't stab me with that there key. I give up." The man stood slowly and emerged from the shadows, hands raised high in mock surrender.

Beth squinted, narrowing her eyes. "Andy? Andy!" She dropped her key and her purse and ran into the warm embrace of Andy Weinberg, whom she had not seen in more than two years.

"Now that's more like the reception I was looking for," he said, his voice muffled in Beth's hair as he wrapped her tightly in his strong arms.

Beth, still holding him, drank in his familiar scent, then took a step back to get a better look at him. He hadn't changed much in two years; there was a little gray around his temples, and he had maybe gained a few pounds, and he had new glasses, silver wire frames with a rectangular design that set off the brightness of his eyes. Beth decided in that instant that he was settling into his mid-thirties very handsomely. And he looked happy.

"So where is …?" Beth, still in an alcohol-induced and sleep-deprived haze, searched her brain for the name. "Dianna? Is she here in Heidelberg?" Beth glanced around the lobby, looking for another silent figure in the shadows.

"No," Andy said evenly, looking down. "We broke up. Almost six months ago."

"Oh, I'm so sorry," Beth said, covering her mouth. "I thought you two were engaged."

Andy nodded and sighed. "We were. Had set a date and everything. She had bought a dress, the synagogue was reserved, the china pattern was picked out, the whole schmear."

"What happened? Did she get cold feet?" Beth hoped she wasn't being too inquisitive. In truth, she was desperate to know more.

Andy shook his head. "I was the one with the cold feet. I woke up one day and realized that as much as I loved Dianna, and I really, truly did love her, I could not marry her."

"Why not?"

"Because Beth, she wasn't you."

Beth was speechless. "I … I …" she stuttered.

"I know this must be a shock," Andy said, taking her by the hand and leading her to the nearby lobby chairs, where they both sat down.

"How did you even find me?" Beth asked, rubbing her tired eyes. "Here in Heidelberg? You tracked me down halfway across the world?"

"It wasn't that hard," he said. "I called your parents and they told me you'd just left the CIT. I called your old boss at the CIT and she told me you were in Heidelberg. She even gave me the name of the hotel. So I can't take credit for having done much Sherlock Holmes sleuthing."

"Are you staying here in Heidelberg?" Beth asked.

"Yes, here at the hotel." Andy nodded toward the staircase. "But don't worry; I've booked my own room. I know it's presumptuous of me to think that after all this time I can just insert myself back into your life."

"Let's go upstairs," Beth suggested. "We've got a lot to talk about, and this lobby isn't exactly the most inviting spot in Western Europe."

Ten minutes later, Beth and Andy, both dressed casually in sweats, sat cross-legged on the double bed in Beth's room, laughing and drinking wine which Beth had ordered up from room service. Beth couldn't believe how easy it was to catch up; after a few awkward questions, the two were talking as if they had never been separated.

Beth filled Andy in on the details of her search for the truth about Sasha and her discovery of her great-uncle Stefan, while Andy related his growing success as a partner in his law firm and his difficult breakup with Dianna.

They had just finished a hilarious reminiscence from their college days, when Andy's face suddenly turned serious. "Beth, I need to know: do I have a chance with you? That's the real reason I came all the way to Heidelberg. I want you back. I'm sorry I left you back there in Paris." The words poured out of him in an anguished rush.

"I was so hurt at the time that I couldn't see past my own pain. I couldn't think about what you wanted." He stopped and took a deep breath. "But now, time has passed, and I can see that I love you, and I want to spend the rest of my life with you. I don't need a final answer from you right now; I know I can't expect that. Hell, you could have a boyfriend or be engaged for all I know. I just realized that I couldn't live the rest of my life without telling you how I feel, and seeing if you feel the same. So that's all I'm looking for right now: an answer to whether I have a chance. Or have I lost you forever?"

Beth's mind reeled. "Andy, this is so sudden. A few hours ago I had no idea where you were or what you were doing, or whether you had any feelings for me anymore at all and now …"

"I know, I know," he reassured her. "That's why I don't want to pressure you. I just want to know if it's possible."

"I know I never stopped loving you," she confessed, smiling as she touched his clean-shaven cheek. "I've dated; I had a serious six-month relationship, but I haven't felt the same way about anyone else as I felt about you. We spent our youth together; how can anyone else replace that?"

Andy smiled broadly.

"But, and this is serious," Beth continued. "My commitment to finding the truth about my grandmother hasn't wavered in the last two years. If anything, it's stronger. I quit my job at CIT and this is my go-for-broke moment. If I don't find the answers in the next few months, I probably won't find them at all."

"I understand," Andy said, refilling Beth's wine glass.

"When we parted ways in Paris, I asked you to put yourself second to my quest." Beth pursed her lips. "Now, I'm asking you to do the same thing again. Andy, I haven't changed about that."

She feared his answer, but he just smiled. "You haven't, but I have," he argued. "What I admire about you and what frustrates me about you at the same time is your stubbornness and determination in the face of all odds. But I can live with that now. It's your zest for life and your spirit that I fell in love with thirteen years ago, my Gypsy girl, and that's not going away."

For one dizzying moment Beth imagined Andy was about to pull out a ring and propose to her again. She was very relieved when he didn't. Her feelings for him were undeniably strong, but she wasn't ready to make a commitment on such short notice. She wasn't even sure how she would feel tomorrow, once the sun had come up and the alcohol had worn off. Beth wanted to say, "And by the way, dear, it isn't appropriate these days for you to call me *Gypsy girl*. *Gypsy* is considered by the Roma to be a pejorative term. Today it is Roma or Romanies." But Beth decided to save it for another time. Hopefully, they would have more time.

"You asked me if you have a chance," she said carefully. "Yes, you have a chance. But Andy, I can't make any promises. The next few months are critical for me."

"Agreed. That's all I wanted to hear." He took her wine glass and placed it on the nightstand, then leaned forward and kissed her firmly on the lips. The kiss swiftly turned more passionate and they began to devour each other, making up for lost time. It was amazing how well their bodies seemed to remember one another, even after so much time apart. Before they knew it they were fully engaged and throwing clothes wherever they landed. Finally Beth came up for air and, gasping for breath, she remarked wryly, "I guess you didn't need that separate room after all."

Two days later Beth left Heidelberg for Auschwitz, accompanied by Andy. This time she didn't need to lean on Feliks. Through her contacts at the CIT she had gotten a visa to enter Poland for "research purposes" and it was surprisingly easy to add Andy's name to the visa as a "legal expert" who could verify documents. She was somewhat uncertain about letting Andy come with her on such a personal journey, especially when a visit to a Nazi concentration camp could only bring up painful issues for him as well. But he was determined to support her, and she had to admit that spending time with him again was proving to be a great pleasure, mentally and emotionally, not to mention sexually.

Beth and Andy left early in the day and traveled by train from Heidelberg to Krakow. At Krakow's Plazow Station they boarded the train to Oswiecim/Auschwitz via the small town of Skawina. The journey from Krakow to Auschwitz took only fifty minutes but seemed to be transporting Beth and Andy back more than forty years. At the train station in Oswiecim they found the local bus number 24 with the word "Muzeum" in stark letters above the front window. This was the bus to Auschwitz.

On the bus, seated near the front, Beth and Andy silently held hands. This seemed to be no time for speaking, or perhaps a situation for which there simply were no words. Both seemed to feel each other's thoughts and the reality that they were making a journey that a few decades earlier would have ended in almost certain death for both of them: he a Jewish man and she a part-Gypsy woman.

Beth tried to, and then tried not to, imagine what it would have been like to have traveled this route forty-forty years earlier. Oswiecim seemed like a staid and rather ordinary large village or small city of about forty thousand inhabitants with nothing to distinguish it, save a handful of old

Catholic churches and the ruins of a castle. The area around the town was a center for industry and trade, and everything appeared a bit shabby, but over all quiet and well organized. How could the worst outrage ever perpetrated against humanity have taken place next door to such an unremarkable and everyday place? Beth's stomach began to churn. Some of these trees, these very trees they were passing, trees that were tall and thick-limbed and leafy, had to be the same trees that had stood silent watch as tens of thousands, even hundreds of thousands, of innocent men, women, and children were transported to their deaths. The stones in this road, these smooth and simple cobblestones, had no doubt borne the weight of endless wooden donkey carts and Nazi trucks and forced marches, absorbing the last free steps of exhausted, confused, and terrified prisoners of the Third Reich.

Beth tried to repress the tears, but they began trickling down her cheeks. Andy noticed and reached over to comfort her. "Are you sure you want to do this?" he whispered in her ear. "We don't have to, you know."

Beth took a deep breath and steadied herself. "I have to do this," she explained. "For Sasha. I have to see the place where she suffered so much. I must do this to honor her memory."

The bus dropped them off a few minutes' walk from the entrance to the former concentration camp, the massive factory of death. One of the many things that shocked Beth was how close the camp was to the city of Oswiecim. "There's no way people didn't know," she said, shaking her head. "It's not like this was hidden off in a forest, or in the middle of nowhere. People passed by here every day. They had to smell the smoke from the crematories; on windy days the human ashes must have fallen on their clothes and their faces. But what could they do against the Gestapo and SS? What could they do?"

Andy and Beth stopped when they reached the front gate and saw the massive and ominous slogan in arched metal, *Arbeit Macht Frei*—Work Will Make You Free. Both Beth and Andy were pale-faced and resigned as they crossed the threshold of their ominous destination.

They joined a tour group and followed silently as the guide led them and the others through the remains of the camp, explaining that on July 2, 1947, an act of Polish parliament established the Auschwitz-Birkenau State Museum on the site of what was left of the Nazi concentration camp. Huge areas of the death factory had been destroyed by the Nazis before they retreated from advancing Allied forces.

"This Polish army garrison transitioned over the course of three years into Europe's largest and most efficient extermination and concentration camp," the guide, a tall, solemn-looking man, explained, sweeping his hand across the backdrop of the camp. He went on to describe the eighteen prisoner blocks and exhibits that the group would be able to view.

The guide led the way into the courtyard of Auschwitz I: the first part of the camp to open; the first place where experiments with the deadly poison Zyklon B took place. Auschwitz I included such noteworthy sites as the camp commandant's office, most of the SS offices, and the central jail, including the notorious Block 11, where solitary confinement led to certain death.

As Beth and Andy and the other members of the group walked from exhibit to exhibit, their shock and horror grew. Even the most well-read of them was not prepared for the sight of six-foot high piles of abandoned shoes, millions of pounds of shorn human hair, storehouses full of suitcases and belongings, and photograph after photograph of tortured, emaciated, brutalized, dehumanized human beings.

The guide called the tour group together in the courtyard and pointed out the "killing wall." This was a partition where thousands, even hundreds of thousands, of people had been executed by the SS firing squads. "Often it was an exercise in target practice for the SS," the guide explained. "There didn't need to be a reason for killing at Auschwitz."

Then the guide pointed across the courtyard to a lone gallows and said, "That was the favorite hanging place of Rudolph Hoess, one of the commanding officers of this camp and one of the world's most notorious mass murderers. He was a Catholic man who lived in a large home nearby with his wife and children, carrying on his life as if all were normal. He was made to answer for his crimes at Nuremberg."

After viewing several other exhibits, the group arrived at Block 10, which had been Dr. Josef Mengele's clinic. The guide explained how Mengele had hummed opera tunes as he performed horrific scientific experiments on children, especially dwarves and twins. The tour group was not allowed inside the clinic, which was a relief to Beth. She couldn't fathom viewing visual images of what had taken place inside there.

The group moved on to Block 11, the underground prison, the cold dark cellar where prisoners who had been sentenced by the punishment tribunal were kept until their turn came to go before the firing squad. "But most of the prisoners never made it to the firing squad," the guide explained. "They simply starved to death during their internment." Beth shuddered. Sasha might have been incarcerated in this dungeon and died here.

Beth walked down one of the long, darkly lit corridors. Only one cell at the end had any sort of light—a very small window at the very top of the wall. The thought of anyone being held in such a dungeon horrified Beth.

Following the tour of Auschwitz I, the group took a shuttle bus the three kilometers to Birkenau, the second area of the vast expanse known collectively as Auschwitz. At Birkenau everything, especially the slaughter of humans, had happened on a massive scale. Most of the machinery of mass extermination was located at Birkenau, along with several hundred primitive wooden barracks where the prisoners had slept, often several to one bunk. In these cold, drafty, disease-infested barracks up to two hundred thousand prisoners were incarcerated at a time, waiting to be killed. Birkenau was where most of the prisoners first arrived and where the selection process took place on large ramps just inside the gates.

The vastness of Birkenau was staggering; the camp was the size of a city completely enclosed with electrified barbed wire fence. Each section of the camp contained its own kitchens, laundries, infirmaries, housing for the SS, and, of course, the ubiquitous watchtowers that were manned by rifle-carrying officers twenty-four hours a day, seven days a week. Birkenau had run as a factory of death, built to handle a constant turnover in population. Here, up to a thousand Sonderkommandos had been assigned to ensure that the process moved quickly and efficiently from one center to the next in each of the five crematories.

The process began in the *Badeanstalten*, the bathhouses, where prisoners were gassed, then moved to the *Leichenenkeller,* the corpse cellars, where the bodies were stored, and finally ended in the *Einascherungsofen*, the cremation ovens. Beth swore to Andy that she could still smell ashes, even after forty-three years.

As the stunned and deeply moved Beth and Andy continued through the camp, Beth realized that the guide never mentioned a word about the approximately twenty-three thousand Gypsies who had died at Auschwitz. The guide's script focused solely on the Jewish and Polish Holocaust victims. This angered Beth, but then, what could she expect when not one Gypsy had been asked to serve on the Holocaust Commission?

When the guided portion of the tour was over, Beth knew she had to see the Zigeunerlager, or barracks designated for the Gypsies, the block named on the map as BBlb2. This was where Stefan and Melina had been housed, along with thousands of their fellow Gypsies. Beth and Andy made their way to that part of the camp and found what little was left of the original complex. A few crumbling stone chimneys represented the thirty barracks that had held more than ten thousand Gypsies at any given time.

Beth walked to the center of the courtyard, where, in the beginning at least, Gypsy families were allowed to gather. For a brief period of time the Gypsies were given a small amount of freedom, compared to the Jewish detainees. The Gypsies were allowed to stay in family units and make music, sing, and dance. The children were allowed to play together. Beth tried to imagine the music of the men's violins, the ramblings of the children, and the rustling of the women's long, colorful skirts as they danced with passion and abandon, defying the dark forces swirling around them.

Beth found a quiet spot beneath a tree and sat down on the ground, drawing her knees to her chin and wrapping her arms around her shins. She stared, glassy-eyed, out across the grounds and toward the crematories. Andy came and sat beside her, wrapping his arm around her shoulder and pressing his head to hers.

"I know now; I really know," Beth whispered.

"Know what?" Andy asked.

"That my grandmother could not have survived this place. As strong as she was, she could not have survived. For a long time I believed I might find her, alive and well, with a story of magical survival, of how she beat the odds. But now, seeing this hell on earth, seeing what she endured, malnourished and pregnant, I don't believe there is any way she could have lived through it. My father was right. I must accept that she is dead, that she died here in this devil's camp or somewhere nearby. I just wish I could somehow connect with her, even for one split second, so that she would know that I came looking for her."

CHAPTER FIFTEEN

Auschwitz, Poland
Summer 1988

Following their exhaustive, and exhausting, tour of the huge complex of Auschwitz-Birkenau, both Beth and Andy found it difficult to speak. Both were overwhelmed by what they had seen and heard. The actual evidence of the Holocaust had never been so real to either one of them. Andy, for his part, was disgusted and would have preferred to have gone home and put it all behind him, but Beth found the experience had made her even more determined to get to the bottom of what had happened to her grandmother.

"Are you still with me in this?" Beth asked, gazing at Andy's pale face and tired eyes as they lay in their narrow twin bed in a small hotel room above a tavern in Krakow.

"Absolutely," he said wearily, pulling the blanket to his chin and curling beneath the covers. "Wherever you go, I will follow. But I'd be lying if I didn't say that I'll be glad when all this is over."

Their next step, after a night of fitful sleep, was to figure out where Sasha had been taken after the Nazi officer had removed her from Auschwitz in the dead of night. Under the German occupation of Poland, Polish farmers were required to supply produce to the German staff and SS officers assigned to the Polish concentration camps. The farmers and their families were allowed to keep only minimal items for their own survival. When the camps ran low on staples such as bread and milk, soldiers were sent to nearby farms to seize these precious commodities, leaving the local population near starvation, and devastating the farm economy and infrastructure.

If there were any truth to the story that a German officer had buried Sasha and her baby at one of these farms, Beth was determined to find the spot. The villagers in the area might remember the officer and have heard rumors of Sasha and the baby. Through a CIT connection in Poland, Beth was able to obtain an official listing of Polish farmers who had requested compensation from the German courts for their financial losses during the war. Beth was surprised, and somewhat relieved, at the small number of farmers who had actually made claims after the war. Limiting herself to those farmers who lived within a reasonable night's drive from Auschwitz-Birkenau, she created a "must-see" list of places to go and people to contact.

In the lobby of their hotel in Krakow Beth and Andy met their English-speaking guide and driver, Pan Ferkowski. He was a man in his sixties, of average build, with stiff gray hair and a gray goatee. He wore blue jeans and a navy blue vest over a plaid shirt. In addition to Polish and English he spoke German, which he had learned during the war at a labor camp in Dwory. He was a friendly, gregarious, and energetic man, which helped to put Andy and Beth at ease.

"I suggest we begin this morning and move one kilometer at a time, proceeding outwards, until we find the farm you are searching for," he explained, fanning his broad fingers before him.

"Perfect," Beth replied, rolling up the sleeves of her white cotton shirt and pulling her hair back in a rubber band. "Perfect," Andy concurred, tying his hiking boots tightly at his ankles and pulling up his heavy cotton socks.

The first few days of their journey were long, hot, and arduous. Pan managed to stay in remarkably good humor; but then again, he was being well paid for his efforts. Beth and Andy, on the other hand, had nothing but hope to drive them forward. The three went from door to door, often on foot because many dirt roads in the Polish countryside were not passable via automobile. They trudged through heavy fields and crossed narrow muddy streams, only to have doors slammed in their faces.

This was a poor part of Poland, and it was clear that the Communist regime, now in its fourth decade of dominance, had not made life any better for the poor struggling people who worked the land. The government had finally given up all attempts at collectivism and had left the farmers to their small plots of land. Many of the farms lacked even the most basic modern equipment, and work was still being done with axes, picks, and hoes. Local produce was still transported to market by horses and wooden carts, which were often seen moving lazily down the road. In some ways Beth thought it rather romantic. Noise was minimal, the pace relaxed, and life pretty uncomplicated.

On the fourth day, with bandages covering their blistered heels and toes, Beth, Andy, and Pan stopped at a roadside picnic bench to eat the box lunches they'd brought from the hotel. Beth tried to enjoy her sausage and cabbage sandwich and the peaceful countryside, but her mind kept returning to thoughts of what had happened on this very land forty years earlier. Thousands of people had been executed and buried here, perhaps even buried directly beneath Beth's sore feet.

"You are not eating your lunch," Pan commented, watching Beth's face.

"I'm not as hungry as I thought," Beth replied, handing half of her sandwich to Pan and the other half to Andy. "Here, take the vodka as well." Vodka went everywhere and with everything in Poland, and everyone seemed to like it. Perhaps, Beth mused, it helped to soothe both the wounds of a troubled past and the uncertainty over the future.

"We'll share the vodka," Pan insisted, raising the metallic flask in an impromptu toast. "It will be good for you to have a drink."

Beth smiled in spite of herself. "Maybe you're right, Pan," she replied. She drank down her water and poured a shot of vodka into her empty cup, wishing she had a little vermouth and a couple of olives to enhance its flavor.

Later that afternoon, when the sun was low in the sky and the wheat fields burnished orange and gold, the three arrived at a small peasant village that was about two hours by road from Auschwitz and close to railroad tracks. Beth wondered if anyone living in this village in the 1940s had seen the haunted, terrified eyes peering out of the locked railcars as they sped by, carrying prisoners to Auschwitz. Did the villagers choose not to look, or did they see, but then look away?

They reached an old stone farmhouse, set at the end of a long dirt driveway off a country road. The house was small and appeared abandoned at first glance. They almost decided to bypass it in their haste to finish covering this area by nightfall.

"No, we better take a look," Beth argued. "You never know when we're going to find our needle in a haystack."

After they had knocked for several minutes, a middle-aged woman with thick brown hair answered the door of the farmhouse. She was dressed in a white apron over a long gray skirt and a faded yellow sweater with small lavender flowers embroidered on the pockets. The brown leather sandals that covered her gray stockings were worn and dusty. Pan spoke to the woman in Polish.

"We are looking for the people who lived here during the war. Can you help us?"

The woman's eyes narrowed in suspicion, as she steadfastly clutched the door. "We don't talk to strangers here," she responded firmly. "We prefer to keep to ourselves."

She began to close the door, but Pan, reacting quickly, stuck his foot in the doorway.

"Please," he pleaded, raising his broad hands, "these two young people are from America and they are looking for a missing relative."

Suddenly a tired, high-pitched female voice came from inside the farmhouse. "Let them in, Irina. I will speak with them."

"But Auntie …"

"Let them in," the voice insisted, stronger this time.

The woman opened the door, bowed at the waist, and reluctantly beckoned the three visitors to enter. The house was so small that nearly the entire interior structure was visible upon entering: a kitchen, a sitting room, and a small bedroom in back. In spite of the smallness of the farmhouse, it was a cheerful and comfortable-looking place. A vase of fresh sunflowers sat on the kitchen table and a brightly woven rug covered the wooden floor in the living area.

An elderly woman sat in a rocking chair in the corner near a woodburning stove. A beige shawl, ragged at the edges, was wrapped around her shoulders. A black scarf covered her head and framed her thick silver hair. Her cotton dress was a faded brown, and she wore black socks and black slippers. In her gnarled hand she held a handmade cane of birch. Her face was pale and doughy, its numerous lines and furrows softened by a generous dusting of pressed powder.

"All these years," the woman said sadly, shaking her head and rocking slowly back and forth. "All these years, I knew. I knew someone would come for answers some day."

Beth felt the hair rise on the back of her neck. She glanced at Andy, whose face had paled. Had they just found their needle in a haystack?

"Please sit down," the woman said, pointing with her cane to a worn old sofa across from her rocking chair. Silently Beth, Andy, and Pan moved to the sofa and sat down side by side, hands clasped in their laps as if they were misbehaving children waiting to be disciplined by the school principal. Sunlight streamed in from a back window, bathing the cottage in light and casting the old woman's shadow before her on the wooden floor.

She asked Pan to translate for her. He nodded. The woman began speaking and Pan's translation was perfect and nearly simultaneous to her carefully chosen words.

"My name is Gerta Klinsmann, and I am eighty-six years old." She nodded in the direction of the middle-aged woman who stood warily beside the kitchen table. "That is my niece, Irina. She lives with her husband in the village, but she comes every day to look in on me. My husband, Dirk, died many years ago. Irina worries when people come to the door; she is afraid that strangers will try to rob me. Irina, bring our guests what is left of the coffee."

"I can assure you that these young people did not come to rob you," Pan explained. "They are looking for information about a woman who may have been buried in this area during the war." Pan paused and cleared his throat. "Madame, what did you mean earlier when you said that all these years you knew that someone would come for the answers?"

Gerta began to rock more quickly back and forth, her anxious foot tapping a frantic rhythm on the wooden floor. "I am a Polish woman, born and raised in this region. But my husband, Dirk, was a German. There are many Germans here and we lived peacefully together for years, but the war made things difficult. Dirk had a nephew, Gerhardt, who was a Nazi SS officer at Oswiecim. Gerhardt came to visit us here every few months or so, bringing grain and vegetables and goats' milk to supplement the little we had to survive on at the time." The woman paused, her pale eyes lost deep in the past.

"I didn't know Gerhardt well; he didn't speak Polish. But my husband was always very fond of him. It was May of 1944, when one night, actually around four in the morning, Gerhardt came to the house and woke us from a sound sleep, pounding frantically on the front door with his fist. 'Let me in. Let me in,' he demanded. My husband rushed outside and

Gerhardt opened the trunk of his car to reveal a woman in labor, struggling to give birth. The two men helped her out of the car and brought her into the house."

Irina, Gerta's niece, took a spot behind the older woman's chair and placed a steadying hand on Gerta's shoulder, as if to warn her to stop speaking. "No, Irina, it is all right. These people deserve to know." Gerta patted her niece's hand and resumed her story.

"The pregnant woman was a Gypsy woman and she had come from the camp where Gerhardt was an officer. She was terrified and in pain, so I tried to soothe her. Eventually she told me her name was Sasha Karmazin and that she had two sons already, teenage boys living in Warsaw. I tried to calm her, but she was in great distress."

"Then what happened?" Beth asked breathlessly.

"I tried to deliver the baby myself, but it was too difficult." Gerta shook her head. "The woman was so thin and the baby was breech. I sent Dirk into town to fetch the midwife. I did not think the woman or the child would survive until the midwife arrived. But Paula, bless her soul, had worked many miracles in the past, and she was able to take the baby through a Cesarean. It was a little boy, tiny, no more than three or four pounds." Gerta cupped her hands to show the small size and smiled at the memory.

"Dirk, bless his soul, sat with the little one by the fire here, in this very rocking chair. I warned him not to get too attached to the child, for he surely could not survive."

"How long did the Gypsy woman—my grandmother—survive?" Beth asked.

"Oh, she did not die," Gerta replied.

"What?" Beth was speechless. "But … but you said she could not survive."

Gerta nodded. "I did not believe she could. The midwife did not believe she could, not with all the blood she lost, the surgery, and the infection coursing throughout her body. By all rights, she should not have lived. But she held on through the night and into the next day. By the second day she was able to drink water and broth. By the third day, she was able to eat some soup and nurse her baby."

"The child survived too?" Andy asked in amazement.

"Yes. He was small, but feisty. She named him Mikisha, after a favorite uncle."

"What became of them?" Beth asked, leaning forward, nearly touching the old woman's knees with her own. "Are they still alive?"

The old woman folded her hands in her lap. "Sasha and Mikisha stayed here with us until the war ended." Gerta looked away sadly. "Then Sasha gave her baby up for adoption to a local couple and returned to Warsaw to look for Henryk and their sons, Karl and Dimitri. It was hard to see Sasha and Mikisha leave us; Dirk and I never had any children of our own, and Sasha and Mikisha were like family to us."

Beth's mind raced. "A local couple. Adoption. So Mikisha was raised here, near Oswiecim?" Beth did some quick figuring. "Born in 1944, he'd be forty-four now; early middle age. He is my father's half-brother and my uncle. Here in Poland! I must see him. Where is he?"

Gerta looked away uneasily, pursing her thin lips. "Understand, he does not know his past. He was a toddler when the family took him in, and they raised him as their own. He was told he was the child of Polish villagers who died of typhus just after the war. The family changed his name, gave him a good loving home, and raised him as their own. You mustn't interfere."

"But he's part of my family; my flesh and blood," Beth insisted. "He's my father's half-brother and Dimitri's half-brother as well. He's got family in America, sisters-in-law and nieces and nephews and a grandnephew! He deserves to know the truth. You have no right to deny him that." Beth's face was hot and red with passion. She clenched her fists to keep them from shaking.

"Beth, do you have the right to destroy this man's life?" Andy asked softly in English. "After forty-four years, out of the blue, you're going to tell him that everything he's believed his whole life is a lie? Do you have a right?"

Beth, shocked, swallowed hard. Not since they had gotten back together had Andy challenged her so directly, or even disagreed with her. "I know it will be difficult, but it's for the best," she argued. "I know that if the tables were turned, I would want to know. Wouldn't you? Isn't the truth always best in the long run?"

Pan did not translate this conversation to Irina and Gerta, as Andy responded, "Would I want to know the truth that my father was a Nazi bastard who raped my Gypsy mother and got her pregnant at Auschwitz, then brought her to a rural farmhouse to die? No, thanks, that's information I'd rather live without," Andy said, his blue eyes blazing.

Beth looked around the room, her gaze moving from face to face: Andy, Pan, Gerta, and Irina. They looked back at her quizzically. "Is that what you all think? That this man should not be told the truth about his past?"

Immediately after Pan translated the question for Gerta and Irina, everyone nodded. Beth was crushed to think that a lost member of her own family was as close as the town half a mile away. But she would never meet him, or shake his hands, or touch the face of this miracle man who had somehow survived against all odds, born to a starving prisoner in a makeshift operation in an old stone farmhouse in the dead of night.

"What about Sasha?" Beth asked softly, unclenching her fists. "You said that after she put the baby up for adoption she went to Warsaw to search for Henryk and her sons. Did you ever hear from her again?"

Gerta nodded sadly. "Yes. Several times, in fact. She wrote to say that when she reached Warsaw she found a city destroyed. Her husband had died and the whereabouts of her sons was unknown. Most people believed they had been killed too, along with most of their classmates. Sasha was heartbroken. The only things that had kept her alive through Auschwitz and her time here had been her love for Mikisha and her deep hope that someday she would return to Henryk and her sons. But then, with Mikisha living with a new family, a family who could give him so much more than Sasha ever could, and her first family gone, she lost her will to live. She began to regret ever surviving Auschwitz; it seemed to have counted for nothing.

"Dirk and I, in our letters, tried to cheer her up, and convince her that God had a plan for her life, and that she still had a reason to live. Our words must have held some sway, because soon after that Sasha joined a convent and dedicated her life to serving the Lord."

"Is she … still alive?" Beth asked, swallowing hard.

Gerta shook her head. "I do not believe so, no. The last we heard from Sasha was 1961. Twenty-seven years ago. Sasha was living at a convent in Krakow and she asked us to send her a photograph of Mikisha, who was then seventeen. It was no easy task, I assure you, to sneak a photo of him without his knowledge. But Dirk was able to do so, while Mikhail," Gerta stopped suddenly, and her hand flew to cover her mouth as she realized she had revealed the name his new family had given him. "Well, there are several Mikhails in this area," she reasoned, color flooding her cheeks.

"It's all right," Beth counseled. "I'm not going to contact him. Please, continue."

Gerta took a deep breath. "My husband managed to take the photograph from the field behind where the boys were playing football on the school pitch. Mikhail was quite a good athlete! He was a tall lad with sandy blond hair, broad shoulders, and strong features."

Beth immediately saw a vision of her father as a young man; the half-brothers clearly bore a strong physical resemblance to one another.

"Irina, bring me my jewelry box," Gerta instructed her niece. The niece grudgingly went to the bedroom and returned with a rectangular-shaped box covered in worn red velvet. Gerta opened the box, rummaged through the items, and withdrew a tattered black-and-white photograph that she handed to Beth, along with a yellowed envelope. "After we sent the photo of Mikhail to Sasha, she sent us back a letter, along with this photo of herself."

Beth gazed at the photo and it took her breath away. The woman facing the camera head-on looked exactly like an older version of Beth. Sasha would have been fifty-four years old in 1961, but the woman looked older. Her eyes were huge and dark, deeply set and ringed with circles. Her hair, still long and thick, was shot through with streaks of silver-white, emphasizing the rich blackness of the hair surrounding it. Her nose was high and regal, and her cheekbones were still firm, even as wrinkles were carved into her forehead and the sides of her chin. The face was an arresting combination of sorrow, pride, defiance, and beauty. Beth felt as if she were looking directly into her own future.

As Beth passed the photo to Andy and Pan, she turned the envelope over in her hand and read the return address from the Ursuline Convent in Krakow. Beth knew that was where her next stop would be.

"When did you last hear from Sasha?" Beth asked Gerta.

"That letter and photograph was the final time," Gerta replied sadly. "We wrote and wrote, but we never heard from Sasha again. It was as if she had disappeared from the face of the earth. I suspected it might be the Gypsy in her soul that led her to wander again. I think if she had died in Krakow one of the sisters there would have written to tell us."

"Mrs. Klinsmann, you have been so generous," Beth said, gathering her thoughts. The old woman was clearly tiring, and Beth needed to extract some last pieces of the puzzle before time ran out. "I can't thank you enough for your kindness and your honesty. You've answered so many of my questions, and given a great gift to me and to my family. But I have one final question. Did Sasha ever speak about her experiences at Auschwitz?"

Gerta's face paled and her eyes grew watery. "At first, no. She would say nothing about what she had seen, or what had been done to her there. But often she would wake up screaming in the middle of the night. Dirk and

I would try to comfort her, but it was as if she couldn't see or hear us. Her eyes would be open, but she was blinded by the terror behind her eyes. We held her in our arms and rocked her, stroking her hair as it grew out from stubble.

"It was many months later that she began to speak, haltingly, of what had happened. The men, women, and children gassed in the showers, the bodies piled high outside the crematoria. The experiments done in Dr. Mengele's lab. Horrors. Horrors, horrors, horrors." Gerta shook her head, choking back bitter tears.

A sudden thought occurred to Beth. "Your nephew—Gerhardt—what became of him?" Beth couldn't imagine that he continued visiting his aunt and uncle with Sasha and his illegitimate child living there; proof of his past and of his crime.

"Oh. He died," Gerta said matter-of-factly, regaining her composure. "Just after the Nazis abandoned Auschwitz many of the officers fled, fearing the advance of the Allies. Gerhardt got as far as Munich on the way home to his family, but when he heard that the Fuehrer had died and the war was all but over, he took his pistol, went out in the woods and shot himself. My husband was heartbroken. He really loved his nephew. I don't think he ever truly believed that Gerhardt was a Nazi, or that he had forced himself on Sasha."

"Was Sasha relieved when she learned that Gerhardt was dead?" Beth asked.

Gerta shook her head vehemently. "No, no, no. She blamed herself, felt his death was somehow her fault. He was a source of much confusion for her. She hated him: hated the violence he had done to her, the way he had defiled her body. And yet, he did save her life and the life of her child. He could have easily killed her at any moment; life was cheap at Auschwitz. But he took a great risk to bring her and the child here. Sasha did not want to see Gerhardt ever again, but she did not wish him dead. I think that was just one of the many, many burdens Sasha carried in her soul."

"There is a man in America, a professor who writes books," Beth said, choosing her words carefully. "He has done some research into the Gypsies at Auschwitz and he claims that Sasha was a collaborator, that she worked to help the Nazis."

Gerta's eyes widened with rage and she suddenly looked much younger than her eighty-six years. "No, no, no." She shook her head back and forth vehemently. "Never. Sasha Karmazin did not collaborate with the Nazis. She did what she had to do to survive and to help her people; no more. Sasha Karmazin was like a daughter to me. She was one of the finest people I have ever known."

CHAPTER SIXTEEN

Warsaw, Poland
Summer 1945

On May 8, 1945, the Second World War ended in Europe. The war in the Pacific ended three months later. But for Dirk and Gerta Klinsmann and Sasha Karmazin and her baby, Mikisha, the good news of victory was met with more relief than with joy. Sasha had been living with the middle-aged couple for more than a year, and during that time she had healed physically and regained much of her strength. Her hair, shorn to the scalp for so long, had begun to grow out. Although she was still painfully thin, her spindly arms were fuller and her hollow cheeks had softened. And Mikisha was the biggest surprise of all. He had been so tiny and frail at his birth that he barely survived his first few weeks of life, particularly a bout with pneumonia. But now he was round and chubby, with tousled blond curls, an infectious smile, and round green eyes.

The Klinsmanns had been beyond generous, sharing what little they had with Sasha and the baby. For the middle-aged childless couple it was a pleasure and joy to have two lives to care for; to nurture and help grow.

On the day the radio reported that the Japanese had offered their unconditional surrender, the war in the Pacific had reached its conclusion. It was time to celebrate. Dirk and Gerta had no wine or spirits, but a neighbor had given them some homemade beer, which they broke out for the occasion. Gerta pulled from the small garden that she had hidden from the Nazis out by the woodshed some young roots: carrot tops and turnip greens. She made a goat meat stew for dinner and a milk pudding for dessert. They held their cups aloft and toasted. "To the Allies. To the end of the war," their tired voices sang in unison.

Sasha raised her glass and took a sip of the bitter liquid. Instead of being happy, or at least relieved, she seemed nervous and fretful, on the verge of tears. After pushing a forkful of stew across her plate, she cleared her throat and looked up sadly. "Now that the war is over, I must leave," she said.

Gerta was shocked. "Leave? But where would you go? What will you do?" Her cheeks grew red and shiny. "The Nazis may have fled, true, but it is still not safe for Gypsies, especially a Gypsy woman and child, alone in the world. The Nazis have left, but their vile beliefs still remain." She looked to her husband for support, but Dirk's face remained impassive.

"It is my hope that you will find a home, a good Polish home, for Mikisha once I am gone," Sasha continued softly.

Now it was Dirk's turn to look shocked. "You aren't taking him with you?" he asked.

Sasha's eyes filled with tears. "No. I cannot. I love him more than life itself; he is truly the only reason that I am still alive; the only reason I endured what I endured." She took a deep breath and straightened in her chair. "But that is why I must do not what is best for me, but what is best for Mikisha. What can his future hold with me as his mother? His life will be in continual danger. Now that the war is over I must return to Warsaw; to Henryk and my sons. I won't ask you to keep him. You need to enjoy your years together now, without the burden of another mouth to feed." Sasha didn't have to say it; all three knew that she would never leave Mikisha with Dirk Klinsmann, the uncle of the man who raped her, a man who might possibly return after the war and take the child away.

"And I can't ask Henryk to accept Mikisha; physical proof that I was taken against my will and defiled by a Nazi. My husband is a kind and patient man, but can any woman ask her husband to accept that? And if my Henryk is dead, or lost …" her voice trailed away briefly, then came back with renewed strength. "Well, as you say, it is no longer safe to be a Gypsy, even a half Gypsy, in Europe, and a single Gypsy woman with a half-Gypsy child will always be an obvious target. If I keep Mikisha with me, I can't see any good future for him, only terrible struggles and dangers."

She paused. "His eyes are green, his hair is blond, and his skin is fair, thank God. He can easily pass for a Polish baby. If he is raised as such, just an ordinary Polish village boy, he will have so many more opportunities in life. He will have everything that I am not able to give him." Sasha's lip trembled, but she refused to weep. She knew she was embarking on a time in her life when she would need more strength than she had ever called upon before, even during Auschwitz.

Gerta dabbed her eyes with a napkin, while Dirk stared at his plate. Both were silent, understanding the wisdom and self-sacrifice of Sasha's painful decision.

That night Sasha sat on the edge of her bed in the small cottage she had called home for the past year. Her hand trembling, she wrote to Mikisha:

September 3, 1945

My Dearest son,

I hope someday you will forgive me for leaving you. It is not because I don't love you. When I saw your sweet face this morning as you lay sleeping, I thought how beautiful you were, and I felt as though an arrow had been driven through my heart. Surely, if there is a God, this will be the last test He will put me to.

I am leaving because I believe your life will be better if I am not in the way of it. You deserve both a mother and a father; that is something I cannot give you. You also deserve to know in a general way what tomorrow will bring, at least until you are old enough to deal with the uncertainties in life. And I have no way of knowing about tomorrow. You see, times are difficult; there is no work for me here on the farm, and soon there will not be enough food for all of us. A child should not have to struggle with these conditions.

How I have prayed things could be different. I would love to have you close to me, to hold you and touch your soft skin every day, as I did my first sons, until you would get your legs under you and break away, as young boys eventually do from their mothers. What pleasure I would have had in watching you grow up to be the handsome and kind young man I know you will be. But you and I could not survive on the road together. I am no longer acceptable to any of my people, and a single Gypsy woman with a baby in a Gadje world is vulnerable to many evils. I would not put you in such danger.

When you go to school, please study hard—read and write as much as you can.

It is the path to a better world. Though you will not remember me, I am your mother forever—this bond can never be broken.

My deepest love,
Mama

Finished with the letter, Sasha put down her pen and sobbed wretchedly, realizing she could never give the letter to Mikisha. It would not be fair to his new family, and she couldn't risk the chance that he might try to find her. Exhausted and emptied of tears, she tore the letter into small pieces and burned it.

It was a cool September morning when Sasha left the security of the Klinsmanns' farm forever to set out for Warsaw. As Sasha prepared to leave, Gerta gave her a set of three new linen handkerchiefs, embroidered with the initials *SLK* and the dates that Sasha had stayed on the farm. Dirk, the more practical of the pair, gave Sasha a small cloth satchel that she could hide inside her clothing, protected from the thieves and beggars she might encounter during her journey. When Dirk handed Sasha the satchel, she was shocked to feel its lumpy weight and then to open it and find it filled with coins.

Dirk and Gerta were truly touched when Sasha presented them with her parting gift, a small wooden-framed painting she had done of their farmstead, a winter scene of slanted sunlight and fallow, frost-covered fields. Sasha had painted the picture with hand-made vegetable dyes because paint would have been far too expensive.

Sasha didn't leave any gift for Mikisha for fear that any item, no matter how small or how innocent, might inadvertently reveal his mother's Gypsy heritage. Thousands, probably tens of thousands, of children had been orphaned in the waning months of the war and Mikisha would not seem any different from any of the other poor children who arrived in new homes with no name, no identity, and no clues to his past.

As Dirk prepared the wagon for the journey, Sasha took her heartbreaking leave of Mikisha. She cuddled him, she cradled him, and she tousled his golden curls. Fighting back tears, she planted tender kisses all up and down his arms, his legs, and his chubby neck. She rocked him in her arms and sang him every Gypsy lullaby she could remember, snatches of old tunes and nearly forgotten melodies, understanding that this likely would be the only time in his life he would ever hear these songs of his heritage.

Dirk and Gerta watched silently as Sasha ran her index finger up and down, over and under Mikisha's little toes, throwing him into fits of giggles. Sasha tried to memorize her baby son, attempted to imprint every inch of him onto her mind, her soul, and her heart. Even Dirk, normally the stoic German, fought back tears as he watched the poignant scene.

Sasha sighed, pressing Mikisha's wriggling form to her chest. She had seen so many wrenching scenes at Auschwitz, had seen mothers torn from their children, had watched babies pulled from their mothers' arms. She tried to comfort herself with the fact that her situation now was so different; by leaving her child willingly, she was giving him a safer and happier life. There would be no gas chambers in his future.

Taking the dusty back roads and avoiding the nearby village, Dirk drove Sasha by horse cart to the town of Rokosowo, fifteen miles from the farm. No one knew that Dirk and Gerta had been harboring a Gypsy woman and her half-Gypsy, half-German child, and it would be best for everyone if they kept it that way.

As they waited on the platform for the train to Warsaw, Dirk awkwardly cleared his throat. "Write to us," he implored. "And remember, you can come back anytime. If you don't find your family …"

"I will never be able to thank you for your generosity." Sasha reached up to touch his weathered, sunburned cheek. "I will write, and hope to send you good news about my reunion with Henryk and my sons."

The train pulled into the station and shuddered to a halt in front of Sasha and Dirk. Sasha grabbed her knapsack and ascended the narrow metal steps into the train carriage. The carriage was hot and crowded, and Sasha had to push her way through the dark, smoke-filled car. The rail cars had seen little maintenance in the years since the war began and they were filthy and broken down with several shattered windows covered haphazardly with cardboard.

Sasha was dressed in the typical Polish peasant garb of a long dark skirt and a wool sweater given to her by Gerta and altered to fit Sasha's still-thin figure. Her dark hair was hidden beneath a babushka, but even so, several of the passengers recognized that Sasha was a Gypsy. Some called her names as she passed; one woman even spit on her. Others pressed close to the train's sides, anxious not to brush against one who was "unclean." It disgusted Sasha to think that even though the Nazis had been defeated, their evil ideology of prejudice and racism still remained. Sasha knew instinctively how dangerous it was to be a Gypsy or a Jew in postwar Europe. While she had been at the farmhouse, she and the Klinsmanns had heard on the radio numerous reports of anti-Semitic pogroms in Poland and stories of concentration camp survivors who, once freed from their hell on earth, had been murdered by angry mobs. Sasha said a silent prayer and asked the Lord to protect her, even as she thanked God that she did not have little Mikisha in tow.

Hours later, when the train reached Warsaw, Sasha was shocked by what she saw. She knew from news reports that the city had been devastated, but nothing in the radio reports could have prepared her for the reality on the ground. The city had been leveled; tall buildings had collapsed into rubble that spilled over into the streets. Burnt-out houses stood like blackened facades, facing the streets but with nothing more than open space behind them. Bombs had left enormous craters in the earth, huge gaping holes that scarred the landscape like a pockmarked face. Mangy dogs and feral cats ran loose, fighting for scraps, while enormous rats slithered along the damp canals, following the streams of dark water that fed the river. Smoke rose on the horizon, smoke from burning tires and smoke from wood fires, where hungry citizens who were starving in the streets burned paper and furniture and whatever else they could find for warmth.

Sasha was in shock. How could this be Warsaw, a city she knew so well, her home for so long? Where was the Warsaw with its cozy taverns, chic cafes, and elegant restaurants? Where was the Warsaw of proud baroque architecture and clean, straight streets with tree-lined boulevards? How could this, this moonscape, this subterranean, subhuman hell, full of smoke and stink and rubble, be Warsaw?

Sasha felt sick at the pit of her stomach as she considered her surroundings. How could anyone have survived this? How could Henryk and the boys have lived through this nightmare? Sasha left the train at the station at the western end of the city; the station in the city center had been bombed to rubble and trains no longer stopped there. Sasha got off and walked the three miles to Old Town, several times getting lost along the way as streets were either closed, unrecognizable, or impassable due to fire and bomb damage. Several times Sasha took a wrong turn, certain she knew where she was going, only to realize that the old familiar landmark she was looking for no longer existed.

Exhausted though she was after a long day of travel, an even longer walk, and no food beyond the butter sandwich and the cabbage and potato pieriogi that Gerta had packed in a small sack, Sasha ran the last hundred yards of her journey, to the front of the building that had housed Henryk's watch repair shop. The building had been damaged by a bomb and by gunfire from the street, but all four walls were still standing, which was a rarity on this particular street. The glass front door had been painted over and the words "Karmazin Watch Repair" were now covered with some strange Cyrillic script.

Panting for breath, Sasha cupped her hands against the glass and peered inside. It appeared to be some sort of makeshift office with a desk, a filing cabinet, and stacks of papers several feet high. Three men were inside, one sitting behind the desk and two others standing. Sasha began to pound on the glass with her fists. One of the men inside turned around and walked toward the door, but before he reached it, Sasha felt a dark shadow slip in behind her. Suddenly a hand grabbed her upper arm and spun her around, nearly knocking her over. She looked up at a tall man in a Russian military uniform, with cold blue eyes, a bright red beard, and a rifle at his side. He began barking at her in guttural Russian.

"I don't understand," Sasha interrupted, "Francais…Deutsch…Pol-ski?"

"I speak Polish," he said in Russian-accented Polish. "Now you need to leave here immediately. This zone is off limits to civilians." He began to frog-march her away from the front door and back toward the street.

"Wait," she pleaded, her feet barely touching the ground. The Russian soldier was so strong he was able to drag Sasha with one hand.

"Please wait. Just one minute. My name is Sasha Lacatus Karmazin. I was a prisoner at Auschwitz." She hesitated in revealing that, for fear of his reaction.

"Auschwitz? What is that?" he asked. "A prison camp?"

Sasha realized that even after the Allies had liberated the concentration camps the true stories of the Nazis' atrocities were still not widely known.

"Yes." She shook her head vigorously. "In a sense. It was a death camp, where the Nazis killed thousands and thousands of innocent men, women, and children. I myself was held there for a time. But before that I lived here in Warsaw, in this very building, with my husband and sons. My husband's name is Henryk Karmazin and he owns the shop that was here. Please, where is he? Where can I find him?"

Sasha caught a glimmer of compassion in the soldier's cold blue eyes. He stopped dragging her and released her arm. "I don't know," he admitted, scratching his chin. "I have only been stationed here in Old Town for the past month. Let me see if my comrades inside can tell me any more. Please, wait here."

The soldier hiked his rifle over his shoulder and trudged through the dusty rubble into the office. Sasha looked up at the windows on the building's second story. The first window belonged to her kitchen, and next to that was her sons' bedroom. Her beautiful curtains were gone, and the rooms appeared dark. Her whole body ached to think that after Auschwitz, after the rape, after everything she had been through, she had made it back to her home in Warsaw. She was here; all she needed was Henryk and the boys and her journey would be complete.

The soldier returned a few minutes later looking grim. "My comrades have been here for over a year," he explained. "When they arrived, this building was empty. It had been abandoned for many months. They said that it had indeed been a watch repair shop prior to that, but the owner was gone long before we arrived here, and no one knew where. At any rate, he left all his work tools behind."

"Oh." Sasha felt she'd been punched in the stomach. She knew there was no way Henryk would have willingly left the shop without his tools.

"What about my sons?" she asked quickly. "There were two teenage boys who lived here too. Where are they now?"

"I'm sorry, I really don't know." The soldier rubbed his blue eyes and looked weary. "The Red Cross has set up an office on Sanguszki Street. You should go there; they might have more information."

Sasha thanked the soldier and walked away, stumbling blindly through the streets, dazed and in shock. Had she come all this way only to fail to find Henryk and her sons? She needed answers, even if they were sad answers. Not knowing would be the worst thing of all.

Sasha walked on for several blocks until she reached the Church of St. Kazimierz, where both of her boys had been baptized. The front door was open, and she entered.

The main floor of the church had been turned into a makeshift field hospital with injured people, old men, women with babies, and soldiers still in uniform being treated by Red Cross personnel and volunteers. Sasha wound her way through the sick and dying to a nun in a long, black, bloodstained habit. "Sister, Sister, please help me," she pleaded. "I am looking for Father Pawel. Is he here?"

Sasha knew the odds were slim that the parish priest, Father Pawel Kriofski, the priest who had baptized the boys so many years ago, could still be here, but she didn't know for whom else to ask.

The sister nodded toward the altar. "He is in his office, beside the sacristy. He should be there now."

Sasha thanked the nun and rushed through the narrow hallway that ran behind and parallel to the altar. The door to the office was open, and Sasha rapped with shaking knuckles. The priest sitting behind the desk looked up over his half-glasses and a glint of recognition crossed his wizened features.

"Sasha Karmazin? Indeed! It must be! My daughter, tell me, how did you come to be here?" He stood, a stout man, broad through the middle, with laughing eyes and snow-white hair parted straight and combed back with precision. He was the first person Sasha had seen since she left the Klinsmanns' farm who didn't look ravaged and war-torn; here was a soul that had somehow survived all the onslaughts. He stepped briskly toward Sasha and took her in his arms. "My dear! Where have you been? When we heard that the Gestapo had taken you away we thought, we feared … how did you come to survive?"

Sasha relished the feel of his kind, strong arms around her and his comforting presence, but she could not wait a moment longer to ask him her questions.

"Father Pawel, please, I must know. Where are Henryk and the boys? Are they still in Warsaw? Are they safe? I have been to Henryk's shop, but it is full of Russian soldiers now and they don't know where he is and …" Sasha's words came out in a tumbled rush, and her head spun as if she might faint.

A look of sorrow crossed the old priest's kindly face as he took Sasha's hand and led her to a small wooden chair beside his desk. He helped her sit down and then took a seat beside her, clasping her hands in his. He cleared his throat. "I am so sorry to have to tell you this. When I saw you just now, I assumed you must already know … Henryk is with the Lord now, Sasha. He is with our Heavenly Father."

Sasha cried out in pain, and her whole body began to shake.

"I am so sorry." The priest stroked Sasha's hand. "But he is free from all the suffering here, and for that we should envy him. He is in the Kingdom of Heaven now, while we must continue to live in this hell on earth."

"When?" Sasha whispered, her head still spinning. "What happened?"

Father Pawel sighed. "It was several months after you had been taken away. Henryk heard that you had been transported to Auschwitz. Even then it was known that no one who went to Auschwitz ever returned home, and he didn't think he would ever see his boys again either. Henryk was devastated; the grief and stress were too much for his weak heart."

"But what about the boys?" Sasha cried. "Karl and Dimitri? Where are my sons?"

The priest shook his head sadly. "I do not know. Truly, I do not know if they live or if they too died. They were sent into hiding before Henryk died; somewhere in Warsaw, I think. I was not told where; people feared that the Nazis might torture me for information and force me to reveal secret hiding places. So no one told me anything."

"So they might be alive?" Sasha asked, heart jumping.

"It is possible. They may have escaped to safety, or they may have died in one of the many fire bombings during the uprising. All I can say for certain is that they are no longer here."

"But how can you be sure?" Sasha asked, remembering the chaos just outside the church's damaged front door.

"If they had survived, they would have emerged after the war to look for you and Henryk. But no one has heard from either of them," Father Pawel explained.

Sasha's stomach lurched. She wanted to believe that her sons had survived, even if that meant they were far away and she might never see them again.

"And what of Manny?" she asked. "My husband's brother? Surely he will have more information." Sasha instinctively knew that if Henryk had sent the boys into hiding, Manny would have been part of the plan.

The priest shook his head sadly. "He has passed away as well," he said sadly. "About three months after Henryk died, Manny, who was quite active in the Deuxieme Bureau, was stopped in the street by a Nazi officer late one night as he was transporting an important message. When Manny didn't have a suitable explanation for why he was out so late after curfew, the officer shot him in the head, leaving him to die in the street."

Sasha shook her head, too stunned to speak.

"I'm sorry the news is not better," the priest said. "But your survival is truly a miracle, a sign of God's grace. Tell me, daughter, what happened? Where have you been for these years?"

Sasha took a deep breath and steadied herself. "Father, I would love to tell you the story of my survival. But that must wait until another day. I must leave and clear my head. I must try to understand your news."

"Of course." The priest patted her hand. "I understand. Why don't you stay here with us? We don't have much to offer; our resources are limited, but we are serving as a sort of hospital and refugee center. You are welcome to share whatever we have."

"Thank you, thank you very much," Sasha replied. "But I must go now."

Sasha bid the priest a hasty good-bye, left the church, and returned to the wretched streets full of the sick and the dying, the homeless, the starving, and the indigent. When she'd walked these streets earlier, she'd been overwhelmed by the sheer weight of human suffering. But now she walked those same streets of woe and saw nothing, so deep was her own private pain. Henryk was dead and her sons gone. Mikisha, thank God, was safe with a new family who could give him everything that Sasha could not. What did Sasha have to live for? "Why continue this painful act of breathing in and breathing out? For what purpose?" she wondered. "Whom does it benefit?"

Even as a devout Catholic, Sasha had always believed that suicide was a sin. But surely the God who had allowed Auschwitz to happen, the God who had taken Henryk and her sons, could not blame her, could not condemn her, for wanting to end her life. Sasha knew she had no other choice, no other option. Death, which she had been sure would come to her at Auschwitz, the death she had fought against with every fiber of her being, would instead come to her now as her own choice. Death, under these circumstances, would be a welcome relief.

Sasha walked to the river, to a spot she remembered was deep, and dropped her sack on the grassy bank. She hoped that Gerta and Dirk would never learn of her death; she was certain they wouldn't. She removed her worn leather sandals and began to walk down the muddy banks toward the murky, death-scented water. She was not frightened. She filled her head with images of Henryk, of Karl and Dimitri as children, and of the baby Mikisha whom she had so recently held in her arms.

The water rose to her ankles, cold and dirty, swirling in little eddies, but she barely felt the wetness on her skin. She walked further, until the water reached her knees, and the soil at the bottom slipped and shifted. Her heels dug in, searching for a foothold just strong enough so she could take another step. Her long skirt began to billow, ballooning around her as the water touched her hips. Twilight had settled and the city of Warsaw, with its limited electricity, was nearly dark.

Suddenly Sasha looked up and saw an apparition, what appeared to be an angel or a ghost. The female figure—tall, angular, and lovely—motioned Sasha to come closer. The creature's face was pale and ethereal, with ghostly eyes, a tiny nose, and the faintest whisper of a mouth. Tears filled Sasha's eyes as she felt enormous comfort and relief. She would not die alone, as she had feared so often at Auschwitz. A spirit was here to welcome her, to give her safe passage to whatever warmth awaited her on the other side. Sasha held out her hand toward the figure and felt herself falling into endless darkness.

CHAPTER SEVENTEEN

Krakow, Poland
Summer 1988

As the hired car sped through the sunny streets of Krakow, Beth could barely contain her excitement. After meeting with Dirk and Gerta Klinsmann, Beth and Andy had left immediately for Krakow, for the Ursuline Convent where Sasha had ended up after the war. Beth had barely slept at all at their tiny hotel in the center of Krakow, and she was out of bed and ready to go at 5:00 AM, a full hour before the arrival of Otto Lunbonski, their interpreter, driver, and guide.

In her hand Beth clutched the yellowed envelope that Gerta had given her, with Sasha's neatly penciled handwriting. She turned the envelope over and over, tracing the letters with her index finger. Other than the cross around her neck, this was the first thing in her life that Beth had ever touched that had also been touched by Sasha.

Andy didn't want to dampen Beth's enthusiasm, but he was afraid she might get hurt. "The Klinsmanns said they last heard from Sasha in 1961. Your grandmother may have died twenty-seven years ago."

"I know," Beth agreed. "But if so, she will be buried in Krakow. At least there will be a grave. My father will finally know where his mother is buried."

When they reached the convent, Beth barely waited for Otto to put the car into park before she threw her door open and bounded for the steps. Otto and Andy rushed to catch up to her. Beth rang the bell at the massive carved wooden door, and moments later a young nun, dressed in an old-fashioned long black habit with heavy folds and wide sleeves, appeared. She had a child-like face and wore a white veil, signifying she was a novice.

"Good morning. I am Sister Biruta. May I help you?" she asked in Polish.

"We are looking for information about a Polish woman, Sasha Karmazin, who may have been at this convent just after the war," Otto explained.

The young nun did not recognize the name but offered to show the trio to the office of the Mother Superior. The Mother Superior, Sister Sophia, was a tall, patrician woman in a black habit with broad shoulders, a stern face, and dark-rimmed glasses. Beth guessed her to be about seventy, which meant she could have been at the convent during Sasha's stay.

Sister Sophia dismissed the young Sister Biruta and motioned for Beth, Andy, and Otto to take their seats in the chairs in front of her massive oak desk. "You are from America?" she inquired.

Beth and Andy nodded.

"Ah, lovely," she replied. "A chance for me to practice my English. Sister Biruta said you inquired about Sasha Karmazin? May I ask about your interest in her?"

Beth nearly leaped from her seat. "She was my grandmother. My name is Elizabeth Ann Karmazin. My father, Karl Karmazin, was Sasha's eldest son. I have been trying to find out what happened to Sasha. I've managed to trace her location to the farm of Gerta and Dirk Klinsmann, from where she left in the autumn of 1945. The last they heard from Sasha she was here at this convent in 1961. Please Sister, can you tell me what happened to her after that?" Beth's words had tumbled out in a heated rush and she wondered if Sister Sophia's English was good enough to understand everything she had said.

The nun was silent for several long moments, and Beth began to reformulate her questions in a simpler syntax.

"Ah yes, Sasha Karmazin. I knew her quite well," Sister Sophia said softly, her eyes closing behind her thick glasses. "She was a remarkable woman."

"Is she still alive?" Beth asked breathlessly.

"I don't know for certain. I don't believe so," Sister Sophia replied, shaking her head.

"Please Sister, can you tell us everything you know?" Andy asked.

She nodded. "Sasha came here in the autumn of 1945. She had been in Warsaw where she had decided to end her life, when one of our young nuns, Sister Philippa, saw her walking into the river, attempting to drown herself. Sister Philippa reached out to save her, pulling her back to shore. Sasha was so touched she vowed to devote her life to the Lord. In one of Sasha's rare lighthearted moments she joked that she thought Sister Philippa was an angel, sent from heaven to guide her to the other side!

"Sister Philippa brought Sasha back here to Krakow, and she joined our convent. She never became a nun; she never took holy vows. But she worked side by side with us for sixteen years. She was an uncommonly hard worker and had a real gift for languages. She taught for many years in our convent school, educating our girls in Polish, German, and French. She even managed to teach herself English, through books in the library and tutoring from our teacher here. I don't believe there was anything Sasha couldn't do, if she set her mind to it."

"If she was content here, why did she leave?" Beth asked.

"She became very ill," Sister Sophia explained, sighing at the painful memory. "This was sixteen years ago, in 1972. Sasha was sixty-five years old and ready to retire. She had developed severe arthritis and a circulatory disease. The doctors said she had only a year or less to live. The opportunity arose to have her transferred to a convent in Bamberg, West Germany. That convent was connected to an excellent hospital with top-notch doctors, much better than the ones we had here at the time. So we jumped at the chance to have Sasha transferred there. It was hard to see her go, but we knew her final months would be spent more comfortably there."

"Did you ever hear from her again?" Andy asked softly.

Sister Sophia shook her head. "No. We were very lucky to get a government permit for her transfer, but because she was now in the West there was no way for her to contact us, or for us to contact her. It is my belief that Sasha Karmazin, God rest her soul, died peacefully in Bamberg. But at least she died in freedom. For a woman who survived Hitler's Holocaust, there is solace and grace in that."

CHAPTER EIGHTEEN

Bamberg, West Germany
Summer 1988

Beth and Andy spent the night in Krakow and were up early the next morning for a flight over the Iron Curtain, back to the West. They changed planes in Frankfurt, and took the short flight to Bamberg. Bamberg was a small city in an area of Germany once known as Franconia. Although geographically it was located in eastern Germany, politically, like most of that region, it fell under the jurisdiction of the West German government.

Beth, reclining in her cramped economy-class seat, was beyond exhausted; she couldn't imagine being so tired in her life. She felt she'd aged twenty years; she wondered if life would ever seem normal again. She couldn't even think about what would happen when this epic journey was finally over.

The one constant, the thing that had kept her grounded, was Andy. She looked over at him, snoozing in his seat beside her with his head bent at an awkward angle. She reached over and touched his hand. He stirred. "It's okay," she whispered, leaning toward his ear. "You just rest. Thanks, Andy. Thanks for taking this crazy ride with me."

After arriving at the airport they hailed a taxi to the Messerschmitt Hotel, a charming, one-of-a-kind inn with an opulent eighteenth-century exterior and dark-paneled interior. A photograph of Willy Messerschmitt, the designer of the BF109 Luftwaffe airplane, was tastefully displayed on the lobby wall, along with the Messerschmitt family crest. Andy salivated as he read the menu beside the check-in counter. He was sick of sausage and cabbage. Dinner for him at the Messerschmitt would definitely include the Franconian duck, chestnut soup, and eels in dill sauce.

Once checked in, Beth and Andy quickly headed on foot for the Imperial Bamberg Cathedral, not even stopping to eat lunch. Following the foldout map Beth had picked up in the hotel lobby, they found the cathedral, or *Dom*, situated on a hill just across the Regnitz River. Next to the *Dom*, where Heinrich II was crowned Holy Roman Emperor in 1012, was the Diozesanmuseum, and next to that, the museum shop.

Beth looked up at the dizzying spires of the cathedral with its massive towers at each corner and was awestruck by how beautiful the large Gothic building was. It cheered her to think that Sasha had spent the final days or weeks of her life in a place of such beauty and serenity and, most particularly, freedom. In recent days Beth had found herself weighing Sasha's life, trying to balance the good with the horrible, the blessings with the pain. This place at least seemed as if it would have offered some solace and a counterpoint to the horrors of Auschwitz.

One of the wings of the cathedral had been converted into a convent and living quarters for the nuns and museum staff. Beth and Andy knocked on the thick wooden door of the convent and were greeted by the Mother Superior, Sister Assumpta, a tall, brisk, no-nonsense German woman in her late fifties with a long, pale, serious face and a hawk-like nose. Her English was quite good, but her manner was rather brusque. She listened dismissively as Beth explained she had come from America to look for a missing relative.

"I am very busy. Please come back tomorrow. Perhaps I can help you then," Sister Assumpta said, beginning to close the door.

"Wait," Beth begged, holding out her hand to keep the door open. "It won't take long, I promise. I'm looking for information about my grandmother. She was a Gypsy survivor of Auschwitz and she was transferred here from Poland in 1961."

"Oh, you mean Sasha Karmazin?" the Mother Superior asked.

Beth was shocked to hear the sister rattle off the name so easily. "Yes. I am her granddaughter. Do you know of her?"

"Of course." The nun ushered Beth and Andy into the front hallway, where Beth had a birds-eye view of the lofty interior. The doors and the windows of the home were trimmed in dark, heavy wood and the plaster walls painted an alabaster white. Two large multicolored stained glass windows faced one another on opposite walls. At the other end, a large tapestry depicting a deer on the edge of a deep forest hung from the vaulted ceiling.

Sister Assumpta did not invite them any further. "I was teaching here when Sasha arrived," she continued. "She was very sick, of course. But our doctors found some treatment that was still unknown in the East and she was later well enough to teach a few language classes. She was always a pleasure to work alongside, even though she had suffered so terribly in her life." The nun's hardened features took on a surprisingly warm glow.

"Is Sasha buried here on the convent grounds?" Beth asked softly.

"Of course not." Sister Assumpta bristled.

"Then, where is she?" Beth asked, puzzled.

"I'm not certain. She should be upstairs in her sleeping quarters, or perhaps in the dayroom," Sister Assumpta replied.

Beth gasped. "You mean she's still alive?"

"Of course."

"But, but I thought she was terminally ill when she arrived here in 1961," Beth stammered.

"Ill yes, but not terminal," the nun explained. "Our doctors were able to stabilize her. She has had chronic illnesses for the past twenty-seven years, but she endures." A slight smile played at her lips. "There is such a spirit of survival inside of Sasha."

Beth's eyelids fluttered, and she thought she might faint. Sasha? Alive? Beth was so dizzy that Andy had to help her to a nearby chair to sit down.

"Sister, please, could we get a glass of water?" Andy asked. The nun nodded and walked down the long hallway.

Never at any point in this journey had Beth imagined she would find Sasha still alive. It seemed impossible. Sasha would be eighty-one years old now. It was common for women to live to eighty-one these days; that was true, but Sasha's life had been anything but common. When Beth's search had begun she knew only what her father had told her—that Sasha Lacatus Karmazin had been taken from her home by Gestapo soldiers in the Old Town of Warsaw in February 1943. Even when it became clear that Sasha had survived the perilous transport to Auschwitz, and even when Beth had learned that a pregnant Sasha had been taken from Auschwitz in the dead of night and lived out the war on a farm in the Polish countryside, Beth had never seriously considered that Sasha might still be alive today. It was simply beyond belief.

The Mother Superior returned with a glass of lukewarm water, which Beth downed gratefully. "Andy, what should I do?" Beth asked, looking up into his kind face with eyes full of questioning. "I want to see her. I want to talk to her. I want to tell her everything. I want to take her back to Nebraska for Dad and Dimitri and for all of us," Beth explained.

"But I'm afraid," Beth continued. "She's eighty-one years old and physically fragile. What will this news do to her? The shock might be too much. How could anyone live with the knowledge that her sons were alive and well all this time? It will be devastating."

Andy knelt down in front of Beth and looked her straight in the eye. "This has to be your call," he said carefully, taking her hands in his. "I think that if you've come all this way and you don't talk to her, you'll regret it later on. But what you say is true; it will be an incredible shock to her. I can't imagine how she'll handle it."

After discussing it with the Mother Superior and the nurse who ran the convent's infirmary it was decided that Beth could approach Sasha with the bittersweet news of her sons and the past she might have shared with them if things had been different.

Beth's heart was pounding, as a young nun, Sister Michaela, led her and Andy up the narrow winding staircase to the living quarters over the convent. Sasha wasn't in her modest ten-foot-by-ten-foot bedroom so the three went to the dayroom where a number of older nuns sat playing cards or reading the Bible. Beth recognized Sasha right away with her long, thick straight hair, mostly white now, but shot through with streaks of glistening black.

Sasha was sitting on a short wooden stool and leaning over a tilted artist's table. Beth couldn't see her face, but she could see Sasha's hand moving in small graceful strokes across the board. Sister Michaela nodded, and the three opened the door and entered the room. As they approached Sasha, Beth could see that Sasha was painting a picture of birds in a clear blue sky over a meadow full of wildflowers. Sasha appeared so content and serene. Beth wondered again if she were doing the correct thing. "If it were me, I'd want to know," she told herself.

Sister Michaela walked ahead and gently put her hand on Sasha's shoulder. "Sasha, you have two visitors here from America," she said in German. "Would you like to speak to them?"

Sasha nodded, and Sister Michaela pulled three small wooden chairs over to Sasha's board, then motioned Beth and Andy to come closer. Through a small open window, Beth could hear a carillon playing a familiar German anthem, but she couldn't remember the name of it. As the three sat down, Sasha looked at Beth and gasped. Sasha squinted and then her eyes seemed to glaze over. She stood quickly, dropping her paintbrush with a splat upon the floor.

"Weg! Geh weg! Teufel!—Go away, devil!" she shouted in a voice of surprising strength as she backed up quickly, never taking her eyes from Beth. "Leave here, please!"

Sister Michaela stepped forward, trying to comfort her. "It's all right," she soothed. "Sister Sasha, please. These people have come to see you all the way from America."

"Who are you?" Sasha demanded in very clear English.

"Won't you please sit down?" Beth asked gently, reaching out her hand. "We aren't here to frighten you."

"Who are you?" Sasha demanded again, staring at Beth without blinking.

Beth cleared her throat and swallowed hard. "My name is Elizabeth Ann Karmazin," she said slowly. "I am your granddaughter; the daughter of your son, Karl. And this is my friend, Andy Weinberg."

"Impossible," Sasha insisted, shaking her head. "Who sent you here to torment me? My sons are dead."

"No, they are not," Beth explained. She felt tense and panicky; afraid the situation was escalating beyond her control. "Please sit down. I would like to tell you the whole story. It's a wonderful story. You have a whole family you don't even know about."

Andy had not wanted to interject himself into any part of this unusual engagement, but it was obvious that Beth needed support. "Sister Sasha," Andy said gently, his voice warm and calming. "I'm afraid we must have startled you when we entered. Beth looks so much as you did as a young woman. We can't even imagine how you must feel. But doesn't the way Beth looks suggest that she is in fact your granddaughter?"

"I just don't understand," Sasha said, shoulders slumping. "How is this possible?" Sasha looked as if she might collapse at any moment.

"Sister Michaela," Andy asked, "is there someplace we can go to speak more comfortably?"

"Yes, there is. Please follow me."

They all stood and followed the young nun down a long narrow hallway of travertine tile to a cafeteria. As they walked Beth took surreptitious glances at Sasha, just ahead and to the side of her. Although thin of build, Sasha was surprisingly spry and moved well for her age. Other than the circles beneath her dark eyes and a web of fine wrinkles, her skin was smooth and clear. Her hands were strong, her back straight. For all she had suffered in her life, her body had endured.

When they reached the cafeteria Beth saw that it was closed to customers, but several workers were busy cleaning up and preparing food for the midday meal. Sister Michaela took them inside and led them to a worn old sofa and a set of chairs around a coffee table at the back of the room. "I'll go see if there's any coffee or tea in back," she explained with a slight bow, as she walked toward the kitchen.

Sasha sat down in one of the chairs and could not stop staring at Beth. It was as if she were looking at a ghost, or a specter from her past. Beth longed to touch her grandmother, to hug her, to hold her, and to stroke her face. Beth longed to convince herself that the person sitting before her was real and not just a case of Beth's addled, sleep-deprived brain playing tricks on her. But Sasha appeared tense and wary, and Beth knew she needed to be careful, lest Sasha retreat completely.

The awkward silence was painful. Beth squeezed her hands into fists and began.

"Let me go back to the beginning of the story," Beth offered. "I'm not sure how much you know about what happened. After the Gestapo took you away, Henryk and Manny arranged for Karl and Dimitri to go into hiding. They spent time in a warehouse outside of Warsaw and then used forged documents to get to Sweden, then to England, and then on to America. They were fostered by the Olsons, a farm family in the Midwest, who loved them and cared for them until they were old enough to be on their own. My father, Karl, returned to Europe before the war was over and fought the Nazis. While he was there he was told that Warsaw had been completely destroyed, the entire city burned to the ground, and that the Nazis had left no survivors; he also learned of the Gypsy liquidation at Auschwitz. So, you see, he was convinced both you and Henryk were dead."

Beth felt her eyes fill with tears. "You would be very proud of the men they grew up to be. Both married fine woman and raised families. Karl married my mother, Margaret, and had three daughters, of which I am the eldest. Karl and Dimitri stayed in Nebraska and went into business together. They are still there today; healthy and well."

Beth paused to take a deep breath. She looked at Sasha, whose face remained blank and impassive. Sister Michaela returned with a tray full of German pastries, coffee, and tea, which she set down before the group.

"After Karl and Dimitri escaped to England, Henryk died in Warsaw," Beth continued, pouring herself some coffee. Beth was aware that Sasha knew that Henryk had died, but it was still painful to say it. "My father and I learned later that Henryk, with good reason, believed you would die at Auschwitz, and he never knew that his sons had reached safety. Sadly, his weak heart finally gave out."

"Henryk," Sasha said wistfully, showing her first sign of emotion. "He was a good, good man. A kind and loyal man."

Feeling uncertain, Beth looked to Andy, who squeezed her hand in support.

"About your son Mikisha …" Beth said.

"Mikisha? I have no son Mikisha," Sasha insisted.

"It's okay, I know the story," Beth said gently. "He was born in Poland, when you lived with the Klinsmanns."

Sasha stood suddenly and began wringing her hands. "You must leave now," she said. "I'm sorry; you must. We've already spoken too long. I don't know who you are and I don't know why you torment me so. You are not my granddaughter; I don't know who you are."

"But your son ... the Klinsmanns ... we spoke with them ..." Beth stammered.

"Sister Sasha is tired," the young nun interrupted, rising to help calm Sasha. "Perhaps you should come back tomorrow, and you can talk some more."

Beth was frustrated, but accepted the wisdom of the young nun's words. "I understand," she said softly, looking at Sasha. "I'm sorry; I didn't mean to upset you." Beth wasn't sure if she should call Sasha "Sasha," or "Sister Sasha," or what she really desired, the name that had been in her heart all these years, "Grandma Sasha."

Beth reached out her hand and was surprised when Sasha shook it firmly. An electric current of excitement and emotion shot through Beth as she realized she was touching her grandmother's hand and in the process, bridging a more-than-forty-year gap of loss and sorrow.

Sasha squinted, leaned close to Beth, and then drew back as if withdrawing from a flame. Her eyes widened and her jaw dropped. "Tell me, what is that? Around your neck?" she demanded.

Beth's fingers flew to the chain around her neck, and she pulled the cross from the folds of her V-neck sweater. "This was yours," she said excitedly. "This cross and chain. The Nazis tore it from your neck when they grabbed you at the apartment in Warsaw and it flew across the room. Karl found it after you were gone, and he kept it safe for many years. He gave it to me when I graduated from high school sixteen years ago."

Sasha's face, which had turned a deathly pale, suddenly flushed a deep red and she choked out a sob. "No," she cried, dissolving into tears. "No, no, no."

Sister Michaela frowned at Beth and Andy. "I ask you to leave," she said. "Please go. Please let Sister Sasha be."

Beth and Andy gathered up their things and retreated quickly. In the taxi on the way to the hotel Andy held Beth and comforted her, stroking her hair. "I just don't understand," Beth whined. "It's obvious that I am who I say I am—I am Karl's daughter and Sasha's granddaughter. I have so many wonderful things to tell her. So many good stories. Why doesn't she want to hear?"

"It must just be too painful," Andy offered. "I imagine she was content in her life, prepared to live out her final years among the sisters at the convent. Now suddenly she has to confront her past all over again."

"What do you think we should do?"

"Give her some time and some space. Show her we mean her no harm, and we're prepared to be patient," Andy said. "I think she will come around eventually."

Sasha's sleep that night was fitful, filled with images of people and events of the past that she had worked so hard to leave behind, erase from her memory. At dawn she climbed out of bed and dressed, then made a cup of tea from hot water at the sink. Then slowly, gracefully, she moved across the room and sat down at the window of her small bedroom which looked out on the public courtyard of the cathedral. She watched the young nuns stroll to and from their classes, and she smiled as several small children chased a kite that had gotten away from them and landed in the convent's diminutive garden.

It is peaceful here, she thought. *I have made a life with the church and it has brought me comfort; it has been my home and my requiem for more than forty years. I have learned to live with the haunted past. But now these people have come with their stories. How could my boys possibly have survived Warsaw and the Holocaust? And to have made a life in America—thousands of miles from Poland? It makes no sense. Yet, this woman has my necklace, the one my own father made for me—and she knows about Karl and Dimitri and even Mikisha. How could she fabricate such a story?*

The door to Sasha's bedroom opened, and Sister Michaela asked permission to enter. "I came to take you to breakfast and then to your painting."

Through tears, Sasha gazed at the young nun's angelic face and then again out to the courtyard, remembering how she had been saved from the swirling waters of the Vistula River by another young nun many years back, remembering how the church had taken her in when she had nowhere to go and no one to turn to, when she thought God was dead. Sasha looked again to Sister Michaela.

"I need to pray, Sister. Will you come and pray with me before we go?"

The next day Beth and Andy returned to the convent first thing in the morning, but the Mother Superior explained that Sasha refused to see them. Undaunted, Beth and Andy spent the day sightseeing in and around Bamberg, exploring the Bishops' Town and Burghers' Town areas. They toured the Altes Rathaus, the old town hall, the cathedral museum, the baroque palace known as the Neue Residenz, and took a cruise down the Regnitz River. Bamberg was a major tourist destination, and the sights were often breathtaking and especially colorful since it was summer and flowers appeared everywhere. Yet Beth found it difficult to concentrate on anything besides Sasha.

Beth and Andy returned to the convent the next day and the day after that, but still Sasha refused to meet with them. Beth felt her frustration growing. "Andy, this can't go on forever," she argued. "We don't have enough money to spend weeks or even months sitting around Bamberg, waiting for Sasha to warm up to us. Yet, I'm not willing to return home and come back some other time; Sasha's age and medical condition won't warrant that. And there's more at stake here than just me connecting with Sasha. There's the matter of Peter Mavik's book and his contention that Sasha collaborated with the Nazis. If I can't get Sasha's statement on tape and on paper, I can't prevent him from printing those lies in the next edition of his book."

Another few days went by and still they had no contact with Sasha. Beth decided to do the only thing that was left to do. From the lobby of her hotel in Bamberg she placed a collect call to Nebraska. Her heart was in her throat as she heard the phone pick up at home.

"Hello, Karmazin residence."

"Dad, it's Beth."

"Beth! We haven't heard from you in weeks. You said you were going to be traveling, but your mother and I have been worried to death. Where are you? What are you doing?"

"Dad, are you sitting down?" Beth asked cautiously.

"Why, no, should I be?"

"Yes, you better."

"Beth, are you okay? You're not hurt or in trouble, are you?" Karl's voice was tight with concern.

"No, it's nothing like that. It's just that I've got some incredible news, and I think you need to be sitting down to hear it."

CHAPTER NINETEEN

Bamberg, West Germany
Summer 1988

Once Beth had explained to her father over the phone that Sasha was still alive, it didn't take her long to convince him to come to Germany to help her try to break through Sasha's protective shell. She purposely, however, didn't tell Karl what she had learned about Sasha's relationship with Gerhardt Klinsmann and the child that was born from that relationship. She simply didn't feel it was her story to tell.

Fortunately, Karl had kept his passport up to date since an anniversary trip he and Margaret had taken to South America a few years back. Dimitri was elated with the news and wanted to go with Karl, but agreed to stay and take care of the business as long as Karl would later do the same for him. In three days Karl had packed, organized his paperwork, and booked his plane ticket for Germany.

As Beth and Andy waited at the Frankfurt Airport for Karl's Lufthansa flight to land on a sunny Tuesday morning, Beth's stomach was in a knot. She hadn't seen her father since her last visit home many months earlier, and when he emerged through the breezeway she was momentarily taken aback by how rumpled and unkempt he looked. But she took into account the fact that he had just come off a jetlag-inducing overnight trans-Atlantic flight and was still dealing with the unimaginable shock that his mother, whom he had believed died more than forty years earlier, was still alive.

At sixty-two years old, Karl was overall showing little decline. He still ran his business full-time while actively pursuing his hobbies of hunting and fishing. He maintained a height of six-foot-three, with only a slight hunching of his shoulders. His wavy ash blond hair had thinned and grayed, now barely covering the top of his head but leaving a fuller fringe at the sides. He had gained a small paunch that thickened his middle, and his jaw line had clearly loosened, but he was still a vibrant and robust-looking man.

Karl quickly picked Beth and Andy out of the crowd waiting anxiously for the disembarking passengers. His face lit up and he rushed to greet them. He grabbed Beth in a bear hug, squeezing her so tightly she could barely breathe.

"Thanks so much for coming, Dad," Beth said. "I don't think we can reach Sasha without your help."

Karl released Beth from the hug, shook hands with Andy, and scanned the busy, modern airport concourse bustling with well-dressed people of all ages, races, and ethnicities. "After I got out of the army, I swore I would never, ever come back to Europe under any circumstances," he admitted, scratching his chin. "But I never imagined a circumstance like this: my mother still alive and living at a German convent."

From Frankfurt they traveled in a rented Citroen across the hilly landscape of southern Germany back to Bamberg. Andy drove on the autobahn, while Beth sat in the backseat with her father, and filled him in on the details of her long journey, what she had learned about Sasha, and how Sasha was doing now. At times during the story Karl flinched and held up his hand, asking Beth to allow him to absorb what he was hearing. Beth balanced her desire to spare her father's feelings against her need to provide him with a complete picture of the situation.

Halfway through their journey they stopped for lunch. Karl ordered a sandwich, potato salad, and a beer, but barely touched the food once it arrived. Beth nibbled at her own lunch, worrying that the stress of the meeting might be too much for both Karl and Sasha. Their meeting couldn't be anything but bittersweet, combining the joy of reunion with the sorrow of having lost forty-five years of their lives together.

When they reached Bamberg, Beth and Andy checked Karl into the Messerschmitt and dropped off his luggage in the room next to theirs. "The room may be small, but it's cozy," Andy said cheerfully. Karl nodded and sat down on the narrow twin bed, rubbed his face and sighed.

"Dad, if you're too tired, we don't have to do this today," Beth offered. "You can rest now and we can see Sasha tomorrow."

"No, let's do it today," Karl replied, looking up with a wan smile. "To be honest, I don't think I could sleep tonight knowing that my mother is just a mile away."

They left the hotel and drove across town toward the cathedral. When the *Dom's* tall towers loomed into view, Karl asked, "how long has she lived here?"

"Since 1971," Andy replied. Karl nodded, and Beth knew her father was pleased to think that after so much suffering, Sasha had spent her later years in a place of peacefulness and beauty.

Andy parked the Citroen in the public lot behind the cathedral and he and Beth and Karl walked up to the convent door and knocked. Beth grasped Karl's hand in hers, and felt the blood coursing through his palm. She squeezed tightly to show her support, and he looked down at her and smiled.

Sister Assumpta, the Mother Superior, answered the door, and her response was the same as it had been for many days: "Sasha is not receiving visitors today. Perhaps tomorrow." Sister Assumpta began to close the door, but Beth held her hand out to prevent it from closing. "Wait," she pleaded.

"Today is different. Today I brought someone who Sasha needs to see. This is her son: my father, Karl Karmazin. Sasha last saw him in 1943, in the Old Town of Warsaw, as the Gestapo soldiers broke into her home and dragged her away."

The Mother Superior's eyelids flickered for a moment, and she appeared truly touched. "Very well," she replied. "This is a new development. Perhaps Sasha will reconsider. I will tell Sasha and ask if she's willing to see you."

Sister Assumpta was gone for what seemed like a long time, leaving Andy, Beth, and Karl standing helplessly on the concrete convent stairs. "It must be bad news," Karl said at last. "She must not want to see me after all."

"No, I think it's good news," Andy argued. "If Sasha had said no outright, Sister Assumpta would have come back right away. I think this means they're negotiating the terms by which she'll see us."

Beth couldn't help but laugh out loud. "Spoken like a true lawyer," she said.

Their laughter was interrupted by the return of the Mother Superior. Beth felt a lump form in her throat as the clicking of the nun's heels moved closer. It was an agonizing few moments as she appeared before them and opened her mouth to speak.

"Sasha has agreed to see you," Sister Assumpta said. "But I must warn you, she refuses to believe that this man is her son. She insists that her sons died during the war. She is quite adamant, in fact."

"We understand," Beth said, trying to contain her excitement. "And we thank you for giving us the chance to speak to her. We know this cannot be easy."

The Mother Superior guided them to her office, where they were met by the young nun, Sister Michaela. Beth was relieved to see a kind and familiar face. Sister Michaela greeted them and bade them follow her up to the living quarters.

Sister Michaela took them across the polished stone floors to the day room where Sasha sat painting, her table facing the warm natural light that streamed in from the window. Given the angle of the table, Beth was able to see that the painting was nearly finished; it was a beautiful woodland scene complete with thick evergreen trees, bushes of bright red berries, and a family of white-tailed deer.

Karl's hazel eyes darted frantically around the room filled with aged nuns and elderly lay workers. His gaze landed on Sasha's profile, and he recognized her right away, even after forty-five years. Tears sprang to his eyes, and he covered his mouth, stifling a sob. Beth had never seen her father so openly emotional, and it frightened her.

Karl composed himself and looked to Sister Michaela for guidance. The young nun bowed and silently motioned for them to stay put while she approached Sasha. Karl, Andy, and Beth could hear Sister Michaela whispering to Sasha in German while she placed a comforting hand on Sasha's narrow shoulder. Sasha seemed distracted, more interested in her painting than in what the young nun was saying. Sasha finished a few brushstrokes and dipped her brush in water, then wiped off her hands and stood. When she saw Karl, her face betrayed no emotion and no recognition—nothing but a dark, hollow stare.

"Sister Sasha, your friends from America have returned to see you," Sister Michaela said gently in German, motioning the trio to come closer. "You remember Beth Karmazin and Andy Weinberg. This is Beth's father, Karl Karmazin." Sasha took his hand and shook it, looking at him warily.

"Hello," Karl choked out in a whisper. "It is a great joy to see you again."

Sasha said nothing and simply blinked. Sister Michaela led them to the sitting area at the back of the day room and excused herself to go get coffee and tea.

"Thank you for agreeing to see us again," Beth said, settling into her seat. "You are looking very well today."

"I am quite busy," Sasha said curtly. "I would like to return to my painting."

"Of course. We understand," Beth said evenly. "We don't want to upset or disturb you. But we thought you would want to meet this man. This is your son, Karl."

"Mama, it's me," Karl pleaded in Polish. "Please believe me."

"I'm sorry; my sons died in the war," Sasha answered politely in English.

"No, Mama, we didn't," Karl argued, switching to English. "Dimitri and I survived. We hid in a warehouse outside of Warsaw until Uncle Manny was able to get us forged documents. We escaped to Sweden, then England, and then to America."

"That is what you have said, but I cannot believe it," Sasha replied, in a voice more calm than argumentative.

Karl reached into the shoulder bag he had brought from America and pulled out batches of photographs. Unfortunately, he had no photos of Sasha or of himself prior to his arrival in America, where he had disembarked with literally nothing but the clothes on his back. But he did have photos of himself and Dimitri as teens in Nebraska, and photos of Beth and her sisters, and Dimitri's children. Sasha's eyes widened when she saw the photos of Karl and Dimitri as teens, but her mouth remained firm.

"No doubt many orphaned children from Europe were placed in the States," Sasha said, handing the photos back to Karl. "That doesn't prove you are my son."

"Mama!" Karl's voice broke. "Your father's name was Corwin. Your mother's name was Edita. Your brother and sister were Stefan and Melina. You were born in a meadow in eastern Poland in the summer of 1907, and your Kumpania belonged to the Keldari clan." Karl rattled off the facts quickly, his face growing red with exertion.

Sasha nodded. "All that is true, but you could have read those things in archives. Somewhere in Warsaw—maybe in the church."

Karl sighed in frustration. He paused to collect his thoughts before continuing. "When I was a boy my favorite food was beef and cabbage stew. I was an excellent soccer player, while Dimitri was gifted at chess. My best friend from school was a tall boy name Piotr Jagodzinski, and you were good friends with his mother, a tall red-haired woman named Magda. Magda made the best raisin cake in Warsaw! She shared it with us often. We had a pair of white lace curtains in our kitchen window that you had made yourself, by hand. You were replacing them with a heavier pair when the Nazis came and took you away. Could I possibly have learned those things from a book or an archive? Who would know these things but your son, Karl?"

Sasha's face paled, and her lip trembled. "I'm sorry; I must go now," she said. "I must return to my painting. Please, leave me be. Sister Michaela will show you to the door." Sasha stood and began to walk away.

"Wait!" Karl called out. "Mama! Please!" He began to follow her, but Beth took his arm.

"Dad, you can't," Beth implored him. "We must treat her gently. This is such a shock for her."

"Beth, I'm sorry, I can't let her go," Karl argued. "I can't. Not after all this time."

Sasha had returned to her drawing table and sat down, motionless, closing her eyes and holding her face in her hands.

Karl stood behind Sasha, cleared his throat, and began singing a Gypsy song that Sasha had taught him as a child. *"Prohasar man opre pirende, muro djiben semas opre chengende*—Bury me standing, I've been on my knees all my life …"

Karl's voice quivered, and he struggled with the pronunciation, but he sang with passion and fervor; he sounded like a man who was singing for his life. Sasha continued to sit in her chair. Her back was still turned to them, but they could see her shoulders shaking as she wept, still cradling her face in her hands. Suddenly she turned around and looked up at Karl, her face glistening with tears. "I have lost forty-five years of my life."

Karl knelt down in front of Sasha and gently took her hands in his. "Mama, it's a miracle," he said softly. "A miracle named Beth has brought us together. I've had a good life in America. I have a wonderful family. This is a time for happiness, not for grieving."

"My son, my son," Sasha sobbed and stroked Karl's face, deliberately but gently touching every feature with her hands.

Soon Karl and Sasha reverted to speaking Polish, the language they had in common, and their words flew so quickly that Beth had no hope of understanding what they were saying. But it brought her joy to see them laughing and smiling and weeping, restoring the mother-child bond that had never been completely broken. Sasha's dark eyes glowed with pride, and her smile lit up the room. Karl looked younger and happier than he had in years. At times his features took on the mischievous grin of a charming child. Beth was glad in a way that she wasn't able to understand their conversation. She would have felt she was imposing, putting herself into a relationship that was both so fragile and so personal.

After Karl and Sasha had been speaking for a while, Beth tapped her father on the shoulder and took him aside. "Dad, I know this will be really hard, but there are some questions that you need to ask Sasha. About the allegations in Mavik's book."

Karl looked distressed. "Do we really have to talk about that now?"

"Yes, I think so. Just to be safe. It's the last piece of the puzzle, and Sasha seems to be open to talking right now."

Karl nodded his agreement and returned to Sasha. He and his mother continued conversing in Polish, but Beth could tell the subject had changed. Sasha's face darkened and her forehead furrowed. Beth feared she might storm off again, but Karl was kind, gentle, and patient, placing his arm around Sasha and encouraging her to speak freely. A few times both Karl and Sasha were reduced to tears.

After about twenty minutes Karl patted Sasha's hand, stood, and approached Beth. "She told me everything," he explained. "I have it here on your recorder. It makes me sick. As her son it was very difficult to hear this, and it will be more difficult to repeat it. But I know you are anxious to know, and you deserve to know. All the pieces fit. A few weeks after Sasha arrived at Auschwitz, she was sent to work as Gerhardt Klinsmann's personal assistant. She cleaned his office, made his lunch, that type of thing. He raped her repeatedly, and eventually she became pregnant with the son whom she called Mikisha. The relationship with Klinsmann was never consensual; Sasha knew she would be killed if she rebuked him, so she used her relationship with him to improve the lot of her fellow Gypsy inmates. Often Klinsmann would allow her to take his uneaten food and table scraps back to her barracks."

"What of Hans Frank?" Beth asked. "And the allegations that she had an affair with him?"

"He visited Auschwitz several times while Mama was there. She was often in charge of the other translators, so she had cause to be in the officers' mess hall while Frank, Hoess, Himmler, and the others were meeting. Hans Frank assaulted her once, but he did not rape her. She was not his mistress, and he did not father her child. And then there is this." Karl handed Beth a letter addressed to Sasha Lacatus Karmazin at the Ursuline Convent. It was yellowed with age and dated December 10, 1946. "Sasha had Sister Michaela retrieve it from the files here."

Dear Sasha,

As you know, I do not read or write, so I have hired a young Polish girl to write this letter for me. I trust she will make me sound more well-spoken than I am. I have come to see you twice since the war, but both times I was told you were not accepting visitors.

I was surprised and pleased to learn you had survived Auschwitz. You must know by now that the Gypsy camp was liquidated on August 1, 1944. I was too sick to move, and so the Nazis left me in the barracks for dead. When the Russians came, they took me in until I recovered.

Although I was disappointed that you didn't follow Gypsy tradition, I always respected your courage. At one time, when you and Emil were young, I had hoped that you might take to each other and become man and wife. But my son would not have been a good husband to any woman. He was untrustworthy and selfish. When he was young, I tried to improve these weaknesses; I so wanted for him to succeed me as the Shero Rom. But as he grew older, I saw what evil he was capable of, and I realized there was nothing I could do to change him.

But I am rambling, and must get to the point of this letter. In the last months at Auschwitz, everyone in the Gypsy complex at Auschwitz thought I was too sick to know what was happening around me, but I was aware most of the time. I heard Emil telling the Gypsy leaders in the camp that you were a lover to Governor General Hans Frank and that you were acting as an informant to the SS. He said you couldn't be trusted, that you were leaking information about the weapons we were hiding. I didn't believe you could do such a thing, but I was too weak to interfere. Then later I heard Emil whispering to an SS officer that the SS was being duped also, that you were an informant for the underground at Auschwitz. I begged Emil to stop talking, to leave you alone, but he rebuffed even me. He said he sought his revenge against you in Warsaw when he turned you in to the Gestapo, but things didn't work out as he had planned. This time he was going to succeed.

Eventually Emil's treachery reversed itself and turned in on him. One night, one of the kapos Emil had been selling drugs to came to the camp to get penicillin. Emil was proud that he had been able to steal it from the evil Dr. Mengele. They divided the drug, and both of them injected it into their arms, thinking if they took it, they would not catch the diseases that were killing so many in the camp. But something went wrong. Mengele, suspecting the penicillin was being pilfered from his clinic, had replaced it with a deadly poison. Emil and his fellow kapo yelled for help as they begin to swell and then to have seizures, but no one came. I was too sick to move. Emil had brought pain to everyone for so long, I said a prayer for him through my tears and closed out the noise.

There were rumors the next day in the camp that you had somehow killed Emil, even though no one had seen you for days. I tried to tell everyone that this was not true, but unfortunately, many in the clan thought my fever had caused me to be delirious.

Perhaps with this letter, you can exonerate yourself from the Auschwitz accusations and untruths should they ever become a problem for you. I hope you have found peace in your life.

Mar Dep, Shero Rom of the Keldari

Karl looked over at Sasha as Beth finished the letter. "With the details we have now from Dirk and Gerta Klinsmann and this letter from Mar Dep, there should be no problem proving that Mavik's assertions are wrong," Karl said.

"I know, Dad, but I never dreamed what I would find when I began this journey. I never realized the complexity of the decisions that had to be made by people caught in a circumstance of time, a time when their lives depended on a nod to the left or right, or on simply trying to survive to the next hour or the next day."

Karl put his arms around Beth, holding her close. "I don't know how to thank you. Not only did you find my mother, you cleared her name. No one will read lies about her again."

"I know," Beth said as her eyes filled with tears. "I'm just so grateful that I had this opportunity, and I am so happy for you."

Karl returned to Sasha's side, and they sat together, turning the conversation to more pleasant topics. As Sasha and Karl continued laughing and talking, Beth stepped away and stood at the window, looking down at the courtyard and its well-tended gardens below. She pressed her palms against the glass and felt the sunshine warming her skin. Silent tears streamed down her cheeks. Andy walked over to her, placing a comforting hand on her back. "What's wrong?" he whispered. "Why are you sad? This is the best of all possible outcomes."

"I know." Beth sniffled and turned to face him. "I'm not unhappy about this reunion, or about how any of this has turned out. I found Grandma Sasha. Alive! I reunited my father with his mother; a task that seemed impossible. I have the proof to show that my grandmother did not collaborate with the Nazis. It's all wonderful beyond belief."

"But?" Andy asked.

"But, now what happens?" Beth replied.

Andy scratched his head. "I don't know. That's up to them. It would be wonderful to bring your grandmother back to the States, but at her age she may feel more comfortable staying here, where things are familiar."

"I don't mean about Sasha," Beth countered. "This is going to sound terribly selfish, Andy, but I mean about me."

"You?"

"Yes. What happens to me?"

Andy looked confused. "What do you mean?"

"Where do I go from here? Personally and professionally? For years I have been looking for the truth about Sasha and for the past several months, my whole life has been dedicated to that effort. And now that journey has ended. I've exhausted my time, my energy, and my money; I gave up my job, everything. I don't regret any of it, not one moment. But I'm not sure what's next. Andy, I don't have a job, I don't have a car, I don't have a place to live, and I have almost no money left. How do I start my life over again at the age of thirty-three?"

Andy smiled. "Beth, listen. How hard can it be to find a new job after everything you've accomplished? Whatever you do from here on in will be easy compared to the obstacles you've already faced. You're smart, you're talented, and you're resourceful. Your resume would blow any employer away."

"Andy, you have such faith in me," Beth said with a sigh. "And I realize now how much of our relationship has been about me. I wish there was something I could do to repay you for sticking by me."

"You can," Andy said blushing. "Beth, this journey has been incredible for me too. It's been a struggle in so many ways, but wonderful and illuminating as well. I feel as if I've been a living witness to history. I guess I'm kind of talking in circles here, but Beth, I don't want our journey together to end."

"What are you saying?" Beth's heart began to pound.

"I'm saying that I want to spend a lot more time with you. On a permanent basis. Beth, I know I promised not to push you, but how do you feel about marriage? I mean, how would you feel about an engagement, leading up to marriage?" Andy stumbled over his words and blushed a fierce shade of crimson.

Beth smiled through her tears. "Andy, I think I understand. And the answer is yes. Yes, I will marry you. This adventure is finished; it's time for a new beginning."

"That sounds like my Gypsy girl," Andy responded as they threw their arms around each other and embraced.

Beth looked over at her father, still engaged in an animated conversation with Sasha. Then Beth whispered in Andy's ear. "How are we going to tell my dad? He just found his mother, and now he's about to gain a son-in-law! I'm not sure how much more family he'll be able to handle!"

Andy wrapped his arms around Beth and gave her a long, intensely passionate kiss. "We've got time," he said as the kiss ended. "We've got all the time in the world."

Manufactured By: RR Donnelley
                    Momence, IL USA
                    July, 2010